DEAD CATS,

POTATO SOUP

AND

A NAKED MAN

SHORT STORIES BY
AYLEENE ARCHER THOMPSON

ILLUSTRATIONS BY PATRICIA THOMPSON

Printed in the United States of America
Published by Seacoast Publishing, Inc.

Library of Congress Control Number: 2005937160

ISBN 1-59421-019-5

To obtain copies of this book, please write or call:

Ayleene A. Thompson
3233 Bonny View Drive
Birmingham, AL 35226
205-822-4492

DEDICATION

I dedicate this small collection to Patricia, Wayne Evan and Treba;
to Teresa, Trebs and Eric and to Haley, Zachary and Wayne Edward.
My special love goes to the Duck Man who made it all possible.

For Clarke and Anne Nall Stallworth,
who lit the fire and fanned the flame.

CONTENTS

DEAD CATS AND THE WAY THINGS ARE	9
IF I MAY COME HOME AGAIN	17
GRANDPA'S SCOREBOARD	27
THE PEANUT BUTTER COOKIE CAPER	32
THE SEATING ARRANGEMENT AT MOLLY'S HOUSE	34
POTATO SOUP	43
MY GREEN THUMB	51
SHOPPING CART RAGE	53
A GOOD DAY ON THE MOUNTAIN	55
YOUR EYES AIN'T BLUE NO MORE	62
THE GREAT HEAVENLY LIGHT	64
RIDE A WILD PINTO TO RUBY FALLS	70
LIMERICKS	77
MY LOVE AFFAIR WITH THE BIG YELLOW BOWL	78
THE ANNIVERSARY KISS	80
THE WISTERIA TREE	83
GETTING TO KNOW HER	90
GARVAS MAHONEY'S MIRACLE	100
LYDIA FRANKLIN'S POSITIVELY LAST HOME-COOKED HOLIDAY DINNER	107
LOVE IS WARMER THAN AN ELECTRIC BLANKET	112
A GENTLE ART	115
THE TITHING	121
IN THAT FAR OFF SWEET FOREVER	128
HOT AIR BALLOON RIDE IN TANZANIA	140
PLACES IN TIME	142
WORDS UNSPOKEN	145
THE REDEMPTION OF LAMAR BILLBERRY	151
THE UNIQUENESS OF AN IMPERFECT DIAMOND	157
CIAO, ELVIS	165
ONE LAST DANCE	173
THE DUCK MAN	177
THAT CHRISTMAS	179
WORM MONEY SATURDAY NIGHT	183

COPPER PENNIES AND SUNNY DEW COLA   191

CURRENT DAVEY O   200

DEELIE   205

DIALOGUE WITH THE Q.O. MAN   211

THE NAKED MAN ON MY PORCH   217

SWEET HONEYSUCKLE MORNING   222

MOON WALK   229

DEAD BUTTERFLIES   236

APPLES   243

WHERE ARE ALL THE CARING PEOPLE?   245

REQUIEM FOR A REFRIGERATOR   250

BUDDY   253

THE DAY THE PRETTY BIRDS CAME   257

THE WINNOWING   267

INTRODUCTION

Life is a journey, every traveler a story.
My make-believe characters sometimes come to me on tiptoe in the
middle of the night, tapping on the door of my imagination;
others barge in without knocking.
Stories are everywhere waiting to happen. Threads of plots dangle from bits
of conversations overheard at the malls, in grocery store check-out lines...is
Annie really going to marry Mark after being jilted by Raymond?
A few of the stories are scenes from childhood years long ago. I am the little
girl who truly felt the fires of Hell in "The Tithing," the child whose rotten
brother clued her in about Santa in "That Christmas" and the one who
learned something about life and growing up in "Dead Butterflies." My
grandpa Archer is the hero in "Anniversary Kiss." The tale was a legend in
my family for all the time I can remember.
Most of the other stories play around with familiar emotions from
loneliness and love to fornication and forgiveness.

DEAD CATS & THE WAY THINGS ARE

January 2

Dear Callie,

Muriel died last week, poor old Muriel. I found her behind the crape myrtle bush, her little feline legs stuck straight up in the air like four yellow striped tent stakes. I'm glad I don't believe what my great-grandmother Ramona used to say. Remember that summer we visited her and she told us that a dead cat brings bad luck, same as breaking a mirror or washing your hair on the first night of a full moon?

It is only six weeks until I see you. Thanks for planning to drive all the way from St. Louis to be my matron of honor---again. Do you think it is poor taste for me to wear the dress I bought when I was going to marry Raymond? Although it has been packed away in tissue for the last five years, it is in excellent condition except for a tiny stain near the front hemline. I feel sure nobody will notice; they will be seeing me mostly from the back. I must lose ten pounds so I can fit into it, but that will be easy now that the holidays are over.

Muriel would have been sixteen years old in the spring. I still think about the semester we sneaked her into our dorm, a fuzzy little kitten, and you tried to train her to crap in the toilet. Mark is leaving work early today to help bury her as I feel I can't go through it alone. Weather here in Alabama has been unseasonably warm, so I put her in a zip top storage baggie in the freezer until I can cope with deciding where would be the right place for her. It should be near the crape myrtle, I suppose.

Love,
Annie

Mark, home before I am, is wearing old tan corduroys, a Crimson Tide sweat shirt and his fishing boots. He stands next to the crape myrtle bush, one foot braced on top of the spade he has shoved into the ground. I think he is incredibly sexy, his gray eyes squinted against patterns of sunlight scrolling across his face each time the wind whips the branches of the oak tree.

"Shouldn't we wait for Muriel to thaw?" he asks.

"It won't matter. Be grateful the ground isn't frozen." I can't stop crying while I wrap her for the last time in her favorite blanket, a piece of my old angora sweater. The heavy clods of red clay make hollow thumping sounds dropping on her coffin, a computer packing box I found in the closet and lined with white quilted satin.

Mark says let's go eat supper at the new fast-food place on the highway. We sit facing each other over red-checkered vinyl stretched taut under a square of glass. The copper lamp hanging over the table sways when I bump my elbow against the wall, and the light drops little pinpoints of rainbow colors on the bubbles fizzing in my soda.

Mark seems absorbed in the double order of fries he arranges in front of him. He salts, dips in catchup, re-salts while I push a plump cherry tomato through a tunnel between Bibb lettuce and the cucumber wedges.

"Are we totally locked in on the February 14 date?" He asks the question as though he has just thought of it.

I say of course we are locked in: church, minister, the three-tier cake with red sugar roses, Callie driving in from Missouri–everything. So, is there a problem, I want to know?

"It's just that I ran into Cindy today at lunch. She may have to be up in Nashville," he says.

January 9

Dear Callie,

I can't recall your meeting Cindy. She works at Dunn Electronics with Mark, although in another department, and I forgot to mention she's who we asked to sing, "Roses Are Red, My Love" at the reception. Can you believe we would choose an old tune from the 1950s or whenever? But it seems appropriate, since we are going with a Valentine's Day theme. Mark still likes the oldies, "Roses" being one of his favorites. I guess we've both made concessions; he agreed I would be foolish to buy another wedding dress.

But back to Cindy, who in addition to her regular job also sings on week-ends with a local band on TV and has recently cut a demo with a group out of Nashville. We may have to ask someone from the church choir to take her place at the reception if her recording session comes up next month.

I've lost another pound, almost, but still have to hold my breath to zip past my middle. The swatch of taffeta you included in your last letter is exactly the perfect shade of pink for your dress, but I'm sorry you are too far into pregnancy–well, of course, not sorry you are pregnant, but I do wish you could still wear what you bought when I was going to marry Raymond.

Fondly,
Annie

P.S. Love to Ralph and little Teddy

It is raining, a bleak mid-winter evening that claws at the windows, whining to be let inside. We are having a discussion about relationships and marriage, doing Chinese take-outs in front of the fire. Mark has mastered chopsticks, routing bean sprouts and chunks of chicken from carton to mouth in a perfect flow of motion. A log on the grate showers sparks across the stone hearth. I untangle my long red skirt, the one he says makes me look like a flamenco dancer, and get up to close the fire screen.

"The girls in the office are giving a lingerie shower for me on Tuesday," I tell him when I come back.

"We've been together three years," Mark is saying, "so what difference is a wedding ceremony going to make in the way we are, the way we feel?"

"It will make me feel less temporary," I say.

"Relationships can be rock solid." He switches off the lamp on the end table, leans back against the sofa pillows. "Jake, one of the guys at work, has been in a relationship with the same person for ten years. I call that permanent as most marriages."

"Well, I want to be married and do it with all the fuss and feathers, all the bells and whistles."

"Aha," his smile seems half playful, half serious, "are we talking to the last girl in the office with no wedding portraits, no lei of ginger blossoms from the honeymoon in Hawaii?"

January 16
Dear Callie,

Mark seems to be having a lot of second thoughts, but I believe this may be normal for a man who has side-stepped marriage until age thirty-five. What do you think? It's not like he is hiding out a wife and children in another city, the way it was with Raymond. But I won't go into that.

I may have to make some alterations on my dress. Satin is such crawly fabric, and I can't seem to shed enough weight to keep it from riding up over my hips. However, my February period will have come and gone by the 14th, and that will take care of a couple of inches in my waistline; you probably recall I retain a lot of fluid before my period. I'm glad Mark doesn't feel threatened by my choosing to wear the dress. I do so love the style and the twenty-eight tiny loops and self-covered buttons down the bodice. Wouldn't it be a shame to just let it rot away in storage?

Sorry Ralph has the flu. Feed him plenty of chicken soup.

Fondly,
Annie

Mark has gone to his office the last couple of Saturdays to catch up on a project. This morning after he leaves, I walk outside to watch patches of wispy clouds flit across the sun, playing hide and seek with the gum tree's shadow stretched over the browned lawn. Muriel's favorite toy, a green rubber mouse, lies trapped in the thick stubble of a boxwood. I feel a sudden restlessness tug at me, a sense of not wanting to be alone, and decide I should deliver the gift I've bought for Cindy when I thought she was going to sing at the reception. It is a little gold chain, which I could save for a birthday, but I think it will be fun to give it to her now, sort of a good luck charm for when she goes to Nashville.

Cindy lives at the end of a lane branching off a county road. A tall pine, shaped like a fat Christmas tree, hides the view of the house until all at once, there it is: a white bungalow at the end of a sloping flagstone drive. A hedge of untrimmed holly borders it all the way to the carport where her black and white van is parked. Snuggled next to it, like a contented lover, is Mark's red Honda.

My brain slips into slow motion while I get out of the car, walk up the steps to ring the bell. I hear laughter inside, the patter of feet. Mark opens the door. He is barefoot and shirtless, tugging at the zipper on his fly. He will catch his death of cold, I think.

January 20
Dear Callie,

Sorry I could babble only incoherent gibberish into the telephone; I have a pot of coffee and two Xanax under my belt now, so I believe I will be able to tell you what happened. The wedding is off, not postponed as you first tried to interpret the meaning of my hysterics. But at two a.m., whose brain is functioning? Putting it bluntly, I have been screwed again without benefit of clergy. Isn't it strange I am able to write what I cannot bear to say?

Just now, when I stopped writing and went for another cup of coffee, I started thinking again about Ramona's dead cat theory and remembered something else she believed to be true: finding the right person to love is just a matter of luck, and some people never seem to get it right. It's the way things are, she said.

Well, Mark asked me to call him at work when I am ready to talk. I said he can come get his things today.

Always,
Annie

"I hope you don't mind the U Haul parked against the front porch," Mark says when I open the door. "It makes it easier getting stuff out."
It is Sunday. His face wears the dark stubble that comes when he doesn't shave until noon. His nose is pink from the cold wind and he shivers when he walks inside.

"Damn heater quit working on the way over." I notice he has on new sneakers and a lightweight gray sweat suit that obviously belongs to someone larger than he. His shoes and jacket, I realize, are in the hall closet.

I think maybe it is not normal that I suddenly sense a calmness, heart pulsing slowly and my hands steady as I close the door behind me. I wonder if I am one of those people who, just before running amuck, feels in total control?

Mark stops in the den, looks at the dead ashes in the fireplace and asks if I want him to bring in some wood and start a fire. When I shake my head, he sinks down into the red corduroy wing chair across from me on the sofa.

"It's not easy to know where to begin." He holds his hands across his knee, fingers laced. "I didn't set out to hurt you, Annie. I never meant to do that."

I watch how the hazy winter sun slants through the windows to draw a line between us while he explains that nothing ever happened between Cindy and him until a couple of weeks ago.

"Not until I panicked when I realized I couldn't commit to marriage."

"But why didn't you tell me, say that you couldn't?"

"I tried. You wouldn't hear. I wanted to go along with it because I love you, I honestly do, but my love comes without conventional bonds and fetters holding us together." His fingers shake as he lights a cigarette. "The way we were."

He stacks his computer, fishing gear and camera inside the U Haul and stuffs his clothes around them.

"Anything I forgot, you can keep or throw out; whatever." He walks half way across the porch, buttoning his jacket, then turns to me. "God, Annie, I'm sorry."

I think it is the sunlight stinging his eyes that makes it look like he is crying. The numbness inside me seeps away to make room for the ache I have not felt until now. When I go back inside, I see the envelope Mark has left on the table.

January 26

Dear Callie,

After Mark came to pick up his things, I found he had left a check to reimburse me for his part of the wedding expenses–we had agreed to go halves on flowers, cake, champagne, etc. Also the enclosed amount to you is to cover cost of your dress and getting shoes dyed to match. He says I should let him know if it is not enough. I thought I had it together, you know, until I saw him again. Did I mention I tried primal screaming afterwards and that it actually helped? The girls at the office refused my offer to return the lingerie, so here I am with a drawer full of satin teddies and also the gift from my boss's wife–I'm sure I told you about the set of black velvet handcuffs and matching whip.

I am considering donating my wedding dress to the Junior League thrift shop. The yellowish stain is more noticeable that I realized, and under close inspection, I see several loops on the bodice have started to fray.

Sorry to hear Teddy toppled off the seesaw and broke his front tooth. He will grow another one, but do keep an eye on him in case he develops an abscess.

With love,
Annie
P.S. Do you think I should get another cat?

IF I MAY COME HOME AGAIN

*S*ince Kevin moved out of their a apartment and took Strumpet with him–Strumpet was, after all, *his* cat–the city seemed to close in on her.

Every day since he'd left, Liz had watched the streets inch closer to the sidewalks when she stepped off the downtown commuter bus; this morning the tall buildings on the corner swayed and tilted in her direction. She buried her nose deep in the fur collar of her coat, but without raising her head saw the towers of brick and glass push toward her as she hurried to her office at Payne Williams Advertising Agency.

When she went home in the evening, the emptiness stretched in front of her like a wide rubber band. She moved quickly from entry to kitchen, flipping light switches, touching leaves of the African violets and ferns on the white wicker stand in the hall. She sat down on the side of the brass bed, shook the long strands of hair from her face. The yellow glow of the light overhead made her squint; she turned it off and lay back, her eyes fixed on the patch of ceiling Kevin missed with the paint roller last spring. She had memorized in the darkness where it was.

The keening of the wind outside the windows mingled with the sound of sleet pelting against the panes. Fragments of music from a radio in the next apartment sifted through the walls and she pressed her fingers against her forehead, trying to weave the notes into a song she remembered. The clock clicked off the minutes, her shoes dropped with a thud, the bed squeaked when she moved. All of the familiar sounds are still here, she thought, but where are the smells?

Later she taped a list of the absent scents: Strumpet's litter box, the stupid vanilla scented candle Kevin burned at night after she smoked her last cigarette; Strumpet's tuna farts, Kevin's sneakers, the bed sheets after they made love.

She labeled the tape The Week After Kevin and played it back once before she erased it.

She heard voices, hers and Kevin's, coming from the TV set she had unplugged because she no longer turned it on. Kevin said, "It's nothing to do with what you did or didn't do. I wanted to go out with her."

"Is she prettier than I am?"

"I honestly doubt her looks had anything to do with my feelings."

"Does she smoke? I know how you hate my doing it and other things like leaving caps off toothpaste, shoes under the coffee table. Is it because you find her better in bed?"

"Christ, Liz. Don't. Let's just agree I'm a louse and let it go at that because I don't have an answer. I'll move out, okay? Maybe I just need some space."

"Was there ever a time you wanted to marry me?"

"I guess the time never seemed right, except once. That week-end at the ski lodge I wanted to marry you. You were celebrating the start of your period, which was late, but I found myself wishing you were pregnant."

"You never told me."

She turned her back on the TV, and now she could no longer see him or hear his voice.

Liz had begun to dream of the house where she grew up and of the wide streets lined with oak and birch trees, the five and dime store and the moonlight that floated like streamers of yellow ribbons on the lake at the edge of town. She used to park there under a willow tree with Stanley Overstreet, and once with Rex Dalhart. The stars glistened and danced that night, so close she wanted to touch them, to hold them in her hands and listen to them sing.

Her father had caught her with Rex after her mother sent him out to look for her. The beam of his flashlight flashed against the car's windshield, her panties were draped over the rear view mirror. Pink with lace insets, she remembered.

After Kevin had been gone for ten days she wrote to her parents:

Dear Mom and Dad,

I have been wondering if I may come home again. It has been two years, closer to three, since we've seen each other. I know from your letters, Mom, that your feelings about me haven't changed. I'm not asking for your approval of my life style, but I want to come for a visit. I want to see Pam and the babies. Maybe later I'll come back to stay. Kevin and I are not together now, and I am no longer living in sin. You were right, Mom. Kevin decided not to buy the cow when he could get the milk for free–I believe this is your favorite homily about sex without marriage.

Her mother wrote a week later:

Dear Elizabeth Anne,

Your father and I have prayed about it and decided that the Christian thing to do is let bygones be bygones. How I wish you had listened to our advice when you were a young girl. It would have saved us and yourself from so much grief and misery. I have turned your bedroom into a nursery for Pam's and Eugene's babies when Pam brings them to sleep over. Did I tell you Eugene is running for the state legislature? He has the support of organized labor and the anti-abortion people, so we feel he has a good chance to get elected. He bought the Turner's house down the street, and your sister is happy living close by us. She is such a good little wife and mother.

Liz bought an airline ticket and arranged to take off work the first two weeks in January. When she finished packing, she stood barefoot on the bedroom carpet and watched little black specks hop on and off her legs.

"Why don't you call the exterminator?" her neighbor from the next apartment asked when she came to borrow an herbal tea bag and a tablespoon of honey.

"It's enough that all of Strumpet's smells are gone," Liz said. "There's nothing except her fleas to remind me that she was ever here at all."

Tears stung her eyes when she got off the plane and saw her parents waiting. Her mother erect, pale blue dress, black-checked coat, and her father grayer, more stooped than she remembered.

Liz laid her head on her mother's shoulder, smelled the soapy cleanness of her, 99 & 44/100% pure.

"You look thin," her mother said. "Are you on another one of your nothing but Oreo cookies diets?"

"My job keeps me thin," Liz said. "Sometimes I forget to eat."

Her father kissed her on the cheek, asked if she had a smooth ride. She slid her arm around him. His body tensed, his brown corduroy shirt rough against her face. She moved away awkwardly. *Forgive me father for I have sinned.*

"You have suitcases?" he asked. "I'll load them in the trunk."

Pam came from her house down the street, carrying the oldest child, Meggie, on her hip and pushing a dual stroller with the youngest ones zipped inside woolly pink snow suits. Tufts of brownish hair, like pin feathers on a pair of baby mockingbirds, poked from their caps. Pam handed Meggie and the stroller to her mother at the front door and ran to throw her arms around Liz.

"I baked a double fudge cake in honor of your first night at home, but Meggie knocked it off the counter. It's in the middle of the kitchen floor, frosting side down."

Liz held her close for a moment before sitting down beside her on the sofa in the living room. She tasted the salt of tears welling in the back of her throat. *Oh Pam, you've found it. Soft pink babies and double fudge cake. You listened to Mother's Theory.*

"I thought Eugene was coming," her mother said. "I made hot rolls."

"He said he would stop by this evening after the campaign meeting is over," Pam said.

After supper, while her sister put the babies to bed in the nursery, Liz went to the room where she would sleep. She stumbled in the darkness over the bag her father had left on the floor in front of the closet. A trail of light moved back and forth on the window panes when the wind sent little wisps of clouds sailing across the three-quarter moon. She pressed her nose in the folds of the white muslin curtains and remembered, in the mingled scents of bleach and spray starch, the long winter evenings of her childhood.

Pam slipped in quietly from across the hall, turned on the small brass lamp on the night stand. She dropped down on the side of the bed, her hands in her lap, fingers laced tightly. "Talk to me, Liz. Just talk–tell me about the lights and the music, the people rushing in and out of the shops. Do you have a Bloomingdale's charge card?"

"Yes, but I seldom go there."

"Sorry I haven't written lately, but there's not much in my life to write about these days except morning sickness and shitty diapers."

"I've missed you." Liz grinned and pulled a green chintz-covered armchair close to the bed.

"Me too. I've tried to reason with Mom after she said she didn't want to see you while you lived with Kevin, but you know there's no winning a point, and Dad doesn't dare disagree with her." Pam picked a piece of lint off the leg of her slacks and without looking up said, "You must hate me sometimes."

"Oh Pam, why would I?"

"Miss Goody Two-Shoes. I always toe the mark, but don't ask me why."

"I couldn't have made it without you. Remember the night of the senior prom?"

"Oh God, yes. Mom sent Dad out to look for you after somebody telephoned her with word that your date had a couple of beers stashed in the trunk of his car."

"Rex Dalhart, and it turned out he actually had three 6-packs, and I'd have never been able to crawl back inside the house if you hadn't helped me."

"The flying cactus bush was in full bloom under your bedroom window," Pam laughed. "Mom almost caught me picking thorns out of your butt when she made final bed check."

"She tells me you're a terrific wife and mother."

"Mom sees what she wants to see. Tell me about Kevin."

"He moved out. He's seeing someone else."

"Are they sleeping together?"

"I think so, but let's talk about you. How do you feel about Eugene running for state legislator?"

"He has the 'Life Is Sacred' group in his corner, and I am a walking campaign slogan with three babies hanging on my coat tails. I feel used, that's how I feel."

"Well, three children," Liz said. "That's a nice family."

"Not for Eugene. He says he will leave me if I use birth control. God, sometimes I wish *he* would sleep around." She put her hands over her face and began to cry. "Liz, I think I'm pregnant again."

"Oh honey, I'm so sorry." Liz leaned forward, smoothed the straight brown hair back from her eyes and held her close.

"I'm scared, sis. I can't leave him and strike out on my own. I'm twenty-seven years old, and all I know how to do is roll over and spread my legs."

The next morning Liz left a note on the refrigerator door: Can't sleep. Going for a walk. Don't wait breakfast.

Cold wind bit at her hands and face, but a trickle of sweat ran down the back of her sweat shirt as she jogged. Two cars drove past her, their headlights like eyes searching the new dawn.

The OPEN AT 10 O'CLOCK sign still hung on the door at the five and dime store. She studied the fan-shaped arrangement of thermal blankets inside the windows. Knitting yarn was on sale this week, hard candies and Christmas cards half price while they last. She painted a foggy, wet circle on the glass with her breath

Across town, the lake sparkled in the first brightness of sunrise. Ducks, the green-headed ones who wintered there, sat huddled together on the bank; Liz wished she'd brought bread to throw to them.

She hunched her shoulders against the cold and walked around to the other side of the water, where the willow tree grew before it had been chopped down to make room for a red seesaw and two swings. She sat down in one of the swings and looked at the stump where the tree had stood. *There should be a bronze marker here: On This Spot Elizabeth Anne Fowler Got Laid By Rex Dalhart, Fastest Pecker In The West.*

She leaned her head back, back until her hair trailed the ground and swished like stalks of autumn wheat across the frost-crested grass. The sky was a deep blue, rosy streaked with morning, but when she closed her eyes the stars were there.

Her mother would be up by now, she thought, still breathing hard after the long walk back from the lake. She wiped her feet on the mat by the back steps before she tapped on the door and went inside.

"You should have told her," her father's voice came from another room in the house.

"I didn't get a chance to tell her yet. How did I know she would take off this morning at the crack of dawn?" The smell of coffee, a clattering of cups on the kitchen counter, the swish of her mother's long blue robe as she turned to face her.

"Tell me what, Mom?"

"I wanted to tell you, I thought you should know that while you are here people may ask you about your husband. I've told our friends you are married to Kevin."

"Well, of course, I'll never let them catch you in a lie, Mother. If I have a conversation with a neighbor, I'll mention Kevin my husband frequently, but you should fill me in. Do we live three flights up over a bakery, or shall I casually bring up the chauffeur and our yacht?"

"You've no cause to be mean-spirited, Elizabeth. Everybody knows you were wild as a buck growing up." Her eyes brimmed, spilled in tiny rivers down her cheeks. "I just wanted people to think that you are settled now with a home and husband. Just like Pam."

"Let it be, Emma," her father called from the bedroom. "You said you'd put it to rest now."

"God only knows why I didn't have a stroke that day you sashayed home from college and announced you were going to live with Kevin," her mother said. "It seems I've spent half my life worrying about you. I know you think I'm hard and mean, but I doubt I have had a dozen good nights sleep since you were fifteen and ran off with that gypsy fortune teller's boy at the state fair."

Her father drove her to catch the late afternoon flight. Liz sat between him and her mother.

"I thought you were staying for another week," he said.

"My work piles up if I'm gone too long."

"Did you have a good visit with Pam?" her mother asked. "You were at her house for a long time last night."

"I guess we had a lot of catching up to do."

"I've said and done some things you don't appreciate, Elizabeth Anne, but it has all been for your own good. It's not that I don't–"

"Mom, I called Kevin last night."

When they got to the airport, her mother reached out and smoothed the collar of Liz's jacket. She felt the pressure of the hand, heavy as a stone on her shoulder.

"I'll just sit here in the car," her mother said. "I hate watching airplanes leave."

Her father walked with her to the departure gate. Sunlight played against the windows and made the day seem warm.

She said to him, "After Kevin left I told myself: maybe this is not what I'm looking for. I need to move back home, marry a hardware salesman or someone solid like Eugene, have a crop of kids."

"What about Kevin?" he asked.

"I don't know. We've still got to iron some things out, but I've got my head together now, and I know for sure I don't want to marry someone solid like Eugene."

When she started to board, he turned to her, touched her cheek. "I remember," he said, "when you were six and I'd given you your third spanking for playing in the street. I asked why you kept disobeying. You said you just got tired of being good."

She dropped her carry-on, put her arms around him and felt him hold her close before he moved away. When she looked back, his face was a blur through her tears.

She heard him call out to her. His words were lost in the space between them, in the other voices around them, but she thought he had said "I love you."

GRANDPA'S SCOREBOARD

*M*y grandmother's eyes, a tad out of focus, fluttered like a pair of pale blue butterflies searching my face for a spot to land.

"Who are you?" she asked as I pulled her chintz-covered recliner closer to her bed and sat down. "I can't seem to recollect if you are the one who don't like men or if I got you mixed up with one of Bernice's girls."

" I'm Suzanne. I'm Zoe's daughter–you know, the one who is married to Phillip. He's the boy with the red hair that reminds you of Gramps."

"Of course you are. I recall everything now." She slid lower on the mound of pillows where sunlight slipped through white lace curtains to dot the veined trails on the back of her hand. "I am getting old, you know, and it is hard to keep up with the comings and goings of all you grandchildren. You must be the one with that pair of twin boys who trampled down my petunia patch last spring."

"I'm the one who doesn't seem to be able to get pregnant, Grams. We've been trying for four years and no luck yet."

She fixed her gaze on me, reached out and gave my arm a little squeeze before nodding off.

Grams died a week later quietly and without a struggle, leaving her world in order. It was like she just floated away, Mama said.

Monies from the sale of her big old Victorian house were equally divided among her seven children, with each grandchild inheriting parts of her treasures. The remains of her bilious green 1931 Packard went to my brother who had salivated over the automobile since he was a teenager. Aunt Bernice's daughter, the one who doesn't like men, was the recipient of Grandpa's antique pistol collection. Jewelry, china, silver and paintings were distributed among the remaining twenty grandchildren.

To me, she bequeathed the first piece of furniture she and Gramps bought when they set up housekeeping–the bed where she first slept on her wedding night and where she slept for the last time the night he died. Phillip agreed that Grandma's bed should replace the lumpy sleeper sofa in our guest room.

"It would be a shame not to use it," I reasoned.

"Ugly as it is," he walked across the room and stood looking at it after we had heaved and tugged to get it set up, "it has a lot of character."

It had been more than twenty years since I last saw it. I guess I was age five, maybe six at the time and was visiting Grams while Mama fin-ished her Christmas shopping. It was a cold, raw day; I imagined the pel-lets of sleet were little white creatures pecking on the windows, begging to come inside.

"The weather's not fit for you to play in the yard," Grams said.

She promised to let me help make gingerbread for supper, but after awhile I got bored with waiting for her to come with me to the kitchen and so I set out to go exploring in the room that I knew was forbidden territory.

The bedroom was closed before I was born, shut off from the rest of the house since Gramps died. There was no lock on the door; it opened with no more than a slight squeak when I gave it a push and slipped inside.

It set at an angle near a row of long narrow windows, the biggest bed I had ever seen. Dark mahogany with massive posters at the foot and a tall headboard with doors that slid open when I pulled a small copper handle. Even now, I remember feeling my heart start to pound faster when I dis-covered a heart shaped box inside containing locks of hair tied with ribbons, a rose pressed between pieces of tissue paper, some cuff links and a locket with a picture of Gramps in his navy uniform from World War Two.

Behind a row of books at the back of the headboard, I found a square of brown paper thumb tacked to the wall. I wriggled my hand behind it and my fingers touched rough splintery places cut into the wood just as Grams walked into the room.

"What does this say?" I pointed to rows of letters and numbers.

"Well," her lips curved up in a little smile and she sighed as though resigned not to scold me, "your Grandpa called it his scoreboard. Some day when you are old enough to understand I'll explain what it means."

She put her arm around my shoulder and stood beside me for the longest time, smiling her far away smile before replacing the paper and leading me toward the kitchen.

"Let's go make that gingerbread," she said.

A quarter of a century came rolling back when I saw the bed again, sitting here in my own home. A shiver of child-like anticipation ran along my spine as I slid open the doors on the massive old headboard and eased my fingers along the back wall. The square of paper was in the place I recalled, yellowed and dog-eared but still there!

Phillip came to peer over my shoulder, bent down to ask, "Searching for hidden treasure?"

"I don't know. Maybe I am. I remember that Gramps carved something in here, but it's too dark to read what it says."

Phillip found a flashlight and let a small beam of brightness play across rows of crude but still legible markings:

September — June 26

March — December 6

November — August 9

February — November 11

April — January 3

January — October 13

March — December 25

Next morning Phillip looked at me over the top of the sports section of the newspaper as I poured another cup of coffee.

"I keep thinking about those carvings," he said, "about what they could mean. Do you attach significance to the fact that each row of dates covers approximately nine months?"

"Oh my God! Grandpa's scoreboard! We've found Grandpa's scoreboard."

"Clue me in."

"Grams never got around to explaining it to me; she said some day when I was old enough to understand, but it isn't too hard to figure, is it? Seven rows of dates, seven children."

"Why that sly old devil." Phillip's eyes sparkled. "You mean he kept scores of all his home runs?"

"It seems he did. I know my mom is the oldest. Her birthday comes on June 26, and I'm pretty certain Aunt Bernice was born on December 6. Fits, doesn't it?"

I didn't wait to stack the dishes in the sink before calling Aunt Bernice.

"What a nice surprise." Her voice was bubbly, as always. "Nobody ever calls me on a Saturday. Too busy, I reckon."

"Actually, I'm checking the family birthday list and I wondered if you could help me with some dates."

"Well, of course you know when your mama was born. I'm next in line, December 6, in case you want to throw a surprise party for me. But it's your Aunt Belle who has the really special day. Hers comes on December 25, and do you know she has always hated sharing the limelight with Jesus."

"I imagine it was hard for her to accept," I said.

"I always thought that giving birth on Christmas Day was Mama's sly way of getting out of having another birthday party," Aunt Bernice said, "and being the last one to come along, Belle has been spoiled rotten all her life, don't you know, but you don't have to repeat what I said."

"I won't breathe a word."

Phillip was still chuckling when I hung up the phone.

The following spring after Grams died, we decided to redecorate our bedroom, and so we moved our sleeping quarters into the guest room while the workmen painted and laid the new carpet.

"Grandpa probably used his trusty old pocket knife to whittle his scoreboard," Phillip mused that first night we crawled into the big old bed. "I might stop by Sears next week and check out one of those gadgets used for wood carving. Just for luck," he added.

Some time during the night I saw Grams etched in a gauzy light that shone across the foot of the bed. Later, when I awoke from my dream, she had vanished along with the fragile threads of light spun by the moon against the windows.

For a long time I lay without moving, holding my breath, not wanting to break the spell. I lay quietly in the darkness remembering the smile on her face, remembering how she had smiled at me as though she knew a secret I had yet to learn.

THE PEANUT BUTTER COOKIE CAPER

*O*n a mild winter afternoon, my husband and I watched a little bandit-face raccoon amble to the edge of our back yard patio and stand watching as though expecting an invitation to share a cup of tea. After a few minutes of eye to eye contact, it walked away to disappear in the shrubbery. We didn't spot it close up again for the rest of winter, although we caught glimpses when it came to the bird feeders to share sunflower seeds with the cardinals, jays and chickadees.

In April, we began our " baby bird feeding" program, stuffing holes in the suet logs with a mix of hamburger and chunky peanut butter. The holes, which we filled at night after the birds went to bed, were licked shiny clean by morning. So our evening watch began.

One night, there it was—we saw the dusky shadow of a 'coon shinnying up the metal pole where the suet log swung in the moonlight. After a few more visits, the little critter seemed to decide there was no need to scurry away when we approached. As it waddled off one evening after a dinner of fatburger, we agreed on a name: we would call it Bill.

My husband had the video camera ready when Bill showed up again. The little fellow performed like a circus acrobat. Hanging upside down, it clamped both back feet to the top of the log while using its front paws like a pair of nimble hands to transfer the suet from the holes to its mouth. When a full view of its little pink belly came into view, I heard a chuckle. "How about we change the name to Hillary?"

By the end of the month, Hillary had become a master beggar while reaching her paw through a small opening in the screen. She never tried to place her mouth against it. The food passed from my hand to hers, and it was like brushing the fingers of a tiny human. She seemed to enjoy the touch and learned to "pet" me through the screen by laying her face close to mine or rubbing her back against it like a cat. It was almost a spiritual experience to connect with a little wild creature in this way.

And then she discovered cookies, peanut butter cookies. When friends came for a visit and brought a tray of the home made goodies, we foolishly handed one to Hillary. After that, there was no turning back. The conniving little 'coon was an instant peanut butter cookie junkie.

When the gift cookies ran out, my husband was off to Bruno's for a store-bought pack. He came back with an expensive, top-of-the-line brand, so I shopped for the next batch, cheapest I could find. "A 'coon is not a galloping gourmet," I said. Wrong.

On that night when my husband gave one of the el cheapo cookies to her, she took it gently, as usual, paused, smelled, and handed it back to him. Then she turned away, bowed up her back and stalked off into the night, her tail held high.

THE SEATING ARRANGEMENT AT MOLLY'S HOUSE

*M*olly never meant to tell a soul Harold had come back. Watching him materialize out of the darkness had, at first, made the goose flesh crawl on the back of her neck, but now she had grown accustomed to suddenly waking to see him sitting in his easy chair beside her bed.

He looked like the same old Harold she buried six months ago: steel-rimmed eyeglasses, reddish hair–what there was left of it–and his gold Masonic Lodge pin gleaming in the lapel of the black coat that hung to the bottom of his underpants. He was without trousers because he had once grumbled that possibly he would spend eternity wearing a damn pair of pants that rode up in his crotch, so Molly instructed the undertaker to drape the white satin coverlet in the coffin to cover the bottom half of him at the viewing.

She decided to keep Harold's visits secret, but the words had slipped past her tongue when Grace said the time was right for Molly to get on with her life. Grace was her best friend who telephoned in the evenings just when Molly finished her Lean Gourmet TV dinner and curled up with a Rona Morris paperback, her mind zeroed in on ruggedly handsome Lawrence O'Halleran. Lawrence was the hero in Rona's series of romance novels, and Molly had read non-stop to page 297 of his latest adventure, *Passion In Paradise.*

This morning, Grace dropped in unannounced and sat down in the sun room.

"Phyllis is growing like a weed," she said, looking at the brass planter of philodendron in front of the window.

"Phyllis gets just enough light to keep her leaves happy," Molly smiled as she laid out linen napkins with two cups of coffee.

"I've been thinking, Molly. Now that you've got Harold's insurance check, you can go see some of the sights you are always reading about in that sack of books you cart home from the library every week." Grace stirred a second squirt of cream in her coffee. "I never catch you without your nose buried in a tale about some romantic place at the ends of the earth."

Molly's pulse leaped at the words. She felt herself drifting to a moon-drenched beach where Lawrence stood like a Viking god near the pounding surf, his powerful shoulders silhouetted against swaying palm trees. *He turned, swept her in his arms. "My darling, my darling," he whispered. His dark eyes smoldered with desire.* [Page 128, *Passion In Paradise*].

"Molly?"

She realized she had heard Grace's voice repeating that she should get herself ready for a vacation. Her heart still raced as though she had run for miles down a sandy beach.

"Well," she said, "I guess it would be lonely, going some place without Harold."

"Now I don't mean to sound cold blooded, Molly, but Harold is gone. Time's come for you to get on with your life."

And that was when Molly blurted out she saw him again last night.

Grace's mouth snapped open like a trap door.

"What do you mean *again* last night?"

"He's back, Grace. Harold's been coming back lately to sit in his easy chair."

Grace drew a quick shuddering breath and put her arm around Molly's shoulders.

"Don't you remember, dear? We buried Harold last March."

"I know that. But sometimes I wake up in the middle of the night and he's here, in his black coat and underpants, lolling big as life in his easy chair beside my bed."

"Molly, we know there's no such thing as ghosts."

"We're not talking ghosts here, Grace. It's Harold, flesh and bone. He's back. Yesterday I caught a glimpse of him at the bird feeder." Molly pointed to the big willow tree outside the windows. "You may recall if Harold wasn't nodding in his chair, he was sitting out there on the picnic bench waiting for the red birds to come eat their supper."

"I suppose it's natural, you thinking Harold's in his chair, since it is where he spent most all of his time." The spoon clattered in Grace's saucer when she got up to rinse out her cup. "But now that I've absorbed the shock of what you just told me, I realize your mind is playing tricks on you."

"I know Harold when I see him," Molly snapped, "and I washed his underpants enough years to recognize them, too."

"Listen to me, Molly. You get rid of that chair. Soon as it's not in the house, you'll stop imagining you see Harold. What you need to do is get yourself set to take a trip." Grace stood for a moment looking at Molly, reaching out to pat her cheek before closing the door on her way out.

Molly sighed as she sat thinking about when she used to sit with Harold in the evenings and see the cardinals come dropping down on the feeder like crimson leaves flung by the wind.

"Wouldn't it be wonderful, Harold," she would say, "to just flap our wings and fly away somewhere, anywhere?" There was still the longing, the ache inside her, when she remembered Harold peering over the top of his eyeglasses, mumbling, "Nothing out there's no better than what you got right here at home."

Molly slipped into her pink flowered nightgown soon as she finished listening to the 8:00 news. The skies had rumbled all day, and now rain pelted against the panes, trickled away in shining rivulets through the darkness. She closed the curtains and climbed into the big four poster; the reading lamp spread a rim of brightness over her white hair on the pillow.

She opened *Passion In Paradise* to the last chapter where Lawrence had come to say goodbye to the woman he loved. *He stood gazing across the lagoon, shimmering sapphire in golden moonlight, then turned again to the slim brown girl. She reached out trembling arms to him. His dark eyes smoldered with desire.*

Molly shivered, loving the way Lawrence's eyes always smoldered with desire. The jangle of the telephone beside her bed made her jump and forget where she was on the page.

"I've been over in Atlanta a couple of days, seeing that specialist about my gall bladder," Grace's voice vibrated in her ear, "and I can't sleep a wink tonight until I know if you still think you are seeing Harold."

"I haven't set eyes on him since I got rid of his chair."

"You sold it while I was gone?"

"I gave it to Goodwill and bought a chaise, blue chintz with Bird of Paradise flowers on the cushions. It's here, beside my bed, same spot where the chair was."

"Well, you did the right thing. While you're about it, bring Phyllis out of the sun room and set her over in that empty corner across from your bed. A green plant gives you something to look at instead of just lying there seeing things that aren't real."

Molly laid her book beside her and tilted her glasses to rest on top of her head.

"I told Goodwill to hold on to Harold's chair for a few days in case I want it back. He did love it so."

"Meaning no disrespect to the dead, Molly, I wonder he didn't take it with him. You did what you had to do and now you can stop thinking you see Harold."

"It wasn't imagination, Grace, but I haven't seen him since I gave away his chair."

"You see? I told you so. It was you looking at it all the time, studying about him sitting there like always."

"But he *was* here, Grace, and I know it was him I saw out by the willow tree."

"Well, you just might have to get that willow chopped down if that's what it takes to preserve your sanity."

"I appreciate your advice, Grace."

"What are friends for?" Grace asked.

Molly said goodbye and switched off the light. She had started to doze off when she remembered tomorrow would be Sunday. If she got up early, she would have time to study her lesson from Song Of Solomon, Chapter 2, Verses 10-11: *My beloved spake and said unto me, Rise up, my love my fair one and come away. For lo, the winter is past, the rain is over and gone.*

In the fuzzy glow from the night lamp in the hall, she squinted to see the outline of Phyllis' leaves stenciled against the window panes. Her eyes followed a sound she heard, the movement of a shadowy form across the new chaise.

"Harold?" she questioned softly, "are you back again?" She felt neither fright nor surprise, only a prickle of guilt for having given away his chair, leaving him with no place to sit.

The figure stirred, and Molly saw the blurred profile of a shaggy head and powerful shoulders.

"Mr. O'Halleran?" she whispered timidly, "is that you?"

He towered above her when he stood, came to take both her hands and bent to brush his lips against her fingers, one by one.

"Oh my," she gasped, certain that her heart had stopped. "Is it really you, Mr. O'Halleran?"

"Call me Larry." He looked deep into her eyes.

Molly didn't recall falling asleep, but she awoke to a dappling of sunlight on the windows. She yawned and turned on her weather alert radio just as the announcer said it was 9:27, under clear skies, Sunday morning temperature at 51 degrees.

Her head started to spin as she bolted up and saw that the chaise was empty, undisturbed as though no one had sat there. She sighed and eased out of bed, her legs wobbly as an old stepladder. No need hurrying now to make maple pecan waffles for Lawrence, no point studying Bible verses;

Lawrence was gone and she had slept right through Sunday School.

She picked up a leaf Phyllis dropped on the floor during the night. "Poor Phyllis," she stroked the sickly yellow veins while waiting for coffee to perk, "I believe you are pouting."

Soon as she drank her coffee, she pulled Harold's old denim jacket from the hook behind the door and buttoned it over her nightgown. She tasted the crispness in the outside air; a scattering of wet leaves, shiny as brown patent leather, squished under her shoes.

A buzz of voices cut through her thoughts. She saw her young neighbors in their yard next door, heard them talking while they staked the tall clumps of chrysanthemums, heavy with yellow and bronze blossoms, along the chain link fence. While she stood listening to their chatter, Molly heard a sound behind her. It seemed to come from somewhere in her house, a scraping noise, like heavy furniture dragging across the floor. Maybe Harold slipped inside and she failed to see him, or was it Lawrence come back for his maple pecan waffles?

"Lawrence?" she called, walking through the empty kitchen, then into the bedroom." Harold, are you in here?"

She saw Harold's old chair was back where it had always been before she gave it to Goodwill; Phyllis sat in her place in the sun room across from the blue chintz covered chaise.

Molly eased down on the side of her bed to rummage through the sack of library books she kept under the end table. Frowning as she looked at first one and then another, she realized she had picked up a sack belonging to some one else; there wasn't a Rona Morris in the lot. On one of the covers she saw the face of a man with curly auburn hair and neatly trimmed mustache, not a whit like Lawrence. *His deep blue eyes filled with pain as he saw the flickering lights of Heathrow. Free at last, Wycliff Pennington had returned to London to begin life anew, returned after serving fifteen tortured years in a hellish prison for a crime he didn't commit.*

Molly's lips moved silently except for occasional little clucking sounds. She had come to the part where Wycliff had been falsely accused of the murder of his wife, Pamela, when Grace's telephone call snapped right through her concentration. Grace said she just wanted to know for sure Molly didn't miss Sunday School this morning because she was depressed about Harold not coming back.

"So, are you thinking about taking a trip like I suggested?" Grace asked.

Molly propped the receiver against her shoulder. She closed her eyes and wafted away, her blue chiffon caftan billowing around her like gossamer wings propelling her from room to room. She smiled down at Harold, asleep in his chair beside her bed as she bent down to tuck a brown woolen afghan around his bony knees. Blowing a kiss to Lawrence on the chaise in the sun room, she patted Phillys' healthy green leaves before floating back to the den to wait for Wycliff.

"I asked if you are going to take a trip," Grace's voice interrupted. "Are you listening to me?"

"A wing chair and foot stool would be nice by the fireplace, don't you think so, Grace?" Molly could almost smell the burning logs. "And I must remember to buy a tin of Earl Grey."

"Molly, what on earth are you babbling about? I'm doing my level best to get you off to see some of those wonderful places you're all time dreaming about."

Grace's voice still droned in her ear as Molly let the receiver slide back into its cradle and reached in the sack for the last book, *Ecstasy In Istanbul*. Her eyes widened.

One silken caress of Ismere's lips against hers, and Fatima was consumed by uncontrollable fires of passion. The blue waters of the Aegean lapped around their feet. In the distance, the call to evening prayers hovered above the minarets silhouetted in moonlight, their shadows reaching like slender fingers toward heaven. Fatima tossed back her long ebony hair and entwined her arms around Ismere.

Molly dropped the book in her lap and leaned back against the cushions on the bed where she sat. Prayer rugs, bazaars overflowing with silks and glittering jewels–it all seemed so far away. She sat upright, letting a thought filter through her mind. If she gave Goodwill her mama's old upright piano that was in the parlor, there would be space for an ottoman. A long, low ottoman covered in red crushed velvet trimmed with gold ball fringe would be perfect for Ismere.

She plumped her favorite needlepoint cushion under her neck, smiling as she reminded herself that after her nap she must stop again by Harold's chair.

"Harold," she planned to say, "I do believe you have been right all along. There's nothing out there that's better for me than what I got right here at home."

POTATO SOUP

I am flying home, on my way to keep a promise to Josh. Coming back is hard; except for Aunt Serena, there is no one to welcome me. My dad and I have not spoken since that night ten years ago. *"You goddamn queer."*

The Golden Gate bridge has vanished below in the fog. A sudden spark of sunlight bounces off the silver wing as the 747 circles, climbs. My foot touches the brown leather case stashed under the seat. Zippered inside is the squat brass urn half filled with ashes.

The plane seems to hover for a moment before it slices an opening through a layer of pink clouds. I loosen the seat belt, unfold a copy of THE MORNING MONITOR and find the story on page 5.

The death of artist Josh Callahan has been attributed to AIDS, according to a report released by the coroner's office. Callahan, a native of Texas, has lived in the San Francisco Bay area for the past ten years. His work has recently received acclaim of major art critics. Callahan's ashes will be flown to his home town of Varona, Texas. Accompanying the remains will be his long-time companion, Max Murdoch. Murdoch has been unavailable for comment.

My flight ends at Dallas. I have a couple of choices of how to get from here to Varona; catch the next Greyhound or rent a car. So I pick up a set of keys at the Hertz counter and head the dark green Escort through the maze of concrete ramps circling the airport. The road winds past Texas stadium, Home Of The Texas Cowboys.

"You can be a pro quarterback in five, six years, Max. You got the magic, the glory shining right down on you. There's a scholarship, for Christ's sake, begging for you at the university."

"It's not what I want, Dad."

"The hell it ain't. You been bustin your butt with a football since you was six years old."

"But it wasn't for me; it was to please you. I want to study drama, maybe get a TV series. Josh knows this guy out in California who can help me get started."

"Good God, Max. That Callahan kid got kicked off the team this year because he's a fairy. He's trash and his sister's a whore, so you sure as hell ain't going with him to California."

A hard gust of wind whips the car sideways, and I tighten my grip on the wheel. Uncle Clint, Aunt Serena's husband, used to claim that the wind out here blew the horns off his pet billy goat in the winter of 1936. I watch the last rays of a pale November sun dart between the branches of the scrub oak trees on both sides of the road. I turn up the radio. Willie Nelson is singing On The Road Again. It will be dark by the time I get to Varona.

It was dark the night Josh and I left. We hitched a ride as far as Wichita Falls with a farmer hauling a load of Jersey cows. Between us we had $10, the clothes on our backs and half a promise of a place with Josh's friend in Los Angeles.

"I'm scared, Josh." *"Hell, I ain't,"* he said. *"Ain't we the best football players in the history of Varona? Didn't Coach wait until after the championship game before he kicked my ass off?"*

"But we're not playing ball now," I said. *"My old man threw me out tonight when he found out about us."*

"Well, shit," Josh said. I been called worse things than queer and I been kicked out of better places. Five, maybe six, before I moved in with my sister back there in Varona."

I force myself not to think about it now, and I don't want to think about tomorrow, about the urn and what I promised Josh. All I want to do is check in at the Wind Song Motel, if it is still in business. What I need is a shower and some sleep.

The night manager gives me a howdy, how yew? when I walk up to the desk. I say fine and I want a single for one night. He takes my Visa.

"You're that—you're Bull Murdoch's boy that went off to California, right?"

"What time's check-out?" I ask.

"Actually, I just remembered we don't have no singles left." He starts to hand my Visa back to me, holding it by one corner. "Now there's this place two blocks down and three over. You might try there."

"I'll take what's available here and pay you for your trouble." I reach in my wallet and watch his milky blue left eye twitch when I lay the bill down in front of him.

"Check-out is at 11 prompt." He is still looking down at the 50 on the counter when I put my Visa back in my wallet and walk away.

I turn up the heat in the room and sit down on the side of the bed. Light from the lamp on the table sketches a circle of yellow around the telephone. Funny, I still remember Aunt Serena's number without having to look it up.

"You hot foot it on out here," she says as soon as I mention I'm at the motel. "I got a spare bed."

I tell her I'll be getting up early tomorrow and no need to disturb her.

"You gonna scatter Josh's ashes at the football field like he asked you to do?"

"On the fifty yard line, where he caught the pass that won the championship game."

"Want me to come with you?"

— 45 —

A lump gathers in my throat. "I guess it's something I have to do by myself, but thanks."

The frost-seared grass crunches under my shoes. At mid-field it is patchy brown, trampled flush with the red clay earth. A rooster crows in the backyard of the cinder block house across the street, another answers down the road. The sky takes on the glow of a hazy winter dawn.

I open the urn, let the greedy wind snatch the first handful of ashes. It catches the next, then the next. Josh slips through my fingers like silver rain until there is nothing left.

There is nothing left.

Aunt Serena is waiting for me. She perches on a Lone Star beer crate in the hall outside my room at the Wind Song. She holds a red and white crocheted pot holder wadded around a terra cotta bowl. Droplets of moisture glisten under the glass cover where wisps of steam curl and wait to escape.

"I figure it's a day for potato soup," she says.

As soon as I open the door, she ducks inside. She sets the dish in the center of the fake marble table beside the bed, turns to me and holds out her arms.

Aunt Serena is the closest I've had to a mother since Mom died when I was nine. She used to have fights with my dad about her taking me to live theater or the ballet when a touring company came anywhere near the Varona area. Dad, who had been All American and probably the best running back University of Texas ever had, said he wanted me to grow up to be a man, not some twinkle-toes sissy.

He made me take the gun. "Every boy's got to learn how to hunt," he said. The rabbit stopped, sat trembling on the side of the grassy slope. "Shoot," Dad said. "Goddam, pull the trigger. Now." We were close to the rabbit. Its long ears flicked back and forth, its eyes like wet brown marbles.

"No," I said and tried to drop the rifle. Dad grabbed my hand,

squeezed my finger hard against the trigger. The rabbit jumped straight up before it fell. Its feet began to twitch, then it was still. Blood trickled out of its nose and mouth.

I gather Aunt Serena close. The top of her head comes halfway up my chest, her hair curls in white little noodles around her ears, fans out in a thin, smooth coverlet over the crown. She smells clean, like a new bar of Octagon soap.

We stand without speaking until she turns away, blows her nose in a loud honking sound. I motion her to the only chair, a fading maroon recliner with a jagged rip in the seat.

The day has turned crisp and blue with bright sun glinting on the window, but I flick on the overhead lamp to highlight her face. It is angular with high cheek bones, still beautiful at 80 years. I see her glance at the jacket draped over the top of my open suitcase.

"I thought you might be staying on for a few more days," she says, referring, I know to a letter I wrote to her just before Josh died. I told her what he had asked me to do, and I said I would like to spend some time in Varona but I didn't want to see Dad. We don't have anything to say to each other, I said.

Looking at Aunt Serena now, I remember how much Josh liked her reply. Her letter spoke, in a spidery downhill handwriting, about how she wished Josh and I still lived close by, especially now that Uncle Clint was gone. She was proud I was going to get a part in the new TV series, she said, and then she mentioned that Josh's sister had moved away without leaving an address. At the close of her letter, she talked about Dad.

"He's changed in the last year or so," she said. "Of course, he is still a horse turd, but Bull has mellowed and he don't know what to do about it."

Josh said he wasn't surprised about his sister; he liked the part about horse turd.

I've never figured out how Aunt Serena with her salty language and feisty ways is considered socially acceptable here in a town that's a little dot on the Texas map between Wichita Falls and the Oklahoma border. I suppose the God-fearing citizens are in awe of her because she still rides a strutting Appaloosa in the annual July 4th Panhandle Day Parade. Or maybe it is because she was married for sixty of her years to Clint McGuirk, cowboy, oil field roustabout and ex-Texas Ranger who claimed he helped gun down Bonnie Parker and Clyde Barrow.

"Recall how your Uncle Clint always brought home a pocket full of candy corn when he came back for a stake-out?" Aunt Serena asks. She reaches across the table and peaks under the lid on the bowl. I want to say to her that my life is cloudy and gray, like potato soup.

My dad used to make potato soup the way Aunt Serena does, with chopped carrots for color and fat black peppercorns for flavor. We were eating it that night after my high school graduation. Dad and I sat down and filled our bowls from the big yellow crock in the center of the table. He said the room was getting dark, so I got up and turned on the light.

I remember standing at the window, watching the summer shower that had started to pelt against the glass. When I sat down again, I decided it was as good a time as any to tell him about Josh and me, spell it out for him.

He let me finish before he said a word; he just sat looking at me. It was like someone had taken soap and hot water and scrubbed all the color off his face.

A jolting clap of thunder rattled the dishes in the corner cupboard as Dad lunged at me from across the kitchen table. The soup crock zigzagged in a yellow blur along in front of him until it tipped over the edge and careened past my chair. His fist caught me on the jaw, and the next thing I knew I was sprawled on my back halfway across the room.

"You was always bringing that kid here, like he was a stray critter you took in. Now you're one of his kind." He stood over me, the purple cording of veins pulsing in his thick neck.

"Now ole Bull's got himself a fairy for a son and I'd rather not have a son at all. So you just go, get on out of here. I never want to lay eyes on you again. You goddamn queer."

"Folks learn a lot as the years go by," Aunt Serena is saying.

"Somebody–I guess it's the one who's stronger–somebody's got to make the first move. Did I ever tell you about the time I found out your Uncle Clint had screwed a woman down in Mexico?"

"You never did," I say.

"Well, it's a long story and I won't go into it all, but I finally had to decide if a one-night stand was worth throwing out a good marriage.

"Clint McGuirk was a handsome devil, but I will say he was not a womanizer; I'd have never stood still for that. He just got drunk one night, got to feeling horny and so he headed for a whorehouse." Aunt Serena squares her jaw like a fighter ready to deliver the big punch. "When he told me about it, I left him, and I said to him that if he even so much as thought about trying to win me back I'd shoot off his balls and use them for fish bait."

She sits with her fingers laced together in her lap. Sunshine streaks through the open blinds and paints slats of light across her hair. Her face, in the years since I've seen her, has taken on the weathered patina of a rich old hand-tooled saddle, but her eyes still remind me of the centers of the black-eyed Susans that bloom wild every summer across the road.

"I never knew you left Uncle Clint," I say.

"Oh, we made up after awhile. Sometimes a hurt has to ripen and mellow for a time before it stops aching," she says.

I look at her and see she is stronger than all the cowboys and roustabouts and Texas Rangers lumped together.

She asks what I am going to do until it's time to start shooting the TV series. I say I haven't thought that far ahead. I don't let her know how my gut balls up in a knot because I'm thinking about what if the tests at the clinic are bad this time. Or the next time.

Aunt Serena unzips her red canvas purse. Her fingers shuffle under a blue can of hair spray and fish out two of her silver spoons wrapped in aluminum foil.

"Let's get at it before it gets cold." She smooths the foil into a square, shoves a spoon in my hand.

The soup is still warm, spiced hot with black pepper. Dad used to make it that way for me; it was how I liked it. Maybe it's the sting of the pepper, the sudden taste of home that starts me thinking about him now.

"How is he?" I ask.

"Not so full of piss and vinegar like he was."

I see her eyes follow mine when I glance down at my watch.

"Lots of fence mending can get done before you have to catch that plane." She reaches out and pats my hand.

I stir the potato soup and watch the orange bits of carrots come swirling to the top. I have not seen the brightness of their color until now.

MY GREEN THUMB

*M*y neighbor is a thoughtful person who shows up at my back door with a plate of cookies or a card on special occasions. When I answered her knock on a sunny spring morning, there she stood, clutching a small flower pot filled with sprigs of ferns and ivy. In the center was a white orchid in full bloom. It wasn't Easter, too early for Mother's Day, and Lordy, had another birthday snuck up already?

"A friend gave it to me. I didn't have the heart to tell her every flower I try to grow just shrivels up and turns brown." She thrust the pot in my hands. "I know you have a green thumb, so I'm giving it to you."

"I'll take good care of it," I hoped my voice didn't sound smug. "And if you should want it back --- "

"Oh no, it's yours. The darn thing would just up and die on me."

So I read the directions on the little tab stuck inside the pot: fertilize lightly, water sparingly. After a few days, some of the ferns and sprigs of ivy started to wilt, turn yellow. Not enough water, I reasoned, but the orchid's petals were pristine white and without a blemish.

It was members of my family who broke the bad news to me.

"The ferns and ivy are the only live plants in the pot," my husband announced after close inspection

"Your orchid is a fake, Mom," My daughter agreed.

For the first time I brushed my fingers across the blooms, blossoms lifeless as pieces of parchment. I HAVE FERTILIZED LIGHTLY AND WATERED SPARINGLY A PLASTIC FLOWER!!!!

Next time I saw my neighbor in her back yard, I thanked her again for the flower arrangement—it seemed the right thing to do.

"I'm so glad you are enjoying it," she beamed. "Is the orchid still blooming?"

"It is just as beautiful as the day you gave it to me."

"I knew you had a green thumb." She smiled and waved and I just didn't have the heart to tell her.

SHOPPING CART RAGE

*I*t was the first day of the new super market's Buy-One-Get-One-Free Sale.

Shopping cart traffic was nearing gridlock by the time I maneuvered my way to the potato chip and cracker isle. I was on tiptoe, searching the top shelf for a package of no-fat nachos when a voice behind me snapped, "You must think you own this whole store."

As I turned and saw an angry face that matched the man's voice, I realized my cart was blocking him.

"Sorry." I moved to one side. "I didn't hear you come up."

"You could have looked before hogging the whole space, lady. Ever try opening your eyes and looking?"

My first impulse was to give his cart a swift accidental bump, but then I thought hey, it's not worth a hassle.

I gave up looking for nachos, picked up my two boxes of crackers and moved on like a meek little ninny. Before losing sight of him, I took a glance back. He was wearing tan slacks and plaid jacket, tie loosened at the neck; his dark hair and moustache salted with gray gave the appearance of the stereotype business person. Maybe he was late for an appointment or was just having a bad morning, I decided, so why let it ruin my day?

A half hour later after worming my way through canned soups, dried beans and pasta, I spotted him again. This time he stood outside the lane of traffic as though waiting for someone. The aisles were jammed, carts going past him, jockeying for the shortest line at checkout. As I started around him, he pulled in front of me and stood blocking the way.

"Hope you're not in a hurry," he muttered.

Seeing this mature man suddenly transformed into a little kindergarten bully, clicked a picture in my mind. I saw my own small son at the age of three or four, pitching a falling-down-in-the-floor temper tantrum. The times it happened was when he was tired, so I would put him to bed for a nap. When he awoke, his world was usually sunny again.

So without thinking of what the consequences could be, I reached out and patted the man's arm and said, "I think you need a nap." Two women standing nearby laughed; the man looked at me without saying a word.

"Well," I told myself, "I guess I got my point across."

After I had walked outside and carted the bags of groceries halfway to my car, I felt a trickle of sweat start to run down my back. Newspapers carry stories most every day about an angry person who goes berserk over a trivial incident, whips out a gun and starts firing. *What if I have connected with a certified looney and he is carrying a gun or knife and he is waiting for me somewhere in the parking lot?*

I looked behind me as I started to walk faster. He wasn't following me. Maybe he was still back inside the store, or was he lurking somewhere ahead of me? My eyes searched the sea of parked vehicles; mine seemed at least a mile away, so nothing to do now except try to appear calm and hope he had gone.

The thumping of my heart had begun to slow as I unlocked the car's trunk. The man was nowhere in sight. Just as I bent down to pick up the first heavy sack of groceries, a voice called, "I think you need some help." When I looked back over my shoulder, I saw he was almost beside me.

Before I had time to prove how loud I can scream, he said, "Look, I owe you an apology. Just because I have some personal problems doesn't give me the right to take it out on you, so let me lend you a hand."

"No thank you."

"Okay," he took a step back. " I just waited around to say I'm sorry."

I finished transferring the last plastic bag of canned soups to the trunk of my car and accepted his offer to park the shopping cart in the return area. Before driving away, I said I hoped things would soon get better for him.

"I'll remind myself to take a nap," he said.

I shook his outstretched hand. We both smiled.

A GOOD DAY ON THE MOUNTAIN

*U*ntil today, only old Jocko McLeod from the farm down the road had come close to discovering her secret. He had seen her coming and going and had once asked why she climbed to the top of the mountain.

"To talk–to check on the blue bird nest." Addie had good days when she thought to hold her tongue, and she had bad days when she babbled. Her encounter with Jocko had come on one of her good days. She was pleased that she remembered to tell only half a truth, the part about the blue birds. "The male has disappeared," she explained. "Haven't seen him in three, four days."

"Blue birds don't nest higher'n half way up the crest." Jocko squinted at her, then at the craggy peak in the distance. "Don't know your real reason for going, but it's a dangerous climb to the top of Bear Claw Mountain for a lady of your years. Begging your pardon, mum."

"It's my business," she had snapped, muttering under her breath, "damn old meddler, always spying on me."

But now, Shawn knew her secret, the reason why she came here to the bluff at the top of old Bear Claw. She did not mean to tell the boy, but he had followed without her seeing him. As she squatted to sit on the big moss rock on the edge of the overhang, she was startled to hear his voice behind her. Today was one of her bad days, so when he asked, she blurted out the truth.

"Why do you come up here to sit by yourself, Grandma?"

"To talk to Grandpa Will." Addie could have bitten off her tongue. She had forgotten to think before she answered.

Her forgetfulness caused most of the problems she'd had since Will died last spring. One day when David, Shawn's father, came by to see her, he found her coughing and fanning the smoke from over the sink where she had flung the charred pan of beef stew.

"Must be getting old," she said. "I don't recollect turning on the stove."

He cradled her for a moment in his arms. "Mom, come stay with us until–for awhile."

"Anybody can forget about a pan on the cook stove." She pulled away and stood back to look up at him.

"I know how much the land meant to Dad, that you want to stay in your own home, but–"

"I'm not aiming to go live in the city and I'm not selling mine and Will's place, if that's what you're fixing to ask me to do."

When she got through summer without heat stroke and winter without setting fire to the kitchen, David stopped nagging her to leave the farm. He came on Saturday afternoons, driving the short distance from his house in Mountain City, to do the outside chores. Sometimes Addie saw him down by the north fence talking to Jocko, and she was sure he was asking the old bugger to keep an eye on her.

David's wife Evie called Addie on the telephone every Wednesday morning at eight o'clock and started the conversation with: "How are you this lovely morning? (no matter if rain was coming down in buckets) and "Now you let us know if you need anything, you hear?" Lately she and David allowed Shawn to spend an occasional week-end with Addie. A good sign, Addie told herself. They think I still have gumption enough to look after a ten-year old boy.

She crept out of the house earlier than usual this morning while Shawn still slept. He won't wake before sunup, she thought, picking her way across the back field where the new crop of weeds covered the stubble of corn stalks. The sky still held a sprinkling of stars when she reached the blue bird box. Will had nailed it to the scrubby pine tree growing at the half way point up the mountain. She heard a stirring inside the box. The female is turning her eggs in the nest, she thought, but where is her mate? There was still no sign of him roosting on his customary branch of the overhanging limb.

The slope turned steep and rocky beyond the pine tree. A dangerous climb to the top, Jocko had said. Addie stubbed her walking stick deep into the ground as she moved upwards, sometimes clinging with her free hand to a sturdy bush or sapling to hold her balance. When she reached the peak, she saw the first glow of morning stretched across the horizon.

"I think that damn hawk ate my blue bird, Will," she said, gathering her skirt around her bony legs as she stooped to sit on the rock. She heard a twig snap behind her and turned to see Shawn, his gray eyes puzzled, watching her.

"But how can Grandpa Will hear you if he's dead?"

"Well, he is and he ain't." Addie wished there was a way to make him understand.

"Does he say things back to you?"

She nodded and patted a place beside her on the stone. Shawn scooted across the damp surface, pulling his knees under his chin, and Addie put her arms around him. They sat without speaking while the sun etched a red-gold rim of fire above the tree line.

"Promise you won't tell? Your daddy will think I'm crazy and he'll take me off to live in the city."

"But why do you want to stay here alone, without Grandpa?"

"Grandpa is here. We can't see him, that's all."

"If you was to come live at our house, could he come with you?"

"Oh no," she shook her head. "He won't leave the mountain. I talk to him during church and when I go places like the grocery store, but he is never there." She pushed back the boy's blond hair and laid her cheek against it. "Bear Claw's been ours for more'n fifty years, and neither of us aims to leave it. Do you think I'm crazy, Shawn?"

"No ma'am."

"It's time to go," she said. "I'll make pancakes for breakfast."
On the way down, Shawn found a handful of blue feathers heaped behind a dead tree stump.

"Suppose it was a fox ate him, Grandma?"

"Most likely the hawk," she sighed. "Poor little blue bird. He never got back to his nest."

She remembered the evening last spring when Will didn't come home and she went looking for him down by the creek. She found him lying on the far bank, the cork of his fishing line drifting with the wind. At first she thought he was napping but his body was cold when she gathered him against her. It was a warm day in April, she recalled.

Jocko honked the horn and leaned out the window of his truck. "I'm driving into town. Need any supplies?"

"Reckon not." Addie set her broom down on the bottom step of her porch. "Got my groceries on Saturday."

"If I see David anywhere around, I'll tell him you're well."

She finished sweeping, then went back inside to get her sunbonnet. She was glad Jocko was gone for the day. He had not questioned her again about the mountain, but she was certain he continued to watch her. He wouldn't let his shirt tail touch his butt before he went tattling to David, she told herself.

The clouds that brought rain last night had drifted away. Addie felt the mid-afternoon sun warm against her back, and she took precaution to walk slowly on the wet pine needles. She had allowed herself enough time to talk with Will and to leave the mountain before darkness made the slippery trail more treacherous. She was halfway up the ascent when her walking stick snapped in the middle, causing her to stumble. The ground seemed to vanish from under her feet.

Addie heard voices. She thought one of them belonged to Will, and she tried to focus her eyes through the blur of colors around her. A sharp pain grabbed at her ribs.

"I can't thank you enough for bringing her here." She realized she was hearing David, not Will, talking to Jocko. "The doctor's coming to look at her."

"I should'a come to you the first time I seen her shinny out on top of the bluff," Jocko said. "She sets up there and talks like there's somebody with her, only there ain't."

Addie remembered now. She had fallen and Jocko found her, brought her to David's house instead of taking her home where she belonged. A hot water bottle and some liniment would have fixed me up good as new if he'd kept his nose out of my business, she thought.

"You could have laid out there all night if it wasn't for Jocko," David scolded when he came to say goodnight. "He went out looking for you when he got home from town and didn't see lights in your house."

"Rubbish," she snorted. "Only had the wind knocked out of me. I want to go back to my own bed."

"We'll talk about it in the morning," David said.

But she saw the look in his eyes and knew.

Addie began to lay her plans. She would find a way to get back to Will and the mountain.

"The bed is very comfortable," she told David after a few days. "My old mattress is full of lumps." (She hoped God would forgive her for lying. There would never be a better bed than the one she shared with Will.) She pretended to go along with Evie's pickey ways of changing the sheets twice a week, of checking to see if Addie put on clean underwear every morning. She would smile and say, "Old ladies forget. We need to be reminded."

By the time Addie's bruised ribs healed, Evie and David had brought her personal belongings from the farm. She laid her silver comb and brush on the dresser and put Will's Bible on the night stand beside her bed. She wished she could talk with Will, but she knew she must keep her wits about her and wait. Wait for the right time and a good day.

One evening when she was playing Monopoly with Shawn, David came and stood behind her chair.

"Mom, I've had an offer from a fellow who wants to lease the home place," he said. "Can we talk about it?"

"Sounds like a good idea to me," she answered, not giving him time to elaborate.

"You're content here with us, aren't you?" Addie was sure she heard the sound of relief in his voice.

"I'm very comfortable," she nodded, counting out her money to buy a hotel on Boardwalk. *My plan is working well. David believes I've left the mountain.*

Evie was helping David and Shawn pack fishing gear in the station wagon one Sunday morning in early September.

"We're taking Shawn and his friends to the lake," she called to Addie. "We'll be home before dark."

Addie felt her body tremble. Is it the right time, she wondered. Will it be a good day?

"Want to come?" Shawn asked.

"I'll just nap in my room while you're gone; you have a good time." She put her arm around his shoulder, touched his hair with her cheek. "I love you, Shawn."

As she watched the car disappear past the curve in the road, Addie remembered that she must call Jocko. Although he was to blame for her having to leave Will and the mountain, she would have to put aside her grudge now that she needed him.

"Good to hear from you," his voice was loud in her ear. "David tells me you're a regular city slicker these days."

"I'm wondering if you will do a favor for me. I need a ride out to my place today, and if you could come and fetch me I would appreciate it."

"Well, sure. I'm at loose ends."

She had counted on it. This morning when David and Evie were planning the fishing trip, she knew Jocko would not be working in the field on Sunday. Her mind raced ahead to what she would say to him.

"I won't be asking to be brought back," she explained. "The children will stop by for me on their way home from the lake." Lying comes easier than the truth these days, she mused.

She was waiting at the curb when Jocko arrived.

"I saw David yesterday at the barber shop," he said after he helped her get seated beside him. "He didn't say you'd be going out to your place today."

"I reckon he didn't think to mention that I need to get the rest of my things together." She kept her voice calm.

"If you want help packing—"

"No, there's nothing heavy to lift."

"I may go over to my daughter's house for awhile." He stopped his truck in front of Addie's porch and turned to look at her.

"Now you're not going climbing, are you?"

"I learned my lesson," she smiled and felt her heart begin to pound. Addie waited for half an hour after she heard him drive away, waited until she was sure he wasn't going to turn around and come back. (Jocko couldn't be trusted not to come sneaking back to spy on her.) .

She stopped at the blue bird house to clean out the old nesting materials, to make room for the new family who would come next spring. The sun flicked patches of light through the branches overhead and she saw the timid speckles of red and gold daubing the leaves in the thickets below her.

She was breathing hard when she got to the top of the bluff.

"City life has made me soft as mush," she scolded aloud as she sat down. The wind sent whispers along the spine of Bear Claw Mountain, and she leaned forward to catch the sound of her name.

"Addie," the voice came to her from below the jagged ledges where the trees stood squat and dense. "Come, old girl."

"It's a good day, Will." She stretched her arms out to meet him.

The only sound was the stirring of the grass heralding the approach of a pair of rusty brown lizards. They crawled across the rock and lay together, sunning themselves in the spot where she had sat.

YOUR EYES AIN'T BLUE NO MORE

*J*hey marry in spring time when the air is crisp and honeysuckle sweet, when leaves on dogwood trees are pale green ballerinas pirouetting in the wind. I, Michael, take you, Jennifer. Sun rays fling handfuls of diamonds across stained glass windows. She looks into his eyes, sees them blue as the April sky beyond the church steeple; the next breath catches in her throat.

They move his things to her apartment because it is closer to where they work. When summer comes, they go camping in the North Carolina mountains, skinny dip under a waterfall at midnight. "I love you," he says.

During the long autumn evenings, they come home and eat pineapple and peanut butter sandwiches. He stacks two on a paper towel and lopes across the room to sit on the couch in front of the TV. She perches on a white wicker stool at the kitchen window, watches the west splash fiery pink, fade to lavender gray. When the light goes, she turns on the lamp she bought on sale at Sears. It traces a yellow-patterned square on the black Formica table.

She comes to burrow beside him. He takes the last bite of sandwich, switches the channel to the football game.

"I had a really busy day," she says. He doesn't answer, leans forward to watch the ball sail between the uprights. She sees his eyes as dull reflections of color flashing across the screen.

She moves back to the wicker stool at the kitchen window, presses her face against the pane. Her eyes search the twilight for a patch of sky. A piece of blue November sky.

THE GREAT HEAVENLY LIGHT

*I*f I could have spoken, I would have told them to stop the pounding and pumping up and down on my chest. There was George and Sharon Anne. George was yelling, "Breathe, Mallie! Come on now. Breathe!" and I believe he expected me to get right up and do it because he said to. Sharon Anne's face was white, her eyes wide. She looked more like a scared little girl than a grown woman.

I wanted to ask the bearded paramedic to please stop blowing his short puffs of breath into my mouth and to put my teeth back in so I could tell George and Sharon Anne to calm down. But at this point I was beyond communication with the living. The pain ran up my left arm and shot out the back of my neck just as George and I sat down to supper. Sharon Anne , who dropped by after work to return the blue silk scarf she borrowed, was walking out the kitchen door as I slumped down in my chair. That's all I recall until I saw this glow that seemed to light up a dark tunnel in front of me. It moved slowly, growing brighter, sparkling like diamonds as I reached to touch it. The Great Heavenly Light! Just as I knew it would be when my time came.

Now isn't it strange that George and I had previously discussed this very subject one night?

I said, "Listen to this, George. Here's a story about a woman who believes the same way I do."

George lay all the way back in his Easy Boy recliner so he could nap through commercials during a re-run of the Alabama and Auburn football game. I sat on the sofa across from him and switched on the reading lamp to look at the new issue of TV Guide.

"A mini-series is coming next week," I told him. "the true life story about a lady who had been pronounced dead and then brought back. She tells about how she saw this bright light that seemed to beckon her to come. It was all so peaceful and beautiful, she claims."

"Bullsh–," George muttered. He said the whole word, which I can't bear to repeat, but it is his reply to anything he doesn't agree with, and he certainly doesn't go along with what he calls religious hocus-pocus.

"Oh, I believe we will all see the light," I told him gently so he wouldn't think I was trying to start an argument. "We will all, saint and sinner, see it when the end comes, George, just before we cross over. Mama called it The Great Heavenly Light. You may recall that her sister Nettie experienced it briefly when she thought she was dying after her hemorrhoid operation."

"Wasn't it Nettie that spotted two UFOs during the July Fourth fireworks show?" George turned his head to look at me over the top of his glasses.

I knew right off he was itching to start something, so I went back to reading the rest of the article to myself. There are two subjects it is pointless to try to change George's mind about. One is Life After Death and the other is The Feminist Movement. I keep my mouth shut on both topics, but Sharon Anne has butted heads with him about the rights of women ever since she wasn't allowed to try out for the grammar school football team.

George comes from a family of heathen, poor man. His mother was baptized Presbyterian but never darkened the door of the church in all the years I knew her. His father was an atheist, right up to half an hour before he died, which was when he repented and accepted Christ. But I have no doubts he did it in time to get into Heaven. Look at the thief on the cross. Didn't Jesus say to him, "This day shalt thou be with me in Paradise"?

Speaking of days, I married George right out of high school in the days when a girl didn't need a brain if she jiggled when she walked. I learned by trial and error about how to pound a piece of round steak with the edge of a saucer to make the meat tender, and if I threw a pair of red socks in the hot water wash, George's white underwear turned pink.

I figured I didn't have one thing going for me until the morning George pointed out my special talent. Sharon Anne, born with colic, cried for six solid weeks and I was up with her day and night.

"You are a good woman, Mallie." he said when he woke me to fix his breakfast, and George is not one to pass out the compliments.

So there it was, like a sign from Heaven. I was good at being good!

From that time on, it just seemed to snowball: each day I was more determined to become a better person. No matter how much I wanted to smack a blister on Sharon Anne's bottom when she fell down in the floor and held her breath, I ignored her tantrums. And after I called George to breakfast three times and he kept on piddling with his stamp collection while loose scrambled eggs turned leathery and cold on his plate, I smiled and whipped up another batch. Not one time did I raise a hand to Sharon Anne or my voice to George.

I tingled with pride when Lottie McCracken from my garden club said things like, "Mallie is such a good person." I'd think about it, wake up sometimes in the night and picture my big mansion in Heaven, wondering what it would be like if I led a perfect life right up to the end of my days. Occasionally I saw myself in repose, my face like an alabaster carving. A blanket of pale yellow roses lay across the bronze casket, sprays and wreaths of carnations and Lilies of the Valley banked the walls and over-flowed into the foyer. Mourners waited outside because there was no room in the sanctuary.

Of course, I never mentioned a word about this to George or Sharon Anne; they would think I was morbid, but I wasn't. I figured a first-class funeral was a worthy goal to shoot for, and becoming a good woman was easy for me. But it was different for Sharon Anne. She never tried to keep peace with George by agreeing with him or just holding opinions to herself. They hardly spoke to each other for a year after she got married and decid-ed to keep her maiden name.George said it was insulting to her husband;

she said changing her name would be demeaning to her and make her feel like a non-person.

To get back to the subject of my funeral, I have to admit I was sick about the arrangements. I went along with burial in mine and George's double plots at Rosewood. George gave me the place facing the road, although I would prefer the one beside the big oak tree, but it was what Sharon Anne came up with later that upset me.

She and George were in the selection room at Peterson's Mortuary and she said to him, "Now Daddy, it just wouldn't be Mama."

"Mallie never expressed her wishes to me about how she preferred to be put away." He turned to look at Sharon Anne. "Did she ever give you her opinion about it?"

"So far as I know, she never had an opinion of her own," Sharon Anne shook her head, "but I can't imagine she'd want to be laid to rest in a double walled $6,000 bronze with embossed silk lining."

"Well, maybe you're right," George finally admitted after Sharon Anne kept hammering away at him about how she is sure I would want everything kept plain and simple. "Mallie would probably rather I give that money to Children's Hospital, have her name engraved on a little plaque over the drinking fountain or something like that." He wiped his eyes and by the time he and Sharon Anne got done simplifying, I was down to a tacky gray model just a cut above the composition board model out on display.

So, there was nothing I could do but pray nobody would take notice of a chintzy coffin when it was covered up with flowers.

Did I mention flowers? I couldn't believe my ears when I heard it, not half an hour after George and Sharon Anne left the funeral parlor and went back to our house. The place was crawling with the neighbors carrying pecan pie in one hand and chicken casserole in the other. And in came Sharon Anne saying, "if anyone is planning to send flowers, I believe Mama would prefer donation to charity." Next thing I knew, Lottie McCracken, corresponding secretary of my garden club, got on the phone. After half an hour, she turned to Sharon Anne and announced that Elizabeth

Barrett Browning Poetry Society and also Ruth and Esther Chapters of Eastern Star would join Busy Diggers Garden Club in giving to worthwhile causes.

"The heart association, I suppose," George said when Sharon Anne asked him to name a charity the money should go to. "That would suit Mallie just fine, I'm sure. We all know she wouldn't want us to waste it on flowers when it could be put to good use. Mallie never asked for nothing for herself."

"She was a wonderful woman," Lottie said and took another bite of whatever it was she carried around on a flimsy paper plate that trailed crumbs all over my clean carpet.

Sharon Anne looked up at George when he walked over to stand beside her in front of the fireplace. "Poor Mama," she sighed. "I think she worked so hard at being good she never really enjoyed being alive."

He slid his arm around her shoulder and then she hugged him while they both had a little cry.

I suppose holding the funeral in the middle of the week when it was raining cats and dogs made a difference in the size of the crowd. George should have set the service on a week-end when people would be off from work. But he had it on a Wednesday and in the main chapel of the funeral home where all the long rows of empty seats stuck out like sore toes.

I looked a sight. The casket lining and limp rayon pillow under my head didn't do a thing for me; off-white, of all things, as if I wasn't already the shade of ashes because the cosmetologist was real stingy with her rouge. Although I appreciated the usual she-looks-like-she-is-sleeping comments when people filed by to look at me, I was shocked when Lottie McCracken whispered to her sister that she never felt comfortable around someone who oozed goodness–that's what she said: "Mallie just oozed goodness at the monthly meetings." Then some of the girls from Eastern Star came up and put in a few remarks, which I won't even stoop to repeat.

George and Sharon Anne ordered a spray of orange gladiolus and some snapdragons of all colors, so that was as close as I got to that blanket of yellow roses on top of my casket. A piddling little basket of Lilies of the Valley was delivered at the last minute from Sharon Anne's real estate office. The gas company where George worked until he retired sent a wreath of bronze mums, but I can tell you the place looked bare. I never thought I would see the day when I left this world with fewer flowers than Eddie Sullivan got. Eddie was the used car dealer down on the main highway. Everybody knew he set back the odometers on half the vehicles on his lot, but last month at his funeral the smell of roses and carnations was so strong it made my eyes water.

Well, live and learn. I no sooner got up here when the Angel In Charge Of Housing Facilities said he was assigning me to one of the less luxurious mansions.

"We have a shortage from time to time in our top of the line models because most of our new arrivals demand the best, but we know we can count on you not to make a fuss." He gave me one of those dipped-in-honey smiles.

"Bullshit," I said.

RIDE A WILD PINTO TO RUBY FALLS

*T*his morning when Kate looked out her kitchen window at the sun rays flickering on the yellowing leaves of the birch tree, she found herself thinking again that she was glad summer was almost over. She had said to Hunter last night when he awoke and found her sitting up in bed, arms wrapped around her long bare legs and her knees drawn up under her chin, "I can't believe I am actually looking forward to getting back to a room full of fidgety eight-year-olds and mountains of arithmetic papers." Suddenly, without knowing she was about to do it, she started to cry. He moved closer to her, pulled her down beside him on his pillow and held her while she sobbed into the soft brown mat of hair on his chest.

"It's all so senseless, her dying because a crazy drunk-- "

"I know, babe," he whispered, "I know."

He fumbled for the switch on the reading lamp and she squinted at the stab of brightness, her eyes blue pools as she shook her head when he asked if she wanted to talk.

"I'm okay, really. Just one of those nights when I can't turn off my brain, thinking about Pop rattling around in that big old house." She yanked a tissue out of the box on the night table, then settled back on Hunter's arm. "I don't think he is coping very well alone. He looks like a scarecrow these days, just puts on any old thing he finds in his closet and would probably exist on bologna sandwiches if Mrs. Deerfield didn't occasionally bring him a plate of fresh turnip greens and corn bread."

"Have you asked him again, now that he's had time to think it over, if he wants to come stay with us?"

"You heard him say *no* when we were at the house two weeks ago. He seems so preoccupied, Hunter. Do you think he's keeping something from us?"

"I don't know what it would be," Hunter said. "He seems to be working through his grief as well as can be expected, but I found him to be in pretty good spirits when I talked to him. He told me he grew enough Silver Queen corn this year to feed half of Cullman County."

Kate, dressed now in faded denims and navy T-shirt, brushed a long strand of brown hair from her face and sighed as she turned away from the window. The uneasy feeling she'd had last night when she couldn't sleep still picked at her mind as she dialed her father's number. He would grumble about her spending money to call him again so soon after she had talked with him a couple of days ago. She asked him to come for a visit while she still had a week of vacation left. "I'll take you out for egg rolls and green tea at our big new shopping mall," she promised.

"That town's done outgrew my taste," he complained, "and I don't like driving all that way down there on the interstate. All them big trucks whizzing by and blowing me off the road."

"Pop, it's just a little over fifty miles. I'll come pick you up and take you back when you're ready."

"Too much trouble."

"Well, think it over. I'll call later and see if you have changed your mind," she had said.

She let the telephone ring a dozen times before she hung up. He might be working in the garden, she reasoned, not wanting to remember what his neighbor, Mrs. Deerfield had told her.

"That poor man is lost without your mother," Mrs. Deerfield said. "He walks past my house every blessed morning on his way to sit out there at the cemetery."

Kate's thoughts were interrupted by the sound of the postman's Jeep chugging up the street. She ran to the mailbox at the curb and stood with one hand shading her eyes from the mid-day sun as she looked at the plain white envelope with her father's return address in the upper left corner. He hates to write, she thought. It was always her mother who wrote to her when she was away at college. Until today, the only letter she'd had from him was two pages of words to comfort her when Patches died. He had written to assure her that the old horse she's grown up with went peacefully and without pain at the end.

"When I bought Patches for you, your mother fought me tooth and nail. I agreed he was too spirited for such a little girl," his letter said, "but oh, how you wanted that black and white pinto. I can still see you now, hair flying in the wind as you galloped him across the pasture. I think you were the happiest child in the world that day, Kat, and I was sad because it was the first step in letting you go."

She cried then as she read it, a woman suddenly turned child again. Afterwards, she packed the letter away in the blue satin-covered box where she kept the newspaper account of the death of her mother, killed in a car wreck last winter while driving home from the grocery store.

Wondering why her father had written to her again, she felt last night's uneasiness return. He is telling me something too painful to talk about on the telephone, the way he told me about Patches. Her legs trembled as she walked back toward the house. She tore open the envelope, dropped down on the back stoop and, smoothing out the single page read:

Dear Kat,

I know we talk on the phone every few days and you will think it strange that I write to you, so I'll get on with what I have to say. I have met a woman. Her name is Sara Bright Star Muldoon. She has a dab of Cherokee blood, the rest Irish. She's more than twenty years younger than me and she is teaching me the bossa nova, at least that's how I think you spell it. She is the exercise instructor for the Senior Fitness class up in Huntsville and that is where we met. I may be in love with her. My best to Hunter.   Pop

"At first I thought it was a joke," she said to Hunter at supper. "I just sat there on the stoop, looking at the words and waiting for the punch line. Numb is how I felt, how I still feel."

Her eyes were puffy and streaked with red. "My God, you don't suppose Pop is having an affair with this–whoever she is?"

"He's a grown man." He glanced again at the letter Kate had laid beside his salad bowl. "I think it's a good healthy sign, the old juices starting to flow again."

Kate pushed her chair away from the table, carried the dishes to the sink and began sharp little jabs at the pasta and cheese starting to crust on the plates. "Well, why can't his juices start to flow with someone like sweet little Mrs. Deerfield? She's a widow and I'll bet she'd marry him in a minute if he asked."

"Maybe he doesn't want to marry sweet little Mrs. Deerfield. Maybe he wants to shack up with Sara Bright Star Muldoon."

"That's gross, Hunter. Really gross. I'm going up there first thing tomorrow and find out what's going on."

Next morning Kate turned down the dirt road beside her father's mailbox. She steered the car's front wheels around a familiar pothole and swerved sharply to miss a box turtle lying like a pile of greenish-brown dung in her path. Past a long row of chicken houses, she beeped the horn when she saw Mrs. Deerfield hoeing in a bed of marigolds and blue ageratum at the edge of her yard.

The old woman brushed her short gray hair from her face and smiled when Kate stopped the car and jumped out to give her a hug.

"You are looking more like your mama every day." She patted Kate's cheek with a hand rowed with thin blue veins, then raised it to shade her eyes as she peered down the road. "I see your papa's truck is back, so he's home now from wherever it was he tore out to a while ago."

"I decided to walk in and surprise him," Kate said. "Maybe cook lunch and wash and iron his clothes."

"Well, it may be a good idea if you call next time before you come because---"

A glossy apple-red Corvette, dust billowing behind it, slid past the flower bed, turned at Kate's father's driveway and parked beside his blue Ford pickup.

Mrs. Deerfield puckered her lips into a tightly pleated "O" and nodded in the direction of the lithe figure unfolding from the driver's seat. "So, like I was going to say, sometimes he's got company these days, and yonder it is right there."

Usually Kate tapped a couple of times on the kitchen door before she opened it and called, "Hey, Pop, it's me," but now she walked around to the front , between the lavender hydrangeas blooming on each side of the stone steps, punched the bell and waited.

Laughter rang from somewhere in the house, her father's deep guffaw mingled with a rich throaty chuckle. She jabbed the button again. The sound of her heart pounded in her ears and for a moment she thought of running back to the car, driving away as fast as she could.

"Just a minute. Keep your shirt on." The laughter was still in his voice when he flung open the door, his eyes wide with surprise at the sight of her.

"Kat!" he exclaimed. "What are you doing, coming in the front way like Sunday company?"

"I don't mean to intrude," she said, starting to turn away. "I really can't stay."

"What are you talking about? Of course you'll stay." He pulled her inside and kissed her, holding both her hands in his. "Sara, come see who's here."

Sara came from the kitchen, moving with light, sure strides. She wiped her hands on a paper towel before she stuffed it into the pocket of her jeans–designer, size three, Kate judged, with hardly extra room inside for a paper towel. She was prettier than Kate had imagined, with a mane of shiny black hair swept back from her face and tied with a red bandana, her skin like milk-white porcelain. Holding out a long slender hand, she said, "Richard has told me so much about you. I'm dying to get acquainted."

"He told me you are teaching him the bossa nova. I can't imagine his wanting to learn it. He and Mom never went dancing." Kate glanced at her father.

"I guess there never seemed to be time for dancing. Too busy making a living," he said.

"Richard has a great sense of rhythm," Sara said. "He is my star pupil."

Kate saw the smile that lit his face, and for the first time today she looked, really looked at him. His gray hair and mustache were barber trimmed. His eyes, behind a new pair of steel-rimmed glasses, sparkled blue as the ageratum in Mrs. Deerfield's yard. He wore neatly pressed dark gold slacks and a green knit shirt, open at the throat.

"How do you like it ?" he asked, tugging at his breast pocket as though reading her thoughts. "Got one of them little alligators on it, see?"

"You look nice, Pop. I'll bet Mrs. Deerfield came over and did your laundry. That was one of the reasons I dropped by today; I thought you might be running out of clean clothes."

"Nope. I washed and dried and pressed the creases in my pants, and it's a pretty good job, if I do say so."

"But I thought she was, you know, helping around the house."

"To tell the truth, Kat, Mamie Deerfield and I had a sort of falling out. She called me a silly old coot when I joined the physical fitness class, so I said she was a bossy heifer set in her ways. One thing led to another."

"Another reason I came was to see if you will go home with me today. We need to have a good visit before I have to go back to work. School opens next week."

"I appreciate the invitation, honey, but I'm going to–is it Tuesday we're going, Sara?"

"To Chattanooga," Sara said. "Bright and early Tuesday morning."

"About twenty of us are riding the train up there, and Sara's taking us to Ruby Falls. You know, Kat, I've never been there. For thirty years I've been reading them SEE RUBY FALLS signs painted on top of my barns, and I think it's high time I go take a look."

"Richard and I are meeting some people for a picnic in the park later today. Stay if you'd like," Sara said to Kate.

Their eyes met for a moment, Kate's blue and troubled, Sara's dark and dancing as she looked up to smile at Richard. Kate saw the sunlight glint on the earrings that dangled like a pair of golden spurs against Sara's long neck.

She said, "Hunter is waiting for me at home. I really do have to go, Daddy."

"You haven't called me by that name since you were a little girl."

"I know. I was thinking back, remembering when you were afraid Patches was too spirited for me. Now I'm the one who is afraid. Will you be all right?"

"Do you love me enough to let me try my wings? Who knows, Kat? Maybe I can fly again."

"I love you." She kissed him at the front door, swallowed the hard lump in her throat. "Be happy, Pop."

A lazy cloud of dust trailed behind her when she looked in the rear view mirror at her father standing in the door, one hand on Sara Bright Star Muldoon's shoulder, the other waving his customary goodbye to her. She could still see the smile on his face.

Mrs. Deerfield's hoe stood propped against a pine sapling like a weary field hand waiting for the first clang of the dinner bell. The bright patch of marigolds and ageratum grew small and pale in the distance as Kate drove slowly, dodging holes and ruts. Halfway back to her father's mailbox, she saw the turtle again. She stopped the car to study his movements, his long snaky head bobbing up and down as he bumped along.

She leaned back, listened and watched the end of summer with wind whipping the blades of browning corn stalks in the fields and sunlight spilling down on the still green leaves in the sweet gum tree.

The sound of hoof beats echoed in her mind. She closed her eyes and felt the surge of the wild pinto once more as she sprang to his back and he galloped away, her long hair flying in the wind.

LIMERICKS

Miss Nude Pageant Queen from Nantucket
Tried to cover her boobs with a bucket.
But the judges avowed
No buckets allowed!
And so the poor girl had to chuck it.

****

A fast-stepping dude from Niagra
Slyly swallowed six shots of Viagra.
In the heat of desire
His zipper caught fire,
Now his gait is a slow shuffling swaggra.

MY LOVE AFFAIR WITH THE BIG YELLOW BOWL

*I*t was a wedding present, this big yellow bowl. My mother's Sunday School class at the Buffalo Gap Nazarene Church pooled their nickels and dimes to buy it at a time when money didn't grow on cactus plants in the yard at our West Texas rented apartment. How I loved it, perched on the orange crate in front of the window, bright as desert sunshine and piled high with dime store wax apples topped with bunches of purple glass grapes. Some day we would have a home of our own and the bowl would have a place of honor on our dining room table. Some day.

During the World-War-Two years, it shared our gypsy life style while packed in a cardboard box or stuffed in a corner of the back seat of the old green Pontiac as we bumped along from job to job over two-lane highways into Louisiana, Mississippi, Arkansas, Florida and finally Alabama. When we settled in our first permanent house in Homewood, I set the bowl in the middle of a spit'-n-polish new dining room table, heaped with bona fide red Delicious apples and a couple of bananas draped over one side.

Years later when the luster began to fade, it served a less glamorous but useful purpose in the kitchen. Sometimes I filled it with a mountain of fluffy mashed potatoes or maybe a hot beef stew for a Sunday night supper until one day I spotted the discolored cracks that had begun to zig zag down the sides. Soon I saw a chip here, a nick there along the rim.

And so its glory years faded, but today it still leads a meaningful existence as the pet's water bowl. It rests on the kitchen floor, an oasis for the thirsty parade of dogs who march in and out of our lives. Once, I recall, it caught the eye of a visiting child crawling towards it. He managed to lap a couple of sips before his mama let out a shriek and grabbed him back by his diaper.

The bowl has lived four lives over six decades--- homeless nomad, dining room centerpiece, kitchen table standby and finally, an humble but cherished water container for the animals. Lately, I see the end is near, for I keep looking at a suspicious brown spot, a crockery cancer spreading along its mottled bottom. Any morning I expect to walk into the kitchen and find it split in half, DOA, its life's blood puddling the floor.

But I have loved it well, my big yellow bowl.

THE ANNIVERSARY KISS

On their Golden Wedding anniversary, Gramps finally did what Grandma always told him to do: he kissed her ass.

My father's five siblings and their families, who had settled from Limestone County near the Tennessee border and south to Mobile, came to my grandparent's home on that sunny, mid-March day to celebrate the occasion. No party, the grandparents had said; not a big dinner where everybody comes traipsing in with green bean casseroles and potato salad. Just cake and coffee.

Chairs from the kitchen and front porch had been lined up along the wall and beside the sofa in the high-ceiling parlor. Everybody talked at once–Eva's adhesions following her gall bladder surgery, Claude's decision to run for mayor of Prichard, and don't the hills around Birmingham look lonesome since they chopped down the trees and built shopping malls?

Pretty soon one of the older grandchildren climbed the rickety stairs to the attic and brought down some 78 rpm records of Glenn Miller's Greatest Hits Of 1940, along with pictures of Gramps in his WW2 Navy uniform. A couple of daddy's brothers drifted outside with their boys to pitch horseshoes in the freshly swept yard where not a blade of grass marred the hard-packed earth. Gramps and Grandma were country folks. No citified green lawn for them.

Aunt Bonnie was the last to arrive. Her bright blue skirt billowing in the wind, she scrambled out of her car with the cake she had ordered from a fancy gourmet shop specializing in party desserts. It was a snowy sheet of confection with spun sugar roses blooming in each corner and the words "Happy 50th" in gleaming gold letters across the center.

"A bakery cake," Grandma snorted. "You can't spare no time these days to make it yourself? Bakery stuff is dry as dirt. Not fit to put in your mouth."

Aunt Bonnie shot me a wink, our secret, soul-mate code. We have both been on the receiving end of Grandma's short fuse and sharp tongue, as had all her children and most of the neighbors.

Grandma had her good qualities. She taught Sunday School class, visited the sick and bought boxes of chocolate mint cookies when the Girl Scouts knocked on her door. The smell of her vegetable soup bubbling on the stove and corn fritters sizzling to shiny brown in a kettle of hot grease turned a blustery day warm and fuzzy. But as my dad pointed out, there were two things you learned about Grandma: she could start an argument with a lamp post, and she would always have the last words. If the disagreement was with Gramps, the last words were: "If you don't like the way I do things around here, kiss my ass."

So, on this day when the family had come together to mark the half century of their marriage, I looked out at the sunshine bouncing off the windows and found myself hoping it was a good omen, wishing for nothing more exciting than a few drops of coffee spilled on the new hooked rug in front of the sofa.

Gramps and Grandma put on their Sunday clothes. She wore her brown silk dress with the ecru collar. The spring scent of laundry starch still clung to Gramps' shirt and his shoes were spit-shined.

"Now if everybody will just keep their seats, me and my bride will go out in the kitchen and make ready the cake and coffee," he said.

When Gramps had closed the door behind him, my dad rolled his eyes. "Want to bet how long it will take for things to start popping in there? I'm saying five minutes, tops."

In less time than he predicted, Grandma's voice ballooned above the buzz of our conversation as she came flouncing out.

"Martha Ann," Gramps stood directly behind her, "Will you please come back in here for a minute?"

"No I won't, and if you don't like the way I cut that dried out cake, you can kiss my---"

She never got a chance to finish before he was suddenly in front of her, standing straighter and taller than I had ever seen.

"Annie," he said, "you have promised me that kiss for nearly fifty years. I know I should collect it in private, but if everybody will excuse me I believe I will do it now."

Before she could move away, he flipped her skirt with the agility of a young athlete, bent low and planted a big noisy kiss on Grandma's scrawny little rear end.

My husband was transferred out of town soon after the celebration, but letters from my mother told me Grandma was still as feisty as ever.

"What Gramps did never fazed her," Mother wrote. "She still tells him to kiss it."

Gramps lived for another ten years, dying a few days short of their sixtieth anniversary. Three weeks later, Grandma joined him. I came back for their funerals, both held in the little church where they took their marriage vows. The preacher said God had reunited them, just as they had been in life. They are together once more, he said, with each other throughout eternity.

After the brief grave side eulogy that followed, I stopped to drop a rose on Gramps' grave where two of our neighbors, their backs to me, stood talking.

"Well," one said, "I suppose they really are with each other by now."

"Yes," the other sighed, "but isn't it a blessing God granted the old gentleman three weeks of peace before she got there?"

THE WISTERIA TREE

*A*unt Spunk is calling from my house, her voice escaping in little raspy puffs through the telephone. "Grandpa has locked hisself in his room, and he says he'll blow the head off the first German spy that opens the door."

I have arrived at Ed's Animal Clinic late for work, stalled in a traffic pile-up on the interstate where a door on the back of a poultry truck flew open and dumped a load of white Leghorn chickens, squawking and fluttering down the middle of the road..

Ed, who is never late, clutches a squirming black and tan puppy under his arm. He shoots me one of his I-can-use-some-help looks as he hurries in the direction of the boarding kennels.

Aunt Spunk is saying, "I tuned in the Good Morning Show and there was our governor, shaking hands on national TV with one of them German people. That's when Grandpa Mac threw the remote at the screen, went wheeling off to his room and locked the door."

"Aunt Spunk, the key is hanging on the hook by the sink." I prop the receiver against my shoulder and smile at the tall blond woman who stands at the check-in window. She holds a cat cage in each hand, cranes her neck to look down at her watch. She doesn't smile back at me.

"Well, I'm not opening that door," Aunt Spunk hisses. "I hear him in there right now, diggin' out that old pistol from under his mattress."

"Just keep calm," I say.

The words have become my mantra since Gramps declared that the Mercedes-Benz automobile plant in Vance, Alabama is a Nazi spy camp.

I try to keep Aunt Spunk happy because she is all that stands between my grandfather and the Golden Sunset Years Nursing Home. She is not really my aunt; she is the neighbor who came from her house down the street to sit with me when I was a little girl. Now she comes to watch after Gramps while I am at work in Tuscaloosa, about an hour's drive from where we live in Greenoaks.

"Oh Lordy! I hear him clickin the trigger!" I can almost see Aunt Spunk's gnarled little fingers clutching at her heart as the quiver rises in her voice. "I better call Chief Eddins."

"Take a deep breath and listen to what I am saying, Aunt Spunk. The gun is harmless unless he drops it on his foot." I have to shout above the yowling that's going on while Ed picks #7 bird shot out of a hound's rump. "You just sit down and have one of the diet Pepsis I put in the fridge this morning. Gramps will come out when he needs to pee. You know how weak his bladder is."

I hang up, realizing she has forgotten what happened back in November at the annual Veteran's Day celebration. Chief Eddins stopped the parade in the middle of Main Street and yanked the clip on Grandpa's Luger pistol, the one he took from the body of a dead German soldier in June of 1944.

Gramps was the guest of honor for this special day when Greenoaks pays tribute to its war heroes. The chief had given him permission to wear the gun holstered on his belt. So, a couple of days before the event, I checked the pistol and discovered Gramps had it loaded and ready to go. I removed the shells and put them in a new place, an empty coffee can on a top shelf in the pantry; I would not know until later that he found my hiding spot and reloaded.

He rode in the red, white and blue Ford convertible that day at the head of the parade, faded old khaki cap set squarely, shoulders erect as he snapped salutes to the people lining the street in the crisp November sunshine. Chief Eddins, mounted on his prize chestnut mare, cantered beside the Greenoaks High School marching band about midway back in the procession.

With a thunderclap drum roll and a clash of cymbals, the young musicians swung into the first bars of Stars & Stripes Forever.

"Yaahoo!" Gramps yelled. He rose to a half crouch, fired off a round of shots in the air and began to chant, "D-Day! D-Day! Bring on the girls!"

The chestnut mare whinnied, reared up on her hind legs and took off, riderless, between the filling station and the post office across the street. She was running in circles around the A&P parking lot when the tuba player, who is also first string wide receiver on the football team, was able to rein her in.

Chief Eddins slapped the dirt from the seat of his new uniform and blew his whistle to stop the parade. He limped up to the convertible, took the gun from Gramps, pulled the clip and dumped the one remaining shell in his shirt pocket.

After the excitement died down, Grandpa said he was sorry he caused a commotion, but he wished he had hit one of them German spies. The chief invited him to come down to the station house sometime to go target practicing, and Gramps apologized for calling him a draft-dodging bully. (Chief Eddins was rejected for active duty in Viet Nam because he had flat feet and a touch of asthma.)

We inherited each other, my grandfather and I, five years ago. I had just ended a bad marriage, and that same year my parents died in a car crash on their way home from a vacation in Florida. So I came back to the house where four generations of McCains have lived and died.

Gramps lost the lower part of his right leg and a small piece of his sanity in World War Two when a barrage of mortar fire from the hedgerows cut him down on Normandy Beach. He doesn't talk about it, except sometimes when he cries out in the night. I go to him, touch his sweat soaked forehead and know he has gone back to a time too horrible to share with me.

"Is it the month of June?" he asks, and I say, "You can sleep now. June was a long time ago."

"Well, no matter." He reaches for my hand. "The sombitch took my leg, but I blew him clean out of them bushes and I got his gun."

Sometimes, especially when the air turns sweet with the first taste of spring, he wheels his chair to the front porch and we sit together after supper. He identifies the calls of the blue jays and cardinals, the robins and mockingbirds who flit in and out of the holly bushes for a bedtime snack of bright red berries. He dozes off in the middle of a sentence, his eyes still half open.

After the birds have flown away to find a nest for the night, I feel locked inside the silence. It is unbroken except for the occasional toot of a passing car's horn, muffled barks of a dog, the airplane flying so high I barely hear the roar of engines. I watch the vapor trail zippering the sky behind it and I think of places like New York City and London—Broadway on opening night, the sounds of Big Ben's chimes. I think of Paris, City of Light.

Light. Greenoaks has two traffic lights and a blinking yellow caution at the highway intersection on the edge of town.

Past the vacant lot across the street I see the tree. It has been growing there ever since I can remember. It is an elm, I think, its scraggly limbs have long since been robbed of meaningful life, strangled by the thick ropes of wisteria vines wound around them. But the tree still stands, defying the final throes of dying as it waits each year for spring to drape its branches in cascades of lavender blossoms.

"She'll bloom out early this year," Gramps' voice predicts. He has awakened and his glance follows mine to the wisteria tree.

I don't know how to break the news to him that I have invited Kurt Werner to eat supper at our house on Saturday.

"No siree bob tail." Aunt Spunk throws up her hands when I hint that maybe she would be willing to cook up a pot of collard greens for my guest. "I don't plan on being in the same house with Grandpa Mac when one of them German people sets foot inside the door." She squints at me over the brown rims of her eye glasses. "Where did you come up with a fool notion like that?"

I explain that Ed, my partner at the animal clinic, and I have joined a group of other business people to form the Citizens Southern Hospitality Group.

"It's an idea someone thought up to make the families and the workers from the Mercedes-Benz plant feel more comfortable while they are here in America." I launch into a part of the speech I have prepared for Gramps. "Some of the group are taking the wives shopping at the malls in Tuscaloosa, inviting the kids over to play; things like that. I decided to ask someone to come to supper for some traditional home-style cooking."

"I never thought I'd live to see the day." Aunt Spunk makes a shame-shame clicking sound with her tongue.

I tell her his name, that his home is near Stuttgart. "We seem to have several interests in common. He reads mystery novels, loves country and western music, and he dabbles in painting. I've talked with him a few times during lunch; he knows how Gramps feels about his people."

"Well, you best come up with a better idea than bringing him home with you," Aunt Spunk says.

Gramps sits in his chair while he listens to the six o'clock news; he argues with the anchorman when he doesn't agree with what he is reporting.

"Mighty fine," he says and I look to see that he twirls the stem of his glass, his eyes reflecting the mellow glow of the evening drink of wine. I have filled it to the top tonight.

"We're having company for supper tomorrow." I take a deep breath and tell him that his name is Kurt Werner and he works at the Mercedes-Benz automobile plant.

"He's a German man," I say.

Gramps glares at me for a moment, then begins to laugh as he slaps the stump of his leg with his left hand. The last sip of wine misses his mouth, zigzags in a red streak down the front of his shirt.

"Well, now," he chortles. "You're smarter than I give you credit for. You bring that spy in here, sweet talk him, and then you git him cornered behind the cook stove, and I'll shoot him down like a possum in the chicken house."

Aunt Spunk is at the back door early Saturday afternoon. "Collards," she explains and lets me peek under the lid of the kettle she balances on a red-flowered pot holder. I see there are two big chunks of fat back floating in the murky green potlikker.

She is wearing her Sunday apron, the blue-checked gingham with eyelet ruffling around the bib. She looks over at Gramps sitting in his wheel chair at the head of the table.

"How's he takin' it ?" She starts whispering close to my ear, then I see her eyes grow wide. The barrel of Grandpa's Luger pokes from under the blanket that doesn't quite cover the stump of his leg.

Kurt arrives promptly at six. He carries a square, flat package and a basket of red geranium. I invite him to come back to the kitchen while we finish preparing the food

Gramps moves closer to the table. Aunt Spunk keeps looking down at the gun and drops the pitcher of iced tea she carries to fill the glasses.

"Keep calm." I repeat the mantra when she follows me to get the mop. Kurt has set the geranium in the center of the table and snips one of the flowers to tuck in the bib of Aunt Spunk's apron. He unwraps the package he brought, a painting in a narrow gold frame, and lays it in front of Gramps.

"The scene is a meadow where my family once had a farm," he explains. "Cows grazing in a meadow near a brook; a peaceful sight and quite good, I think. It was painted by my grandfather."

Gramps doesn't look.

"I never knew him," Kurt continues. "He was killed in the war. My grandmother once told me how he died a hero in the hedgerows of Normandy."

Aunt Spunk rattles the silverware as she arranges and rearranges each knife, fork and spoon beside the plates.

Kurt says, "Let me help get the food to the table." He comes to stand beside me at the kitchen stove.

The ceiling light glints on the barrel of the Luger but Gramps doesn't make his move.Aunt Spunk gets a case of hiccups, the way she does when she is nervous, and then I hear the squeaky wheel on his chair. He pushes away from the table, stops, reaches back to pick up the painting. He says he isn't hungry.

It is Monday.

Kurt sends a postcard from Stuttgart. He has gone back for a two-weeks vacation. It is good to be home again, he writes, and underlines the words. He says he has missed the bustle and bright lights of the cities.

While I wash the supper dishes, I get a telephone call from Ed. He tells me he found a home for the two black kittens somebody dumped at the back door of the clinic; he asks if our date to go bowling tomorrow night is still on. I say I'm glad about the kittens and yes, Aunt Spunk will stay to sit.

We go out on the porch for awhile, Gramps and I. He doesn't mention the painting Kurt gave him. Not yet. His face is peaceful, I think, except for an occasional twitch along his cheek when the breeze fans his hair like sparse strands of cotton on the crown of his head.

I look across the street and the breath catches in my throat. The rays of the sun are beaming directly over the vacant lot, glittering like thousands of lights. I think they have come to dazzle me, come to dance on the lavender blossoms of the wisteria tree.

GETTING TO KNOW HER

*N*ews of her mother's death came at sunset. She remembered later its red-gold rays flashing against the window panes as she fumbled for the key, then hurried inside. A tall blond woman with wide-set gray eyes, Amelia came home early from the office and, while still outside her front door, heard the faint ringing of the telephone.

A quick intake of breath betrayed the calm tone of her sister's voice, and Amelia knew, knew and still she asked: "when did it happen?"

"Oh God, ten minutes ago, maybe–she wanted some note paper from the gift shop." Nola's words tumbled out as though racing for the nearest exit. "I left her propped on pillows, picking at the food on her supper tray, and when I got back to her room I thought she had fallen asleep."

"Is there anyone with you?"

"She still had a bit of strawberry jello in her spoon, and I stood there thinking: *you didn't clean up your plate*. Amelia, I left her to die alone."

"Nola, let me speak with one of the nurses."

A faint crackling sound, then, "Amelia, Ralph Gorman here."

"Oh?" pausing to remember, "Of course, Reverend Gorman. How kind of you to come to Nola at this time."

"I sat with your mother for awhile this morning and happened to be visiting another of my parishioners in the room across the hall when Martha slipped away," he said. "Her going was a blessing, my dear. God's mercy."

In the background, Amelia heard the small routine that had become familiar to her—the starchy rustle of bed linens, a squishing of rubber soles on polished tile floors. Their sounds trickled through the telephone lines and spilled over her fingers as she said yes, it was a blessing. God's mercy. She thought of the sticky sweet perfume of the potted gardenias on her mother's window sill, blossoms white as death against the glass. Her mind pictured the sweep of blond hair in the wig that always seemed tilted off center, perched on the Styrofoam head next to the bedside telephone.

"I'll give you girls a moment of privacy." Ralph Gorman again, then Nola's voice, "Are you okay to drive down tonight? I mean, there's really nothing–"

"Honey, it is two hours from Fort Worth to Oakdale." Amelia cupped the receiver against her shoulders while scribbling a reminder to stop at the cleaners for her blue silk dress. "I've not unpacked since I saw you last week, so I'm on my way soon as I let a couple of people know I'll be out of town. Hey, I love you."

"Love you, too." Nola's voice dropped to a hoarse whisper. "Amelia, why would Mama give Ralph Gorman a letter to mail after her death?"

"A letter?"

"To Marilee Browder."

Amelia steered the gray BMW through the lingering twilight that, in summer, seemed to hang suspended along the flat stretch of interstate. The heat shimmering over the city during the long afternoon had played tag with the sun, followed it across the low rim of hills. She brushed a stray wisp of hair from her face, and through the open windows felt a slap of wind trailing the scent of white prairie clover. The fragrance nudged at memories of open fields, the wild thorny blackberry patch behind the house where she grew up, the musty smell of the rope swing her father hung from a limb of the big live oak. The father who, until his death, nourished the daughters with his love, had always shared himself with them.

Martha just slipped away. God's will. The brief peace that swept over her after hearing Reverend Gorman's voice was replaced now by an aching sadness. Since childhood, Amelia felt awkward in her attempts to crack an invisible barrier that seemed to surround her mother in a fragile cage of glass. Now she would never know, really know, this perfectly manicured and always in control little woman who embraced the small town of Oakdale with her charity, yet held her own family at arm's length.

The hum of tires on the pavement seemed to echo Ralph Gorman's words. God's mercy. Lights from the traffic whizzing toward her began to weave and float across her vision. Her head ached and her eyes burned. She eased off the accelerator and pulled over to park on a grassy spot, to sit motionless behind the wheel, fingers pressed hard against her temples.

Mama's letter to Marilee, the widow of Will Browder who was papa's business partner. Thirty years since Will Browder parked his new tan Buick in the back of the Sears customer lot, covered the upholstery with a plastic sheet and a heavy bath towel and shoved a .44 caliber pistol in his mouth.

What happened that evening began to light scenes in her mind. She saw herself at the age of five, Nola at four. They were at home, huddled in their favorite hiding place in the dark cubbyhole beneath the stairs, waiting to begin the game their father always played with them at supper time. The smell of cinnamon drifted past her nose. Had he made rice pudding?

Mama's voice from the kitchen: "Jeffery, food is on the table."

"Now where can those girls be? Where are my girls?" Papa poking his head inside a pantry, squinting behind Mama's big roll-top desk in the corner. Calling their names in mock dismay while they clung together, holding back their giggles until the right moment to jump out at him like jacks-in-a-box.

A loud pounding at the front door, Papa's brown slippers scurrying past the secret hiding place. A crying sound, muffled words seeping down the hall, someone saying his brains splattered all over the front seat of his car; the bullet about blew Will Browder's head away.

Papa's feet walking back, slowly past the secret hiding place to the spot where Mama's shadow loomed, frozen in the angle of light that glowed from kitchen to dining room; their silhouettes meshing to speak in low whispers.

"Girls, come out this minute and wash your hands and faces." Mama issuing the command.

Papa, suddenly kneeling beside them under the stairs, folding them in his arms, long and thin as marsh reeds. No, oh no, he said. He would never blow his head away like Mr. Browder did. He would always be here to love them.

He kept his word until last winter when he died from injuries after a fall from his horse. He said to Amelia that morning when they were alone in his room: "I can't seem to put my finger on exactly when it was your mama left us, but one day a stranger came to live inside her. I don't know why, but I believe her heart and soul just packed a bag and ran away from home."

His eyes, his whole face, seemed so out of focus that she patted his hand until he looked up at her with a flash of his old smile and said she should pay no attention to what he sometimes prattled about these days; the damn medicine made him talk crazy.

Amelia, recalling her shattering grief at his death, felt a pang of guilt tonight as she merged again with the gleaming ribbon of headlights and drove, dry-eyed, to begin making arrangements for her mother's funeral.

When it was over, after she looked back as she left the wind-blown cemetery where baskets of lilacs shriveled from pale lavender to brown in the mid-day heat, Amelia sat across from the Reverend Gorman at her mother's dining room table. Nola, wearing an off-white linen sheath that accentuated her tan, chose the wine brocade-covered chair beside her sister. The soft hum of a ceiling fan accompanied the swishing rhythm of summer dresses as three of Martha's neighbors tiptoed in to clear away the platters of ham and fried chicken, the bowls of fruit salad topped with little pastel dots of marshmallows. Brown crusted cobblers lined the heavy oak sideboard where earlier Amelia stooped to smile at the scrawled message "Ella Lou's Scratch Angel Food" taped to the side of a crystal cake plate.

"Rest their souls." Ralph folded the white linen napkin and gazed over the top of his steel rimmed eye glasses. "My association with your parents went back many years before either of you were born, but until Martha confided in me during her last hours, I never knew what a truly courageous person she was. Her strength was remarkable."

Amelia leaned back and closed her eyes against the streaks of brightness, the dog days of August heat slipping uninvited through the blinds on the long row of windows facing the west. Oh yes, Mama, you were courageous. *How much courage does it take to say I love you to a pair of little girls? And by God, you were strong. You saved the polar bears at the zoo, kept the county orphanage solvent. You, personally, shoveled dirt to plant the twenty-eight poplar trees in the city park without chipping a nail.*

"I see Nola often, what with her teaching here at the university." Amelia jumped at the sound of Ralph's voice as he turned to her, "but it has been too long since you and I had a chat. I was sorry to hear about your divorce from Roger, but happy to hear you've been made a partner in a Fort Worth law firm."

"Junior partner," Amelia smiled, "and Roger and I are still good friends. He has promised to come with me to Nola's wedding at Christmas time."

"We plan a simple affair, and, of course you must perform the ceremony." Nola's dark brown eyes leveled on Ralph's face. "So now I think we should talk about the letter."

Amelia heard the squeak of the back door close behind the last neighbor leaving the kitchen. The dishwasher made a loud click at the end of the cycle, and as though the sounds of the house conspired to prevent an awkward silence, the grandfather clock in the foyer began to strike.

"Four o'clock already." Ralph nodded as he checked his pocket watch. "Yes, we must discuss the letter. Martha meant my mailing it to be confidential, but I clumsily dropped it on the floor as Nola entered the room."

"What possible connection could Mama still have had with Marilee Browder?" Amelia asked. "Marilee moved away soon after the her husband died and I have no idea where she is, but you have her address and you know what was in the letter, don't you?"

"Martha left Marilee's address with me, yes. I never read the letter, although I do know the reason she wrote it. You will probably find that information tucked away in Martha's records, but come by my office at the church any time if I can help fill in the gaps." Ralph winced slightly as he got up from the chair and tucked his glasses in his pocket. "I'm getting ancient; everything hurts when I sit too long."

The storm that threatened in late afternoon blew in at dark. Ragged streaks of lightening crisscrossed the sky above the stand of scrub oaks outside their mother's bedroom windows.

"We might as well start here." Nola rolled back the top on Martha's cherry wood desk and swivelled the brass lamp so that a trail of light spilled over her close-cropped hair and down on a neat stack of papers. She opened a drawer and sat looking at the compartments arranged with note pads, stamps and rubber bands.

Amelia walked across the room to draw the draperies, stood for a moment to watch how the rain unfurled a watery tent over the black outline of the trees. When she turned back to Nola, she saw the red leather-bound book in her sister's hands.

"Mama kept a journal," Nola said. "Did you know?"

"No. How could I? I never snooped in her things, even when we were kids. Did you?"

"Are you serious? I keep looking over my shoulder tonight, waiting to be turned into a pillar of salt."

Amelia felt her throat tighten as she held out her arms to Nola, the way she had done so many times, and after their tears were spent, she said, "Maybe there's nothing here at all, just her day-to-day thoughts. Should we wait until tomorrow when we've had some sleep?"

"Who can sleep?" Nola had already flipped through several pages. "Strange. There are no dates on any of the entries."

Tornado warnings were out the morning Jeffery left for Oklahoma City. It was a big contract he was going after, he explained, and when I asked he said no, Will Browder was not the one to handle it. Will was to stay and look after the business here.

I suppose it was around eight o'clock that evening when I heard Will's car turn in the drive. Looking out the window, I saw that he had run over the curb and across the triangle of my boxwood. By the time I opened the door, he stood on the stoop waving his arms in the direction of the flattened shrubbery.

"I'll replace your posies." He grinned an apology while he explained he had dropped by to see if the storm had knocked out the electrical power. "I promised ole Jeff I'd look in on you, so would a cup of coffee be too much trouble? It's been one hell of a day; Jeff gone, plus we got this new secretary with shit for brains."

I smelled the whiskey on his breath, but knew he usually took a drink or two before he left the office in the evening.

"It's thoughtful of you to drop by," I told him. "I'll brew a quick pot. Marilee will be wondering what has become of you."

"On second thought," his voice came softly from behind me as I walked toward the kitchen, "make it three bourbons neat. Two for me and one for you, little darlin'."

I felt him watching, felt his eyes like the lense of a camera clicking each movement I made; the slur of his words sent a warning chill up my spine. As I flipped the switch on the pot, I started to reach for the telephone on the wall next to the oven. Will asked what was I doing and I said "I'm calling Marilee to come drive you home."

"Well, goddamn." He tossed back his head and laughed, and I saw the big purple veins cording his thick neck. "Just like my nagging wife. You don't look like Marilee, but you sure as hell must be. That's a poem. Get it? Marilee–must be."

He came at me, grabbing my arms, pinning them against my sides. Will was a big man, well over six feet tall; his grip was like claws of a tiger tearing at my flesh. He whirled me around to face him, and I saw the fevered brightness of his eyes, the pulse throbbing in his temple. As he pulled me to the floor and fell on top of me, I kicked him as hard as I could. I had scrambled up on my hands and knees when the blow across the back *of my neck sent me spinning into darkness.*

Later, I don't know how long it had been, I felt him tearing at my dress, ripping away my underwear. The weight of him pumped up and down, crushing me, his hand clamped over my mouth. The foul odor of his breath was a sour wind filling my lungs. And when he had finished, he didn't speak. The room was silent, so still as though death hovered and time was suspended. .

I pressed my face against the cool whiteness of the tile floor and heard the sounds of him standing above me–the rustle of fabric as he tucked in his shirt, whiz of the zipper, rattle of belt buckle. I lay without moving until the door slammed, until I no longer heard the echo of the grating spin of tires in the graveled drive. No one must know, no one must know.

Three days later when Jeffery walked into the house, I was prepared to tell him I bruised my cheek when I stumbled over a root in the back yard. But I saw the gray sweaty pallor on his face and my heart seemed to flutter and stop. I thought he somehow found out what had happened, but he explained he became ill soon after leaving Oklahoma City. He drove home in severe pain.

Jeffery's appendix had ruptured. By the time he was home from the hospital and we were together again, the first waves of morning sickness washed over me. And I was the good wife. Jeffery never knew that the baby I carried inside me belonged to Will.

Sweet Jesus. Amelia reached for the journal as it slid from Nola's hands. The light seemed to dim as she tried to focus her eyes on the words. "You're right." Her fingers trembled as she turned each page. "There are no dates, no clues to the year it happened."

"So do we want to know which of us is the bastard child of the rapist? Let's burn the goddam book." Nola's voice was flat.

"We've come this far. I think we have to finish it." Amelia began reading where Nola left off.

The night after Will died, I went to sit with Marilee at the funeral home, and I said yes when she asked if it was true that he had raped me. Standing over his closed casket she told me how he came to her on the evening he took his life:

"It was getting dark outside, and I turned on a light just as Will walked into the kitchen. I had begun to wash greens for a salad when, without a word to prepare me, he started to tell me about the night he raped you. He said he believed he fathered the child you gave birth to.

"It seemed the longest time before I comprehended his words, before I heard my voice screaming out at him that I would go to the police, to Jeffery. I said I would go to Ralph Gorman in the pulpit of the church."

"I need your forgiveness," he said.

"You forced your baby on another woman, a baby I ached for but could not conceive. Forgiveness? I will destroy you." I flung my wedding band on the floor where it lay in a shining circle at his feet.

Will just stood there, looking at me with a sadness I'd not seen before. He picked up the ring, dropped it in his pocket. Then he reached out and laid his hands against my face, his big hands suddenly soft and gentle. "Destroy me? Little darlin'," he whispered, "I self-destructed a long time ago."

(I self-destructed too, Will, for it was the same as if you fired the first bullet in me. You left me to wince at Jeffery's touch, to turn away from my children because I was no longer capable of expressing love. I was left to be eaten alive by my shame.)

Marilee left Oakdale soon after Will's affairs were settled. We have kept in touch and she has honored our pact to keep the secret that has festered for so long. Now another malignancy lives in me, and time has come to settle my accounts with the living; only God can judge the dead. In the letter I have written to Marilee, I released her from her promise and asked her to agree that my daughters may contact her through Ralph if they wish.

Perhaps they will want to see you again, I told Marilee. Maybe one day, one of them will want to know more about her father.

Amelia felt the pounding of her heart as she slid the journal back inside the drawer and turned the key in the lock.

Later, while she lay beside Nola in their mother's bed, she closed her eyes and remembered the rays of the sunset flashing against her window panes, the baskets of lavender blossoms browning on the mound of red earth. She thought about tomorrow; she must begin to plan for tomorrow and for the next day and then the day after. But for now, she longed for the comfort of the night to come to her. She lay quietly, waiting to gather the softness around her and hold the gentle darkness in her hands.

GARVAS MAHONEY'S MIRACLE

*A*round midnight, before the medicine had time to kick in, the pain seemed to start at the crown of his head and flow in a river of fire rushing to the soles of his feet. He clinched his fists, inhaling, exhaling in short puffs like the nurse told him to do. Like a woman in childbirth, she had explained, as if he should know.

As soon as the worst was over, Garvas wiped the sweat off his forehead with the back of his hand and eased out of bed to sit in his recliner. He pressed himself against the cushions, drifting between sleep and gauzy awareness until a finger of sunrise pointed the first shaft of light at the windows.

By the time Susan tapped on the back door, he had showered and bunched the tail of the blue plaid shirt inside the waist band of his trousers so they didn't droop down off his hips. "Coffee's made and on the counter," he winced as he moved to his chair at the kitchen table. "I didn't expect you for another half hour."

"I was up early." She smoothed the long denim skirt around her ankles and sat down across from him."You look tired."

"Couldn't sleep. I kept dreaming about Anna the way she used to be, not like at the end with her all vague and not knowing who or what she was."

"It's normal you would dream of Mama."

"I still do, most every night." Garvas sprinkled a packet of sugar in his cup, circling the spoon through the dark brown liquid. "But now I got to get my own ducks in a row. If this new treatment don't work, you know what the good doc says–I've used up all my miracles."

"Daddy, he also said it could buy you some time, maybe eventually a cure. We'll know more after your appointment this morning." She glanced at her watch. "We'd better get on the road in case we get blocked in heavy traffic."

At the medical center, a white-coated attendant ushered them inside where the doctor sat shuffling through a stack of notes on his desk. Before he broke the long silence, he lifted his glasses to rest across the balding spot on top of his head. "I am an optimist, Mr. Mahoney, always hoping for one more miracle, so I've never found an easy way to break bad news to my patients."

The room has gone quiet. I see his lips move but where are the words? What has happened to the clicks of footsteps in the corridor, the hum of elevators going up, coming down?

When the sounds came back, Garvas heard the rustle of the sheet of paper the doctor laid in front of him. "Here are names of a team of specialists in Baltimore who might could help you."

"No." He gripped the arm of the chair. "I can get punched and poked on right here, so I don't plan to go to some other place for more of the same."

"I'm sorry. All I can do now is prescribe medication to keep you comfortable as possible."

"Well," Garvas shook the doctor's outstretched hand, "I'm not a religious man. I've never believed in miracles, but I was counting on this one coming to pass."

"Who can say you won't find it out there somewhere, Mr. Mahoney?"

A light mist hugged the windshield as Susan drove away. They rode for awhile in silence until she said, "Maybe you should try other treatments. Something good could turn up."

"Darlin', the only thing likely to turn up is my toes. So while you're watching the road, I'm mulling something over in my mind. I'm planning my wake."

"Daddy, don't."

"Now hear me out. I want to throw the biggest going-away party that's ever been; have it before I die instead of when I'm waiting to be planted in the graveyard."

"We'll do it, if that's what you want," she said, and after a long pause, "How about inviting everybody to join us at the cabin for barbecue? I'll recruit some help to get the place in shape. Nobody's used it since last summer."

"Good. Plenty of room there for friends and the whole Mahoney clan. Maybe you can get the Sunshine Boys band to come play some music."

For the rest of the drive home he leaned back to think about the cabin. Garvas and his brothers, Pat and Marty, had built it in the middle of the parcel of land inherited in equal shares from their grandparent's estate. Perched on the brow of a slope, it overlooked a lake of clear water filled with bluegill trout and hungry bass. It was intended to be a fishing shack, a place to stow bait buckets and tackle boxes, but over the years they added a deck and a room large enough to hold parties and reunions.

The young members of the family still flocked there for graduation and July Fourth celebrations, but twenty years had passed since the last Mahoney family reunion, twenty years since Marty slithered out of town in the middle of the night and headed out west to live in Nevada.

"How about we set the wake for a week from next Saturday?" When Susan's voice interrupted his thoughts, Garvas realized she had stopped the car in the driveway at his house.

"I'll leave that up to you. Be sure to invite the out of town friends and all the family," he said.

"You said all the family. Does that include Uncle Marty?"

"Hell no, it don't include Marty, and I don't want no sermon from you. Pat has already brought his preacher to come pray over me."

"Marty's my uncle too, and he's your brother same as Pat, but you're too stubborn to let go of what happened, even when you are---"

"Dying." He finished the sentence, looking away from the angry tears glinting in her eyes. "Leave it lay, honey. It's something I can't forgive, something that never should have happened."

Lately, with the sickness gnawing at his bones, it might as well have happened yesterday instead of, how many years had it been? He had tried to keep himself so busy he wouldn't have time to think about it, but days came when he thought of little else. It was the year Marty lost his job up in Huntsville and came to live for awhile in the guest apartment Garvas built above the garage at his and Anna's new house. Susan was starting first grade, he remembered, and times were good in his construction company.

He had finished a project in Atlanta ahead of schedule and decided to drive back home a day earlier than Anna expected him. It was close to midnight when he parked his car in the garage beside Marty's truck. He stopped short of turning the key in the back door lock, fingers stalled in mid-air when he heard voices, Anna's rising to a shrill pitch: "I want you out of here and if you ever set foot inside this house when I am alone, I'll report you to the sheriff." Then Marty: "Aw honey. The kid's asleep upstairs and you know you ain't gettin' your share with ole Garvie on the run day and night. Don't make me force you, baby. It wouldn't be pretty."

When Garvas hurled himself through the door, he saw Anna pinned against the china cabinet, Marty's free hand clawing at the front of her blouse. The room whirled, went black until he looked down at his clenched fists, red with his brother's blood.

The next afternoon when he saw Marty's truck stop in front of the house, Garvas met him on the porch.

"I came to ask you and Anna to forgive me. I had too much to drink and went a little crazy, but I want you to know it was all my idea." Tears started to roll down his cheeks. "I couldn't have gone through with it, Garvas, honest to God."

Garvas turned without a word and walked inside. He came out with his deer rifle pointed at Marty's chest.

Marty's face went pale under the purple welts across his nose and swollen lips. "Jesus, Garvas, I'm apologizing, asking forgiveness. What else can I say?"

"I don't care what you say, but I can tell you what you can do. You can get the hell out and if I ever catch you on this property again I will blow your sorry ass clean across the Chattahoochie into Georgia."

After Marty left town, he wrote letters that Garvas never opened before scrawling Return To Sender and dropping them back in the post box. After a couple of years went by, Pat began to visit him, and each time brought back news: Marty married a Navaho Indian lady; won and gambled away a fortune at the casinos; the Navaho lady divorced him.

Garvas sat in his wicker chair on the porch and unfolded the morning newspaper. He glanced up when he heard Pat's car in the driveway.

"You're looking chipper."

"The medicine is keeping me pretty comfortable." Garvas nodded.

"That's good to hear. I have been wondering if you might feel up to taking a airplane ride. I'm going out to see Marty."

Garvas folded the paper and laid it across his lap. "You have been inviting me to make that trip almost ever since Marty high tailed out of here. What I said last time still goes. I ain't lost nothing in Reno."

"Marty did a terrible wrong to Anna, to the whole family," Pat said, "but she forgave him before she passed."

"Well, I don't, by God. He tried to rape her, would have if I hadn't busted in. Now she's gone."

"He had nothing to do with the tumor that damaged her brain. You have wasted half your life hating your brother and what's it got you?"

"Leave it there, Pat. Just leave it right there." Garvas walked back inside and slammed the door behind him.

He stood in the living room until the sound of his heartbeat stopped pounding in his ears.

The cabin was no longer visible through the long row of windows; two giant magnolia trees, grown from saplings over the years, blocked his view. But now, with the air turned sweet with spring, he pictured himself standing there on the slopes in a grove gone white with dogwood blossoms. Through the eyes of his mind he watched the last tip of sunset flare above the lake and when the wind stilled, heard the trees go silent. The only sound was the music of the water, lapping a hymn to the deer and rabbit.

The jangle of the telephone cut through his thoughts. "Daddy, the wake is all set for Saturday. I've booked the Sunshine Boys for the day and promised them their regular fee with all the barbecue they can eat."

"They play a lot of songs I want to hear one more time," Garvas said.

By Saturday, the rain that came during the night had washed the air clean and left a lazy mid-April breeze to shoo away the puffs of clouds from the sun. When Susan came to drive Garvas to the cabin, she stood looking at him and smiled "Isn't that your good suit and silk tie you're wearing? Kind of fancy for a barbecue, I'd say."

"I figure today is a dress rehearsal. It's what I picked to be laid out in."
Laid out. To make a dead body ready for burial.

He felt the cold dankness of fear sweating his palms, a fear of watching the end of his life unroll in front of him like a tattered old rug. The tick of the clock on the table grew louder. Tick. Another second gone. Tick. *Here I am, God. Can I come in?*

"Look, honey," he turned to Susan, "I ain't near as brave as I let on. I'm scared as hell to die with my heart full of hate. It's festered inside me all these years and I can't find a way to let it go."

Garvas sat in a cane bottom chair, listening to the squawks of jays swooping low over the deck at the cabin. He wondered if the blackberries were in bloom on the other side of the lake. The smell of oak chips smoking on the grill drifted past his nose. From somewhere down in the yard he heard laughter mingled with sounds of the Sunshine Boys noodling a few bars of Blue Bird On The Wing. He leaned forward to watch a car swing into the graveled area down the slope, saw a man get out and stand for a moment, as though uncertain of his surroundings.

"Is that you up there, Garvas?"

A tightness clawed at his throat at the sound of the familiar voice. He cupped his hands above his eyes to squint into the streaks of brightness flashing through the trees.

"It's me," he said.

"If you're packing a gun, go ahead and shoot now. I'm coming up."

"Wait there. I'm coming down."

He made his way haltingly down the steps and halfway along the path stopped to gather his breath. Marty walked toward him, sunlight carrying the long shadows of his outstretched hands. As they met, he looked into Marty's eyes and into a face that mirrored his own, faces grown craggy and antiqued by the years lost between them.

When Garvas opened his arms to his brother, a quiet river of peace washed over him, and from somewhere deep inside rose a cry like the forgiving voice of the earth when a storm has passed.

LYDIA FRANKLIN'S POSITIVELY LAST HOME-COOKED HOLIDAY DINNER

*I*t seems to her that she has spent the better part of the month of November replenishing her spices, picking out pecans for Roxie's and Anson's favorite pie and scouting the meat counters at the super markets for the proper weight turkey to serve ten people. But of course, this dinner will be special because it is her last one; everything must be just right. Fiftysomething years of giblet gravy and cornbread stuffing, and everybody half-chewing the celery sticks without even bothering to taste the flavor of real butter whipped in the mashed potatoes. Just bolting it all down like pigs at a trough so they can get back to the parades and football games on TV. Enough is enough.

Lydia Franklin is seventy-nine years plus two months old. She supposes she feels her age, no more, no less, but how can she be sure?

"I've never been this old before," she tells Anson, her son, who has rushed in and grabbed her in a bear hug so tight she gasps for breath while he says she doesn't look a day older. It's what he always tells her when he comes home for a visit each year. He has arrived a couple of days before Thanksgiving from Clovis, New Mexico, to Gadsden, Alabama in twenty-three and a half hours road time, thirty-four miles to the gallon. Lydia knows the information on the time and mileage will lead to a discussion later about the performance of his new car. Anson is still a little red-headed, freckled-face boy when it comes to cars; his daddy was the same way.

Anson's wife, Tiffany–his second wife, actually–is a scrawny, shadowy little thing who, Lydia imagines, lives on lettuce leaves and that damn bottled water she sucks on all day. She is a good fifteen years younger than Anson, who is forty-five and going gray in the temples and moustache. Tiffany, when Anson is done hugging Lydia, gives her a dutiful peck on the cheek, asks did she put a rinse on her hair to take out the yellowish look it had last year?

"It's got a year whiter," Lydia smiles and sits down on the couch to let Michael, Tiffany's and Anson's little blue-eyed boy climb on her lap. He says he wants her to hug him so he can watch her soft skin wiggle when she holds out her arms.

"M-i-c-h-a-e-l!" Tiffany sounds out each letter. "That is not a nice thing to say to Gamma."

"It's a perfectly lovely thing to say," Lydia tells her, pretending she doesn't know he is describing in five-year old child language how the flesh on her upper arms flaps at half mast when she reached out for him.

Anson says he believes he will go on out back and see if there are any more of the garden tools he wants to take back with him this time.

"You sure you won't need the grubbing hoe?" he asks. "I could use it out back at home."

"I'm sure." She squints through the window into the sunlight to watch him, hands stubbed deep in his pockets as he ambles past the big elm tree by the bird bath. He looks too thin, his pants hanging half off his hips; probably never gets a decent meal, what with Tiffany hell-bent on that body fat percentage theory she tries to explain to Lydia.

She knows Anson is going out to the tool shed to sit on the ragged seat of that old tractor and cry about his daddy. It's the same with her when she sometimes hears a gravelly voice behind her at the grocery store or when she pulls open a drawer in the bedroom and smells a memory come rolling out. It's been two years and she knows. She knows.

She chops onions and celery on the big wooden board that lately had developed a crack down the middle; she thinks ahead to next year. That new restaurant at the mall across the highway advertises home-cooked holiday dinners with seating for family gatherings and convenient parking out front.

Roxie, her daughter who teaches fifth grade at Rainbow City–her husband is career military and won't get back home until January–Roxie charges in through the kitchen door. She is wearing her new red warm-up suit, the early Christmas present she bought herself for twenty percent off at Wal-Mart. She kisses her mother's cheek, asks, "Why are you dicing the veggies on Grandma's old dough board when you have a perfectly good food processor?"

"Because somebody put it up too high for me to reach without climbing on the top step of the ladder, and I get dizzy up there. Besides, it's too much trouble to wash up after I get done."

"Move back so the onions won't make you cry."

"I have already been crying because I'm so damn mad," Roxie says. "Do you know that Charley, my thoughtful son Charley, is going skiing with some of his fraternity brothers from the university instead of coming home? It's bad enough with his daddy stuck off in a god-forsaken hole half way around the world."

Anson comes in trailing wet brown leaves off the soles of his shoes. He and Roxie hug and kiss and swap a couple of dirty jokes right off the bat; Anson asks if she's heard the one about the English teacher who goes into the adult book store.

Tiffany yells out to ask where is the rug shampoo because Michael has stepped in chewing gum and tracked it on the carpet. Lydia calls back that she should first rub a cube of ice over it so the gum will harden and then maybe she can pull it out of the nap.

Roxie pours a diet Coke for herself, a beer for Anson, and says she doesn't see why she can't call up Shirley and invite her to drop in, just for pie and coffee after dinner. Shirley is Anson's first wife, and Roxie says since it has been nearly ten years and nobody's mad at anybody any more, Shirley should be included this time. Especially now, Roxie emphasizes, when Shirley is in the middle of getting a divorce from husband number two and is at loose ends, probably feeling sad to be alone. Anson tells her just don't start raking up trouble with Tiffany. Roxie says okay, forget it and she should have known.

Lydia's baby sister Myrtice and her husband Dude arrive early Thanksgiving morning with two of their grandchildren who are spending vacation with them. Ten-year old twin boys—Lydia can't tell one from the other and who, in her estimation, are capable of leveling a two-story house in half an hour. Myrtice sends them to play outdoors with their ball and warns, "Don't you be rassling around out there in the dirt with your good clothes on."

"Why are you soaking the turkey in the sink?" Myrtice turns to Lydia. "Shouldn't he already be stuffed and in the browning bag?"

"He's thawing," Lydia explains. "I forgot to haul him out of the freezer until four o'clock this morning."

By mid-afternoon everybody is seated around the dining room table, holding hands to form a circle while Lydia asks the blessing. Before she gets to the amen, Michael calls out, "Look, it's Cousin Charlie getting out of his car."

Charley comes in through the kitchen, stands behind Lydia's chair, squeezes her shoulders, says, "Boy, this place sure smells better than the cafeteria. I got to thinking I didn't want to miss out on Gamma's turkey and dressing."

Roxie jumps up, starts to cry before she runs over to hug Charley, and says she might just put a knot on his head for even thinking about not coming home.

Myrtice says soon as she finishes her pecan pie and coffee she would like to go out back to look at Lydia's chrysanthemums and the late blooming petunias. Lydia decides to go with her so she won't have to listen to the football announcer screaming like a crazy man, and maybe seeing bronze and purple flowers will take her mind off Roxie and Tiffany banging her good china against the sink while they clean up, which they always insist on doing. By the time they are done reorganizing her cupboard for maximum efficiency and hiding cups and saucers behind the wooden salad bowls on the top shelves, she won't be able to find everything before next Easter.

Myrtice is set to leave soon as she rounds up the twins and pries Dude loose from in front of the TV. She tells him they can't wait until half time because she promised the basketball coach she would have the boys home in time for a team meeting at six o'clock.

"Good food, Liddy, best dinner you ever fixed," Dude says, which is a long conversation for him. Lydia always finds Dude dull as cold mush, but if he's suited Myrtice all these years it's no skin off her bones.

Lydia says she will take a rain check on the invitation to join Anson and Tiffany at Roxie's house later on. Tiffany mentions that Michael is sound asleep upstairs and Lydia doesn't have to do a thing unless he has to use the bathroom and needs help in aiming in the right direction. Anson says Uncle Dude is right about this being her best dinner ever, asks how does she keep doing it year after year?

"Practice," she tells him.

After they have all gone, she walks through the house, hearing the leftover sounds in the rooms: the drip of a faucet someone forgot to give an extra turn; a floor board in the hall relaxing with a tired squeak. She opens the refrigerator, stacks a slice of turkey breast and some cold dressing on a saucer and sits down in a chair by the window to analyze the flavors. A little more salt, just a pinch, rubbed inside the bird while he browned would have made it perfect.

She looks out across the trees to catch the last of the light, which seems to her to be brighter than usual for the beginning of a sunset. She thinks she might go over to the mall one of these days to check out the food at that new place, although she is willing to wager they put too much sage in their dressing. Restaurant people, Lydia feels certain, don't always trouble themselves to get things just right.

LOVE IS WARMER
THAN AN ELECTRIC BLANKET

*A*gust of biting wind, forerunner of the West Texas "blue norther," whipped through my lightweight coat as I ducked into a cab at the airport. I had come from my home in Alabama to see my mother, who was recovering from a light stroke. I'd forgotten how quickly the prairie country's pale November sky could suddenly deepen, darken even at mid-afternoon, to let the wind play out its fury.

Mama, in her rose printed Sunday dress, greeted me at the front door with her usual twinkle, the blue shine that her eyes never lost. "Couldn't drive out to pick you up since I got this darn crippled leg," she snorted, taking a firmer grip on her walker when I bent to hug her.

My arms, pressed against her frail shoulders, felt the sharp thrust of bone poking against skin. Her face glowed fresh and pink when she looked up at me, and I suspected she had taken more than her usual time today to blush the hollows of her cheeks and camouflage the dark circles beneath her eyes.

She walked through the house ahead of me, flicking light switches, her bird-like motions bringing the rooms alive with brightness. Reflections from the pair of grandmother's old pewter lamps in the hall danced on the piece of crystal in a shadow box as Mama's tiny glass peacock seemed to suddenly catch on fire, the way I remembered it as a child. .

A familiar aroma of homemade vegetable soup, the blend of onions and a hint of sweet basil, wafted from the kitchen. The living room smelled of lemon oil furniture polish and the fresh starch in the curtains at the windows overlooking the rolling hills to the west. Before I could scold her for overdoing, Mama explained about her companion housekeeper, Inez, who "cleans a house from top to bottom the way it should be done."

"And I never did a lick of work to help," she wagged a finger at me, "except for the soup. I made it special because I recalled it was your favorite. Remember the time I didn't fix enough for you to have a third serving? How you cried."

When night came, I helped button her blue flannel nightgown and then we talked while I sat down beside her bed. The norther had churned itself into an angry blizzard, firing missiles of sleet against the window panes. Sounds of the wind's howls under the eaves made me wish I'd thought to pack my woolly sweater.

I noticed that when Mama laid down she covered herself with one of her old quilts, drawing it close around her. When I asked about the electric blanket I sent her on Mother's Day, she confessed it was still in the box it came in.

"It's such a sweet pretty yellow and just matched the draperies," she sighed, "but somehow I keep warmer under this quilt me and your daddy shared for most of our lives together."

She reached for my hand and guided it across the pieces of the Double Wedding Ring pattern she had begun putting together when she was a bride. My fingers touched a scrap of the silk kimono Daddy brought her when he came home from Japan after the second World War. She guided my fingers across a square of white lawn cloth that was once a part of a layette for the little boy who died before I was born.

"And this," she smiled up at me, pointing to a bit of lavender crepe de chine, "this is from the dress you wore to your first piano recital."

"Miss Vida Toney's School Of Music And Dance," I said. "I believe I was the only student who played my whole piece off key."

"But you played with such beautiful rhythm," she smiled. " I doubt anyone noticed." She gave my hand a squeeze before dropping off to sleep.

After Mama died the following winter, I took the quilt home with me. It hangs on her rosewood display rack in the guest bedroom. Sometimes when the night grows cold and the wind howls outside my windows, I turn off my electric blanket and bring her quilt to my bed. It has worn thin and tattered with the years, but I wrap it around me and lie down to sleep warm and cozy under a blanket of love.

A GENTLE ART

My parents put together a hurry up wedding two days before Pop's reserve unit shipped out to join the U.S. troops fighting in Korea. Mom kissed him goodbye, finished nurses training and took a job at Westside General Hospital near Montgomery, Alabama. Before she saw him again, he would be wounded, captured and held for thirty-six months as a prisoner of war.

After he spent another two years in veteran's hospitals in the U.S., he returned to his job with a general contracting company. He and Mom settled in Montgomery, in the big white house were they would live and grow old together. She traded her starched white uniforms for blue jeans and two babies, my sister Beth and me. Although she gave up nursing, she practiced on Pop the gentle art of healing until the day she died.

The morning after her funeral, Beth and I walked into the living room and she started to talk about what we should do if the time came when Pop couldn't look after himself.

"Roger would never agree for him to come live with us." Her eyes were still puffy from weeping and lack of sleep. "You know how Pop always goes for the jugular with him. I mean, just because Rog went on a couple of protest marches during the Gulf War doesn't make him a bleeding commie, for Christ sake."

She perched on the edge of a wicker arm chair across from where I sat on the sofa. We had flown back to Alabama as soon as Pop called. Beth came from her home in San Francisco while I snagged the last seat on a red-eye out of Dallas.

"Do you think she suffered, Johnny?"

I shook my head. "You know what Pop told us. One minute she started walking toward him in the back yard and then, how did he describe it? She just folded and dropped to the ground. I doubt she felt more than a quick flash of pain."

Before Beth answered, Pop walked in. He said he was driving over to the cemetery to bring home the potted plants if vandals hadn't already looted the grave. I followed him out the door until he turned and looked at me the same way he did when I was a little guy and forever tagging along in his shadow, or when I was too chicken to ride my new bike without training wheels. So I just stood there in the cloud of grey dust he left behind, shot down by him again like I was still six years old.

By the time I walked back inside the kitchen, I smelled the coffee perking. I pulled a chair up to the breakfast table facing the windows and watched a feeble sunlight stencil the panes with silhouettes of the gum tree's naked branches. Beth filled two mugs and sat down across from me and we started talking about things that happened when we were growing up.

"Remember that day you took your new cowboy boots for a trial run across the hood of old man Jackson's Mustang?" Her voice carried the hint of a smile.

"Yep. Mom left a hand printed message on my butt. "

I poured another shot of cream in my coffee and looked up to see tears starting to glisten in her eyes. She reached over and patted my arm. "I'm thinking about how angry I was at her when she caught me trying to sneak Danny Hanks into my thirteenth birthday sleep-over party. She grounded me for six weeks, no allowance, and I missed the class trip to Florida."

"Mom took no prisoners, that's for sure," I said. "I got the old six-weeks-grounding-and-no-allowance when the principal kicked me out of school for tossing a firecracker into the girls locker room. That was one time I thought Pop was going to wade in and give me the works, but he just turned away and left it up to her."

Beth asked if I wanted more coffee.

"Thanks, no. I think I'll jog out and check on Pop."

"It's a long cold walk."

"Piece of cake. I work out every day."

A blast of cold wind stung my cheeks as soon as I stepped outside. I watched a line of drifting clouds churn themselves into fragmented figures—a legless poodle, an elephant's trunk sliding away, a wispy Abe Lincoln profile. I lowered my head and cut across the park where Beth and I learned to play tennis when we were kids.

I got to thinking about what she told me one time. She said Pop was like a polite stranger in our house when we were around, that he didn't seem to need anyone but Mom. "He worked long hours to give me *things* I needed," she said, "but he never shared himself. It was sort of like I wasn't really there." She was right. I was never able to get close to him, even after I grew up, although one time I thought we almost connected.

It was when I spent a couple of weeks back home after my divorce became final. I was pretty blown away and feeling a need to touch base with Mom, maybe make one last try with him. At the end of my visit, Mom came down with a bad cold, so Pop drove me to the airport. About half way there while we sat waiting at a red light, he turned to me and said, "War does things to a man."

I waited, but that was all he said. The light changed to green and then I mentioned something about the weather in Dallas and said I hoped my flight would be on time. Whatever he wanted to say didn't matter, I decided. Too many years had gone by.

The wind started to bite through my jacket by the time I looked up and saw the gates of the cemetery up ahead. I spied Pop's truck parked outside the fence where he stood holding a pot of what looked like a pink azalea. I slowed to a trot, watched him turn towards me. He called my name, and I think it was the sound of his voice that made me start to run again, run away from him like a frightened child until my breath was a fire inside me, leaping out of control.

By the time I rounded the back side of the cemetery and stopped for air, I heard the chug of his truck beside me. Pop reached across the seat and opened the door.

"Get in," he said.

He didn't speak for a long time. After awhile he lifted his hands from the steering wheel, sat staring at them.

"I don't know how many people I killed over there or how many towns I helped wipe out. It was war. I was doing my job and they were the faceless enemy until that night."

He rubbed his arm across his eyes as though to clear his thoughts. "I was standing guard duty in the dark, with orders to shoot anything that moved. When I heard something behind me, I whirled and shot. They fell out of the brush almost at my feet, two children not more than toddlers, probably out scrounging for food. The little girl was nothing but a bag of bones."

I swallowed the big lump that hung in my throat and we sat in silence until Pop put the truck in gear and drove on around to where we could see Mom's grave, the baskets of lilies and white carnations browned now by the cold.

"You want to get out for awhile?" he asked.

We walked down the narrow graveled path between the headstones, sat down on one of the concrete benches.

"I spent three years a in prison camp," he said. " I wasn't fit to be called a human being by the time I got out. Tried to kill a guard with my bare hands. Once I got started I lost all control. *God, it felt good.*" He laced his fingers together, opened and closed them. "It was your mama who had to keep you kids in line because I was afraid. But you see," his voice grew soft, "it was her love that kept me from going all the way over the edge."

I reached across the seat, maybe I reached across time, and laid my hand on his shoulder.

"I love you, Pop," I said. I don't know where the words came from.

They might have been there all along, so I told him again.

It was the second time I ever saw him cry.

THE TITHING

*I*t was barely light outside, but Cassie Lee was already awake when Baby Scratch started to crow. Perched atop the stack of railroad ties piled at the north end of the house, the little bantam rooster was beginning his raucous calls earlier than usual.

In the kitchen, Ora Martin had set the heavy crock of flour gravy on the table. She bent to remove a shallow, blackened pan from the oven and stood silently, her hands protected from the searing metal by rags wadded to monumental thickness, while her husband said grace. When he finished, he selected three plump biscuits from the pan, carefully buttering and setting each one on his plate before taking another.

"Breakfast is gettin' cold."

At the sound of her mother's voice, Cassie Lee turned away from the window and took her place on the rough wooden bench at the end of the table.

"I venture she's not come down from the clouds since yesterday," Lon said, "after bein' judged best writer out of all the schools."

"But my essay's got to be the best in the United States to win the big prize money from *Farm And Ranch Magazine*. I was just a winner from Texas, but I don't get no prize money for that."

"Well, no matter. I'm thinkin' your piece will get that hundred dollars for best in the whole United States."

"Oh Papa!" She jumped up and ran to throw her arms around his neck, almost upsetting his chair. "Can I buy Midnight? Please, Papa. Mr. Stevens will sell him and his saddle for a hundred dollars."

Ora poured coffee for herself and sat down next to Cassie Lee.

"Before you and your Pa go throwin' around all that money, I got one question. How many other young'uns you reckon are plannin' to win that prize, already dreamin' about where to spend a whole hundred dollars?"

Cassie Lee shook her head, feeling the gravy settle in a dough lump halfway down her throat.

"Well, they's plenty, I can tell you, so it ain't likely to be no little Miss Prissy from Hawks Gap, Texas." Seeing the bright tears welling in the girl's eyes, Ora laid a rough freckled hand on her shoulder.":Not meanin' to be unkind, but you ain't winnin' no such big contest, not in a million years. It's always goin' to be somebody else, so no use in pinnin' your hopes on it."

"Got as good a chance as any," Lon argued. "She writes pretty, for a twelve year old girl."

"Everybody had to write about the same thing," Cassie Lee wiped her eyes on the back of her hand. "The title is "Why I Am Proud To Live On A Farm."

"Seems to me you got a fine chance. It won't surprise me none if we find that check in the mailbox any day."

Ora raised her head to look at Lon. "They's no sense in you fillin' her head with silly dreams. It's just that she ain't gonna win, no matter how proud she is to live on a farm." She began to stack the dishes, scraping the plates in short, savage jabs with the crust of Cassie Lee's uneaten biscuit. "Dreamin' never got you nothin' but ten years of breakin' your back on a wore out tenant farm and comin' down with a sick headache when you see the man headin' this way for his lease money."

"If she wins, she can buy the horse." Lon's voice was firm, so Ora said no more.

When school was dismissed that day, Cassie Lee didn't stay to help dust erasers and wash the blackboard. She hurried out the door and across the playground, ignoring the catcalls from the small group of boys tossing a baseball.

"Holy Roller," they chanted, "Praise the Lord."

She pretended not to hear, not giving them the satisfaction of knowing that she wished with all her heart that she was Baptist, like most of the children, or even Methodist.

The Martins were members of Hawks Gap Holiness Church where Brother Musgrove held Wednesday night prayer meetings and preached twice every Sunday. In summer, when the windows were open, the singing and shouting at the Holiness revival meeting could be heard across the valley. Brother Musgrove said they had a lot of religion to shout about. Heaven, he said, would be filled with Holiness people while lukewarm pussyfooters burned for eternity in the fires of Hell.

Cassie Lee cut across the back side of the school yard and when she was no longer in sight of the boys, ran all the way to Mr. Stephens' pasture.

He was digging post holes in the sun baked ground along his fence line. His sharp, dark face reminded her of the bronze hawks darting and gliding in wide circles overhead as he smiled and greeted her with a handshake.

"Mr. Stevens, I hear you want to sell Midnight."

"Don't want to, but I got to come up with some cash money."

"If I win the big magazine contest, I'll have a hundred dollars. Will you sell him to me?"

When he nodded, she looked closely at his eyes.

"You won't go back on your word?"

"Ask your Pa if he ever knowed ole Tuck's word not to be good."

She finished evening chores quickly, crumbling corn bread on the ground for Baby Scratch, then filling the lard bucket with wood chips for Papa to start the morning fire in the heater and cook stove. A blustery wind, sweeping across the northern tip of the hills, slashed unchecked at her face and hands. She still shivered after she ran inside the house, although she noticed the beads of sweat rowing the faint line of reddish fuzz above Mama's lip while she hurried to clear away the supper dishes.

Cassie Lee had almost finished the arithmetic assignment for tomorrow when it suddenly occurred to her that she had forgotten about her tithes, about the ten percent of the prize money she would owe to the Lord. Not to give God his share, she knew, was same as stealing. She had tithed when she earned money last fall, dropping one silver dollar and two quarters in the collection plate on the altar. But now the figures she put down on her tablet seemed to leap out at her. With ten percent going to God, there would be only ninety dollars left for Mr. Stevens, not enough to buy Midnight. Mr. Stevens was in a mighty hurry for a hundred dollars because his wife needed to go for her operation.

She did not dare question God; the anger and resentment flooding her mind was a strange emotion. She was in danger of burning in Hell throughout eternity, but more than her soul's salvation, Cassie Lee wanted Midnight.

On Sunday, Brother Musgrove's sermon lasted longer than the usual one hour, and he preached about tithing. Her mouth went dry, the small hairs prickled on the back of her neck as his voice grew louder. *He knows. Everybody knows.* He told about a man he once know who refused to pay his tithes, so God took away his most treasured possession. His golden haired child was killed right in front of his eyes, crushed to death under the wheels of the man's big, fine automobile.

She didn't dare look up for fear her eyes would reveal the blasphemous thought she'd had. She knew Brother Musgrove had been directed by God to preach right at her, to warn her that something awful would happen to Midnight if she failed to heed His word.

The choir sang all three verses of "Sinner Come Home", but Jo Boy Smith was the only one who knelt at the altar to repent. Jo Boy went to altar call every Sunday and sometimes again on Wednesday night, but nobody ever paid any attention to him. He wasn't right in his head because his mother held a neighbor's deformed baby in her arms just before Jo Boy was born.

Cassie Lee remembered one time at summer revival when Jo Boy got excited and wet his pants while kneeling. She had never heard of a grown man doing that and she watched, angry at the people who laughed at him but fascinated as the dark circle spread across the front of him and drops of amber fluid splattered down on the laces of his shoes. But she felt pity for him then, as now, while everybody hurried to shake hands with Brother Musgrove at the front door and Jo Boy still knelt at the altar confessing his sins.

Slipping out the back way, she ran as fast as she could down the road toward home, not looking for Midnight when she passed Mr. Stephens' pasture. Once inside her room, her breath coming in great wheezing gulps, she fell on her knees.

"Oh God, please don't take away my most treasured possession because I had sinful thoughts. It wasn't Midnight's fault. Please don't let something terrible happen to Midnight."

She continued to stop after school at the post office, walking past the picture of President Roosevelt to peer closely inside the glass enclosed cubbyholes. Each time, torn between her desire for the horse and fear of reprisal from an angry God, she was almost relieved when the envelope was not there. As the days dragged on, she became sure that Mama was right, that her dreams of winning had been foolish.

At the end of six weeks she started going home by a different route, not walking within sight of the post office. She would not have stopped by the place again, but on a Friday she went in to look for a post card Mama was expecting from a cousin in Sweetwater. The card wasn't there, but hidden under the monthly issue of *The Christian Herald* was the slender white envelope addressed to Miss Cassie Lee Martin.

Ora and Lon were both sitting by the fireplace when she reached home. She had walked in a daze, not realizing it was almost dark, feeling nothing until she saw their faces.

"Well, my stars," Ora kept repeating. She ran her fingers lightly across the writing on the check, touching each letter as though she feared it might disappear.

Cassie Lee's eyes searched her father's face. "Papa, will God punish me if He don't get his ten per cent?"

"I believe in tithin'," he answered without hesitation. "Maybe some would say it ain't got me much in life, working the land for another man. He's got money and I know he don't pay me my fair share, but in some ways he ain't nearly as rich as me. His wife's left him and I hear his boy has fell in with a no good crowd." He paused to look around the room. "But I got more than most folks realize. Got a place to live inside out of the weather, don't go hungry. Got a good honest woman and the prettiest, smartest girl in the whole United States." He touched her wet cheek gently. "I reckon you will just have to pray about it, Cassie Lee."

By Sunday morning she had made her decision. Tomorrow she would tell Mr. Stephens she could not buy Midnight. But except for knowing that the horse would not suffer because of her wickedness, she felt utterly desolate, even as Brother Musgrove shouted and the people in the congregation praised the Lord for whipping the Devil when he tried to tempt Cassie Lee.

After church, she hung her Sunday dress in the closet and sat in her room to watch a flock of black birds as they swooped down to peck in the plowed ground where the vegetable garden had been planted last summer. She tried to count them, but they constantly shifted and scattered, growing in numbers as more dropped from the sky. Looking toward the fields to the west, she saw a horse and rider coming at a fast trot, clouds of powdery red dust flagging their approach.

"It's Tuck Stephens on Midnight," she heard Papa call.

Cassie Lee stood on the edge of the porch, curling the toes of her good shoes over the ends of the board.

"I have to tell you, Mr. Stephens, I can't buy him." Her face had gone white, but there were no tears in her eyes.

"Can't make no deal today nohow, Tuck." Lon moved close to his daughter, putting an arm around her shoulder. "We don't do no tradin' on Lord's Day."

Tuck pushed back his hat with the end of his finger, his teeth showing straight and white when he smiled.

"Not bein' a church man, I did forget about that, Lon, and I'm sorry. The little lady and me can tend to our business tomorrow.

"But I don't have the hundred dollars any more." Cassie Lee's lips were numb, so stiff she could no longer feel a movement when she spoke.

"I don't hold with the practice of tithin'," Tuck said. "Meanin' no offense, but I figger the good Lord give me sense enough to hang on to what little money comes my way, 'specially in times like these." He rubbed the stubble on his face, his dark eyes squinting almost closed in the sunlight. "But I already heard what you done today, Cassie Lee, so ole Tuck's gonna do some tithin' in his own way. I'm knockin' ten per cent off my askin' price, and you can have horse and saddle for the ninety dollars you got left."

"We can't let you do that, Tuck, much as we're obliged," Lon interrupted quickly. "You got your own problems. I know you can get the full askin' price for Midnight, and he's worth every penny of it." He shook his head. "No sir, we can't let you do that."

"I ain't askin' your permission, Lon. It's between me and the girl." Cassie Lee longed to reach out and touch the soft mane of the horse, but she stood frozen to the edge of the porch. She wanted to throw her arms around Mr. Stephens and kiss his cheek before he rode away, but Mama had told her she was too grown up now to go showing herself off to the neighbor men. So she turned and ran to the corn crib to begin shelling the grain for Baby Scratch. Tomorrow she would have to put down hay for Midnight.

The kerosene lamp was still burning in the kitchen when Ora came in to say goodnight. In the soft shadows she looked almost pretty with her long copper hair brushed and falling loose around her face.

"I believe it's a good omen for the Martin family, Cassie Lee," she said, "you winnin' the prize and bein' able to buy your horse. Maybe it means things is lookin' better for us."

She sat down shyly on the edge of the bed. "Know what I've been thinkin'? I've been studyin' enterin' a contest, too, when the county fair comes next September."

"Oh Mama!" Cassie Lee's eyes were shining. "Your strawberry preserves! You could win. I know you could!"

"I aim to do just that." Ora's voice was determined. "I mean to win me a blue ribbon for my strawberry preserves."

IN THAT FAR OFF SWEET FOREVER

Lyla, hurrying to answer the doorbell, seeing him standing in the circle of brightness spilling beneath the porch light:

"Michael–what's wrong? Why have you left school?"

"Because I need to talk with you."

Gordon's voice, a sleepy yawn from the bedroom: "Everything okay out there?"

Michael, backing away at the sound: "Sorry, Mom. Bad timing."

"Oh God, Michael. Wait. Please wait." Her bare feet taking root in the carpet, eyes swimming in the red blur peeling away from the curb. A squeal of tires at the end of the block.

The night she met Gordon Sinclair on a business flight, Lyla didn't consider beginning a relationship that would take them on a sleep-over in a rented apartment hundreds of miles away. Tall, wheat blond and, according to her boss, the best electrical engineer in Alabama, she had just celebrated a wedding anniversary with her architect husband. Married to Neal Carter for twenty-two years, half her life. Three children bam bam bam: Sally, high school junior, already chattering about prom dress, class ring, new car promised her as an honor student. Nick, middle child Nick The Playboy, eking through freshman year at Florida State; Michael at a small college in

Oklahoma preparing to follow Grandpa Harper's footsteps into the ministry. Michael, her first born who occupied a niche in the tiny grotto of her heart where mothers sometimes lock away secret dreams.

The day her boss asked her to take Sam Davis' place on an out of state construction project, she had come home to find Neal already there and unloading a thick roll of blueprints on the desk in the den.

"That big shopping mall in Saint Louis?" He peered at her over the top of his glasses. "Shouldn't it be finished by now?"

"There have been a couple of slow downs; looks like another three, four months to go. Sam asked to come back home to be with his family; problems with his son, I heard." She paused for breath. "The company is offering an attractive package, better than last time: a bonus plus all the perks including apartment, car, flights home on week-ends when I can get away."

"Missouri isn't far," Neal said. "I can manage things here with Sally. We muddled through while you were in Denver last year."

"I know, but I hate leaving you with full responsibility. A sixteen year old woman child with drivers license can be hazardous to your health."

She saw a familiar grin tug the corners of his mouth. "We'll save a pack of grievances for you to settle in your time at home."

"Touche," she laughed. "I do seem to recall unloading on you when you traveled during those early years."

That night she curled next to him with her head against his chest, hearing the slow gentle tide of breath flowing in and out. In the shadow of her mind she traced the outline of his face–the stubborn dark hair falling across his forehead, the bright blue glint in his eyes. When sleep came, she dreamed a vision of her Grandpa Harper who took her to raise as his own child after her parents drowned in a boating accident in the dark waters of the Warrior River.

Grandpa Harper had served as pastor of the church where she was baptized when she was twelve years old. In her dream she stood before his congregation in her white eyelet pinafore to sing his favorite hymn:

There's a land beyond the river

that they call the sweet forever

and something something something –

She awoke, drenched in sweat, unable to recall the rest of the song.

Lyla spent the first week in Saint Louis starting her job, shivering in a freakish April blizzard and settling in a three-room apartment. She flew home for Neal's birthday at the end of the month, a large German chocolate cake packed in the top of her carry-on.Both boys had already arrived, Nick bursting with the good news that he was passing English Lit.; Michael, who usually headed straight for Nora Bennett's home across town, spending most of Saturday in his room. He and Nora had been engaged, off and on, since high school. According to Sally, Nora was sick of waiting to get married.

On Sunday when Michael didn't come down for breakfast, Lyla tapped on his door before going inside to find him still wearing his old blue pajama bottoms. He lay in a heap of bed covers, one arm flung across his face. She felt a need to smooth the mane of black hair tousled on the pillow, but instead walked to the windows, pulled the draperies and stood squinting into the sunlight.

"I'll go to church with you this morning if you want company," she said. "It's been awhile since I've been there; maybe it would help get my week off to a good start."

"Thanks, I'll pass. Would you please close the curtains?"

"You're not coming down with a bug, are you?" His cheek felt cool under her hand, but she saw the gray hollows beneath his eyes.

"I don't want to talk right now, Mom. Okay?"

She didn't mention their conversation to Neal when she went with him later that afternoon for a walk around the lake near their home. I'll call Michael when he's back in his dorm, she decided. Only happy birthday thoughts allowed today.

"Is it all going well with you and Sally? Truth, please; no cover-up." She stood watching as Neal crumbled pieces of stale bread Sally had hoarded for the wild Mallards quacking along the lake bank

"Nothing we can't handle. And you?:"

"Stressed out sometimes. Walking into a new job is always a challenge, but I love it." She tucked her hand is his and hunched her shoulders against the chill of evening wind that had begun to ruffle the water. "Neal, do you remember Grandpa's favorite old hymn?"

"Good lord, it's been twenty years since he passed away, but I think a couple of lines were 'in that far off sweet forever, just beyond the shining river' or something like that," he laughed. Why do you ask?"

"Honestly, I don't know. Some of the words keep popping into my head and I can't put them together. I suppose I can't bear the thought of losing them."

Lyla meet Gordon Sinclair for the first time that night on a late flight out of Birmingham. Rumpled khaki trousers, a scuffed briefcase on his lap, auburn hair starting to gray at the temples, he barely looked up from the paperback in his hands as she shinnied around his long legs to take her seat by the window. Sweaty and out of breath, she had almost missed the plane. As soon as they were airborne and she could no longer feel the rush of speed, she let out a deep sigh and opened her eyes to look at the string of toy cars moving in a trail of brightness along the interstate.

"My ex-wife thinks he degraded women," the man said. Lyla glanced up to see him studying the author's picture on the jacket of the book she had started to read.

She felt a prickle of annoyance as she reached overhead to adjust the light."I saw him at a workshop, later at a book signing and thought him to be rather sweet and shy. It was just before his last surgery and he looked so frail and vulnerable. Later I sent him a card to wish him well."

The man smiled, indulgently, she supposed, and went back to his reading.

Neal had teased her about sending the card, she remembered, wondering why she would babble on to a stranger.

She had begun to feel drowsy when the cabin lights blinked and suddenly a voice: "Uh–we are experiencing—" Drink cans and bottles flying from the snack cart, darkness: free falling, plummeting faster, faster, all the breath sucked out of her.

In the whirling nightmare she clawed at the blackness; her fingers touched fingers, grasped a hand. Lights flickered on, off, on again as the big craft shuddered and began a wobbly climb. Her senses returned, hurtling toward her like a giant roller coaster; sounds of crying, whiffs of vomit in the aisles, the feel of her dry lips bonded to her teeth. Lights winked from a city close below. Too close below.

"I seem to have lost circulation in my fingers," she heard the man beside her say. She saw she still gripped both his hands as the wheels of the plane touched down for an emergency landing.

"By the way," he said. "My name is Gordon Sinclair."

It was past midnight when they arrived in Saint Louis and he asked, when she stumbled while walking down the ramp to the terminal, "are you all right?"

"I'm working on it," She tried a faint smile.

She stopped at the first telephone to call home and, after saying goodnight to Neal and Sally, saw Gordon motion to her from across the room. He sat at a small orange colored table in a corner of the snack bar, two coffees and a basket of fries in front of him. A quick rush of hunger started to gnaw inside her when she slid in next to him.

"So," his grin showed a chipped front tooth and crinkles around hazel eyes, "here's to a couple of survivors, to me and you, whoever you are."

"Oh gosh, sorry. It's Lyla, Lyla Carter. I'm an electrical engineer at the Big River shopping mall under construction here. My home's in Birmingham. Are you from there, too?"

"Nope. I'm from Joplin; just happened to be in Alabama over the week-end on business. My company has the contract for heating and air conditioning at Big River, so looks like we'll be seeing each other from time to time." He handed her the business card he pulled from his shirt pocket. "I'll be glad to drop you off at your motel."

"Tell you what. I have a car reserved, but look me up at the job and I'll take you out for a drink."

The third time she dialed Michael's room at the dormitory, he answered.

"I'm not sick or anything; it's just that I'm pretty busy," he told her when she asked.

"I know something's wrong, Michael."

"It's personal, Mom. Let it rest, okay? I'll work it out."

Later in the week she had a long conversation with Nick who said he might stay down in Florida during the summer, working as a life guard; Neal called to tell her Sally had a slight accident.

"Is she hurt? I can catch the next flight." The thump of her heartbeat started to pound in her ears.

"Sally is fine, not a scratch, but I can't say the same for the rear end of your car. She backed it into the rock wall behind the gym last night after band practice."

Lyla found Gordon's note with a telephone number clipped to a file on her desk:

Sorry I missed you. If offer of drink is still on, pick out a place and I'll meet you.

Later that evening, she watched him thread his way to the table she had chosen in front of a long planter banked with ivy and philodendron. Seeing him for the first time wearing neatly pressed slacks with coat and tie made her smile as she remembered a phrase Grandpa Harper used to say: "He cleans up real good."

He sat down in the chair opposite her and after the waiter brought bourbon on the rocks for him and white wine for her, he said, "You sure know how to pick a fancy place, Lyla Carter." He raised his glass for a moment to catch the reflection of light flickering around the small crystal oil lamp in the center of their table.

"It's the least I can do to show my appreciation for saving me from cardiac arrest on the airplane that night."

They talked about the job, their conversation flowing easily about labor problems, time schedules.

"Have you always lived in Alabama?" he asked over after dinner coffee.

"In and around," she smiled. "I'm small town, a P.K."

"Sorry. You've lost me."

"P.K., preacher's kid. My grandfather, who was all the family I had, was a minister. We were called Holy Rollers; made a lot of noise at revival meetings. Hell fire and Hallelujah, all that. At one point in my life I planned to become a missionary; I really felt a call to do it, but back in college God and I had a falling out and I decided on a more lucrative career."

"I would never have thought of you as a small town old time religion lady."

"Well, I don't find time for the church these days. I'm afraid Grandpa Harper would say I have lost moral courage, drifted afar, but maybe my son Michael will bring me back to the fold." She set her cup in the saucer and brushed a strand of hair from her cheek. "Tell me about you."

"Not much there. Divorced, no kids. Used to drink a lot more than I do now; my work keeps me pretty busy. Do you like jazz concerts?"

"Yes. Very much."

"The summer jazz jubilee starts next week. It's a festival in the park: professional, amateur, some of it darn good. We can catch a couple of hot dogs, hear some music. My treat."

"I'd like that. Thank you."

Lyla joined Neal for a July Fourth charity golf outing in Memphis. At the end of the day they sat dangling their feet in the motel pool while he updated her on news from home.

"Sally's summer job at Speedy Burger has turned her into a millionaire; she's filled a quart mayonnaise jar with her tips. Nick is off with a fraternity brother for the week-end; he's brown as leather from living on the beach. Michael is spending the holidays at home keeping an eye on Sally."

"Do you know what is wrong with Michael?" Lyla asked. "When I talk with him he always seems preoccupied. I think he and Nora are having serious problems, don't you?"

"Frankly, I hope he breaks it off with Nora. She is putting a lot of pressure on him to get married; I'm glad he decided to stay in Oklahoma for summer session." Neal scooped a handful of water from the pool, dribbled it down the front of her swimsuit. "And you worry too much about that boy."

"I suppose you're right. Nick and Sally are both totally uncomplicated, but Michael, my prototype child–I've never known how to deal with. Maybe I stand a little in awe of him." She sighed, smiling up at Neal. "Anyway, I'll be moving out of my apartment soon and back home again. By the way, the Big River people are planning a banquet next month to celebrate the grand opening of the mall. I'm mentioning it now in case you can make plans to take a holiday, come be my date for the evening."

"I'll try to arrange to get away," he said.

Lyla worked straight through the next two weeks. Late one afternoon, Gordon stopped by as she sorted through stacks of papers piled on her desk.

"Play truant with me tomorrow and I'll take you on a quick tourist trip," he said. "You can't possibly spend time in this grand old city without going to the zoo, taking a ride through the arch on the cog train."

It was almost midnight when they stopped off at the little beer garden about a mile from her apartment. They sat across from each other at a small wooden table where the lights glistened along the river. When the band struck up the last song before closing time, Gordon said, "I'd ask you to dance but I have no idea how to do the polka."

"It's been fun," she smiled, "but I have a big day tomorrow and I have stayed out 'way past my curfew."

"I don't want the evening to end." He brushed the back of her hand lightly with his fingers. "Our first meeting created a special bond between us, you know, and I'm going to hate like hell to say goodbye to you when the time comes."

Lyla cradled the telephone against her shoulder while she listened to Neal's voice.

"Honey, I thought I would be able to get away for a couple of days, but I'm on a deadline to finish a job. I'm really sorry to miss the party."

"I actually don't care much about going," she said. "It will be one of those farewell affairs, you know–creamed chicken and green peas and lots of speeches."

"Of course you should go," he urged. "Good public relations."

"What are you going to wear?" Sally's voice cut in on the other line.

"My long black skirt will do," Lyla laughed. "Maybe I'll spiff it up with a new top, make it suitable for the private club crowd.

"Parking space will be limited," Gordon said. "We can go together in my car, if you'd like."

The drizzle of rain that started earlier had cleared away by evening, making way for the reflection of a slice of orange moon to shimmer in the fountain in front of the club house. After dinner, Lyla circled the room, shaking hands, applauding speeches, stopping to chat until the first notes from the band signaled the last dance, the sweet sad waltz that reminded her of all the goodbyes she had said during the years.

"May I have this one?" Gordon suddenly appeared at her elbow.
He held her awkwardly, stiffly at first before sweeping her close. His breath was warm on her cheek and she felt a tingle zigzag up her spine from the spot where his hand pressed lightly against her back.

They were silent on the drive back to her apartment. The front door lock made a loud click when she turned the key. Gordon stood inside the small entry alcove while she went to answer the ringing telephone.

"Come sit down," she called to him. "Seems I left a folder of papers on my table at the club. One of the employees is bringing it by in about an hour."

"I can go pick it up," Gordon said.

"It isn't necessary. My address is on it; the man who called just now said he comes by here on his way home. He will ring the bell when he drops it off."

He still waited in the entry hall.

She held out her hands to him as she walked by. "I'll put on a pot of coffee, so come talk to me while it brews."

He came to her, grasping her hands tightly while they stood looking at each other without words, without needing to speak.

"I should go now," he said.

Her tears came without warning, filling her eyes so that she saw him through a gauzy mist. She let go his hands and gathered him to her.

"Don't go," she said. "Stay."

Afterwards she slid noiselessly out of bed and in the narrow rows of light through the blinds, inched her way to open and close the bathroom door without a sound. Standing naked under the harsh glare of the ceiling light, her tears flowed again, sweeping away her mascara in tiny polluted streams down her cheeks.

The loud chime of the doorbell made her jump. Was it an hour already since the call from the club? She threw her robe around her, fumbling to tie the sash as she hurried to open the door. The breath caught in her throat. Michael stood in the circle of brightness spilling beneath the porch light.

"Michael...what's wrong? Why have you left school?"

"Because I need to talk with you."

"Everything okay out there?" Gordon called from the bedroom.

"Sorry, Mom. Bad Timing." Michael's eyes grew wide as he backed away.

"Oh God, Michael. Wait. Please wait."

Gordon came to stand beside her as the red tail lights swept out of sight at the end of the block.

"The young man from the club seemed in a hurry," he laughed.

"Oh God, it was Michael. It was my son."

He brought a glass of water, put it in her hands and sat down beside her on the sofa. "What can I say except I'm sorry?"

"You don't need to apologize; you didn't rape me. I sensed your vulnerability tonight. I knew my own,"

"I'm not sorry I made love to you," he said. "Being with you was the sweetest I've ever known, but I did it knowing it was against your principles. For that, I apologize."

She dabbed at her eyes with the crumpled piece of tissue fished from the pocket of her robe. "I do have feelings for you, but I never meant for them to get out of control."

He said, "I've loved you since about five minutes after I first saw you and if you want me, I'll stay. But I love you enough to walk if you want me out of your life."

"I just want my life back. I want it the way it was."

He cupped her face in his hands and kissed her.

The door creaked, its closing echoed behind him. She watched the streak of headlights slide across the window panes as his car pulled slowly away.

Lyla began to walk back and forth, pacing up and down the room. Her thoughts whirled: say nothing to Neal, keep silent. No. Confess, get it out in the open. Say to him: I did a terrible thing to you, to myself, to our marriage vows. Can you forgive me?

A sip of cold black coffee left from breakfast washed a bitter wave across her tongue. Her thoughts tumbled one over another as she tried to assemble them in orderly fashion. Michael will not confide in Nick or Sally; her logic told her. He will not say to his father that he heard a man's voice calling from his mother's bedroom.

Explanation: Oh Michael, it wasn't what you apparently thought. My co-worker who drove me to the banquet had a little too much wine; I urged him to stay until he was fit to drive. My goodness, just because it happened to be a man– In the hours before dawn she slept, sitting upright. The ringing of the telephone awakened her to hazy sunlight starting to jab at her eyelids.

"Lyla." Neal's voice. "I came in on the 8:00 flight. Can you come pick me up?"

"You're here? I thought you were not coming."

When he didn't answer, she felt a cold panic growing inside her. "Neal, what is it? Tell me."

"Just come" he said.

In the private room where a flight attendant had arranged for them to meet, he took Lyla in his arms and told her Michael was dead, that his car had flipped off an exit ramp outside Cape Girardeau, that he died on impact.

"We have to go there to identify the body," he whispered. "Please be strong for both of us. I think I would die, too, if you were not here for me."

She stood mute, too numb to cry, rocking his head against her, his tears falling warm against her breast.

"I killed him," she said at last. "I killed our son."

"I won't hear you say that." Neal wiped his eyes and moved away to stand by the window. "The police clocked his car at more than one hundred miles an hour. You must know how deeply troubled he was when he came to see you last night. I wanted to prepare you but he made me promise I would let him tell you that he had dropped out of school. And about Nora."

"What about Nora?"

"She is pregnant; it isn't Michael's child. My God, he did talk with you, didn't he? What did he say?"

"Yes. He talked. He said, 'sorry mom, bad timing.'"

"I don't understand," Neal said.

It seemed to Lyla such a long time before he turned to look at her.

"I don't understand," he said again.

In the dim light shunted through the panes, she watched the naked innocence fading from his eyes. She watched, knowing she must probe the deepest chasm of her soul to find the courage to kill again.

HOT AIR BALLOON RIDE IN TANZANIA

Throughout the safari, suspense about tomorrow's hot air balloon ride has continued to build. It will be a first time experience for most of us. We are scheduled to go up at sunrise unless rain comes or the early morning winds exceed 10 knots per hour.

Thunder rumbles during the night, a smattering of rain pelts against our tent. I hear the wind thrashing the branches of the yellow fever trees, but by wake-up call at 5:30 the sky is a deep cloudless blue, wind calm.

The two-story high multi striped balloon billows and sways in the breeze while we crawl into the eight-person wicker basket below. Fire from the overhead flame rack swooshes and bellows, readying for lift-off.

Going up is easy, balloonist Captain John Coleman assures us; getting back down in the fun part. He shows us how to brace for landing at the end of the flight when the basket touches down. It will tip over on its side, he says, and bump along the ground until the balloon is brought under control.

We soar up into a pink and gold morning, sometimes floating silently not more than ten feet above a herd of zebra before ascending to skim above the trees. Branches scratch and scrape the bottom of the basket. A flock of green pigeons flutter away as we approach a deep wooded area along the Mara river. Crocodiles lie sunning along the banks; a mama hippo floats half submerged, her new born baby clinging to her back. Hundreds of wildebeests string out to march single file. A lioness plays pat-a-cake with two cubs, our shadow sways above them.

We hang tight for the landing, feel the basket tilt, flip on its side and bounce once, twice before the ground crew brings it to a halt. Captain Coleman explains that the extra bounce came when the basket hit the top of a tall mound of termites.

Down on the ground, the workers have laid out breakfast for us on a bright red tablecloth. They stick Masai spears in the ground at the four corners of the eating area to keep the kite birds from swooping down and snatching the food. Kite birds, we are told, have a great respect for the Masai spears and want no part of them..We sip on champagne from silver goblets, eat French toast, sausage and bacon cooked over the flame racks.

At mid-morning we ride back to camp, then to Nairobi where we leave for home. The flight back to Birmingham is a hard eighteen hours, but along with aching muscles and seventy-five rolls of exposed film, we have brought back memories of an experience in one of the earth's last remaining wild life kingdoms. We have seen a little piece of Africa, home of a proud people whose culture dates back to the dawn of time.

PLACES IN TIME

*T*he cat came to me in a dream, drifting through remnants of darkness into shards of light unfolding around her. Lifting one white forepaw, she meowed a greeting and bounded towards me. I awoke with my heart pounding, my mouth dry. The scene was intense, so real I still saw the amber eyes gleaming, smelled a faintly musty scent tugging at a memory fogged by time, blurry as an old out of focus photograph.

I lay on the bed in unfamiliar shadows of a room, gathering my thoughts until I remembered I was in a hotel in Kusadasi, a tiny fishing village nestled on the coast of the Aegean Sea. I had come here, to Turkey, to join my tour guide for an early morning walk through the ruins of the ancient city of Ephesus.

It was still an hour before sunrise, but each time I tried to to go back to sleep I saw the cat's image; the sheen of her brown and gray striped fur seemed stamped on my eyelids. From my windows I looked toward the sea, nodding in gentle ripples against the shore line. The silhouette of a fisherman in a wooden boat rocked up and down on the rim of the horizon. With the first rays of the sun, a pair of white gulls came to strut the length of a long wooden pier.

I dressed and walked down the path winding through a flower garden to the rocks at the water's edge. A breeze blew warm and damp across my face, blending the salt air with smells of fish and crawly urchins of the deep.

An old man with a ragged blue stocking cap perched on the back of his head knelt beside clumps of red and pink geranium. The scrape of his trowel against a stick or stone in the ground played a raspy percussion to a tune he whistled under his breath.

Then I saw her, the cat, as she was in my dream—brown and gray striped fur, white forepaws, amber eyes. She sat beside a row of bright orange flowers, eyes following me. I caught my breath, unable to move until she trotted over to arch her back against my legs as though to say, "I have waited, I knew you would come." I knelt to scoop her up, my heart racing faster when I recognized the scent of her fur, like a whiff of dankness from crumbling old books.

I sat down on a rock to scratch her ears, hold her while listening to her purrs and the lapping of waves at my feet. I watched the sunlight hit the water with a shower of diamond bright sparks that seemed to ignite a trail of fire reaching as far as I could see.

The cat walked close beside me all the way to the steps at the hotel's entrance. Stroking her once more, I turned to go inside. When I looked back, she had not moved.

Later that morning as I walked through Ephesus, between the pillars of the once mighty Gate of Hercules, I felt a tingle run down my spine. Although I knew I had never been here, I felt I had returned to a time, to a familiar place. A faint sound in the distance was like the creaking of a chariot's wooden wheels rolling across the marble streets. With each step I took, the dream about the cat gnawed at me. Once, I thought I glimpsed her in a shadow behind a broken urn, smelled her scent near a dark niche in a stone column. I waited, expecting to find her perched on a pedestal somewhere around a corner.

The day turned stifling hot with a sprinkle of marshmallow clouds tagging the sun. A powdering of red dust from the excavation digs in progress stung my eyes, blew in ripples across the mosaic paved sidewalks of the old city. Perhaps not more than a dozen other tourists milled about in the area, but as I neared the facade of the Library of Celcus, it seemed I heard the buzz of hundreds of voices. The guide had begun to explain that we were standing in the courtyard where the Ephesians once grouped for political debates and lectures. When he suddenly paused in mid-sentence, I realized he was looking at me.

"Are you unwell?" he asked. "You look quite pale."

"I feel I also stood here at that time," I said.

"You see?" he chortled, "I am very good at my work. I make the ancient past come alive for you, yes?"

It was late evening when I returned to the hotel to pack for an early morning flight out of Turkey. The cat was nowhere to be found. As I made room in my bag for the packets of cinnamon and saffron, the jeweled copper lamp and harem slippers from the street bazaar, I told myself I had to find her. Although I knew it was impossible to take her with me, I had to say goodbye.

I walked through the garden the next morning, hoping to see her along the path. The old man had come back to dig in the flowers. He nodded when I asked if he spoke English. I described the cat and inquired if he had seen it today.

"No, madame. I do not see it. I never see it, only the ones who belong here." He pointed to a fat yellow tom lolling in the shade of a large rock. A couple of half grown kittens chased a red ball in the grass.

"But the cat I tell you about walked with me yesterday, here on the path. Surely you saw it."

He looked back at me and shrugged. "Your travels must take you to many places, madame. Could it have been in another place, perhaps another time when you saw this cat?"

The wind gusted suddenly cold and damp from the sea. I hugged my jacket closer around my shoulders.

"Perhaps so," I turned to walk away. "Perhaps it was another time."

WORDS UNSPOKEN

*L*ast night he told her about the girl.

"It wasn't like I had an affair with her," he said. "An inter-lude, I suppose. Five minutes and it was all over, but since then it has been on my conscience, gnawing at me every time I make love to you."

Logan closed the sliding glass panel behind him and came out to sit beside her in the sun dappled corner of the patio.

"You said you don't want to go out tonight, so I called the Fergusons and canceled." He eased in next to her on the slatted porch swing, hunching his shoulders past the line of wood splinters on the back. "I said you are coming down with a virus."

Joanna nodded, in agreement, he imagined, dipping her head stiffly the way she always did when hurt or angry. Since he told her last night about what happened in Dallas, she seemed determined not to break the tension that stretched like a taut frayed rope between them.

"A virus seems a good enough excuse to miss a wine and cheese party, so I said you've caught a bug of some kind," he said.

The flagstone terrace below them looked out over a grove of trees, pale green and daubed with random patches of snowy dogwood. Their house, gray brick with dark blue shutters, faced a wide street. Horns honked and tires squealed on the pavement near the edge of the front lawn. In the back yard, fat squirrels scampered across the grass and a small brown rabbit came in late evening to nibble on Joanna's clumps of white petunias.

Logan lit a cigarette, cupped the flame for a moment in his palm. Joanna tucked her long denim skirt around her ankles and leaned back from the thin line of smoke trailing in her direction; a reason, he thought, to move farther away from him. He watched the movement of her hands as she dropped them in her lap, laced her fingers tightly together. A spark of sun flashed through the trees, spilled bright as blood on the ruby in her ring.

He had always thought her hands exquisite. If he were artist instead of architect, he would paint them, the porcelain fine fingers, long tapered nails like deep red petals of a rose. He supposed her hands turned him on in the same way legs or breasts or a smile might effect another man; he told her this the first time he took her out. They were in college then and Joanna was dating his fraternity brother, Mickey Scott.

She blushed when he said it, withdrew her hand from his.

"I agreed to come with you because Mickey hates Italian movies and I hate seeing them alone." She tilted her chin, smiling up at him, and he thought that under the marquee lights her hair was apricot sherbet.

"I have tickets to the jazz concert next week," he whispered halfway through the film, feeling a rush of blood to his face. He wondered if his heart knew he had already fallen in love with her, that he could never love another woman.

Last night, while she walked woodenly around him, snatching up sheets and a blanket for the guest bedroom, he said again there could not be anyone but her.

"The girl in Dallas—she was like something that never happened."

"But she happened."

"Except for that time, and I honestly don't remember much about it, I've never been with anyone else since I met you. Even in 'Nam," he said. " The times I went on R&R in Thailand, when some of the guys took on half the whores in Bangkok, I couldn't touch them. Swear to God, not one."

"What was her name, the whore in Dallas?"

"How the hell would I know? I never asked, and if she told me I wouldn't remember. I was too drunk to think of my own name.

"It happened the last night of the convention, after I found out about the promotion. I had sat around in the bar with Chester Miller, getting stinking crazy. Chester and a couple of the other fellows thought it was a great joke, sneaking this girl in, having her in my room when I went up after the banquet.

"Sometime after midnight, I guess it was getting on toward the wee hours, I opened the door and there she was, stark naked, spread-eagle on the bed with a stack of pillows under her butt."

"So you couldn't tell her to get the hell out? Jesus, Logan, I was stuck here at home, nursing an impacted wisdom tooth while you celebrated becoming a VP, humping a whore on a waterbed in Dallas."

He glanced across the swing at Joanna who turned to look at him as though she read his thoughts. She pushed back a strand of hair the wind whipped across her face. Late evening light sifted through the young leaves on an overhanging branch of the persimmon tree, gloving her hand in lacy shadows.

"Why, Logan?" she asked. "It's been two years; why say anything at all? I'd have never found out, you know."

"I was tired of it hanging over my head. The only way to get rid of it was to tell you. I guess I foolishly hoped that, knowing it meant nothing to me, you would say it doesn't matter now."

The sun had dropped from sight, draping a gossamer cape of red and gold across the shoulders of the woods. Logan watched it glow, fade and disappear as though the streaking fingers of evening gathered it back and replaced it with a long gray shroud. A mockingbird flitted to a lower limb, ruffled its feathers and began to sing.

The swing squeaked when Joanna stood up. Her sneakers made a faint swish as she moved toward the door; she drew her arms against her sides and shivered.

"I'll get your sweater," he said.

She shook her head. "I'll go inside now. I've done a lot of soul searching while we've sat here. I was angry last night, my pride wounded, I guess." She turned to him when he came to stand with her, said softly, "you are right, you know. What happened a long time ago shouldn't touch us now. It shouldn't matter."

He ached to feel her close to him. Without thinking, he held out his arms. She slipped into them, standing motionless except for the tremble that ran along her spine when he pulled her close to him. She laid her head on his chest while he stroked her hair, her cheeks, traced his fingers over the outline of her lips. He felt the soft curve of her belly pressed against him, her breasts straining under the fabric of a thin white blouse.

"Make love to me, Logan," she whispered.

They walked together, back inside the house, down the narrow dim hall to their room, and sank down without turning back the bedspread. Quietly at first, then like warriors in combat; lunging, holding, drifting, holding. Outside the open draperies, darkness chased the last shards of twilight across the panes, sent them racing in pursuit of the lost sun.

He lay beside her when it was over, feeling whole again, smelling the sweet musty scent of her, the way it had been the first time they were together after the fraternity dance.

He went alone that night and arrived late, stiff and itchy in a rented tux. The chandeliers in the Crystal Ball Room at the old Strand Hotel gleamed over the half empty silver bowl in the middle of the banquet table. A dozen couples moved across the dance floor, their shadows like disjointed marionettes swaying along the walls. He saw Joanna and Mickey standing at the far end of the room, arguing, Logan knew, from seeing the tilt of her head, the arch of her back.

He poured a cup of punch and when he looked up, Joanna stood beside him.

"Mickey and I broke up," she said.

They danced. He tried to remember the name of it, the sweet slow tune, but he could recall only the sound of his heart drumming in his ears, the heat of her like a low burning fire on his skin.

The music had stopped when he saw Mickey stalking toward them.

"We're leaving." Mickey fished the car keys out of his pocket and took hold of Joanna's arm. She pulled away, stood facing him, her eyes unblinking.

"God damn it. You came with me, you're leaving with me."

"Like hell," she said, and when his hand reached for her again she grabbed the keys, ran out on the balcony and flung them over the railing.

Logan never saw the punch coming; Mickey's fist caught him above the right cheek bone and sent him sprawling across the polished marble floor. He came up swinging.

He took her home. She walked him up the steps of her off-campus apartment, led him inside. A copper lamp, hanging from a chain in the ceiling, dropped a small unsteady circle of light in the middle of the room. He leaned back on the couch while she rubbed ice cubes on the purplish blue lump under his eye and stroked his forehead with her long delicate fingers. He closed his eyes and she wound her arms around him, whispering, "Make love to me, Logan." Over and over she said it, the way she whispered it now while they lay where they fell moments ago.

He felt her breath, coming soft and rhythmical again, brush his face.

"You've been far, far away," she sighed. "Where were you?"

"I was thinking about the night you broke up with Mickey."

"It was a lovely fight the two of you had, but that was long ago on another planet, wasn't it?"

"Listen, I want to tell you–"

She rolled her fingers lightly over his lips. "No more confessions. I don't want to hear."

"No, really. I have to say something I never told you." He moved her hand aside.

"I used to be jealous as hell of Mickey, even after we married. Like when I went off to 'Nam and he was still here, the son of a bitch. I had nightmares about you and him getting together again." He slid his arm from under her head and lay propped up on his elbow, looking down at her face, her eyes luminous in the shadows. "I was more afraid of losing you than of taking a bullet from the Cong."

He felt her flinch, pull away.

Her hand rested on his pillow. He touched it, like carved ivory, cool against him. A tight knot rolled, grabbed and twisted in his belly.

"Joanna." He saw the glint of tears that pooled but had not spilled over her cheeks. "Joanna?"

"Please don't." He strained to hear her voice. "Let it drop."

"Like hell I'll let it drop."

"Some words are better left unspoken, Logan. Don't make me say them."

"I want to know. How many fucking times? Once, twice, fifty? Mickey's place, the sofa? My God, in our *bed*?"

"Once. One time, and it was in our bed, in this bed–maybe on the same sheets. I don't remember. It was a New Year's Eve and I wasn't drunk. I was lonely. God, I was lonely. I called him and he was here, flesh and blood, not an 8x10 blow-up in silver frame on the dresser. He held me and I remember everything. I remember I was safe and warm and for those few moments there wasn't a war and I wasn't afraid. Does it help if I say I'm sorry?"

Logan sat up and groped for his lighter and the package of Winstons on the night table. When the last cigarette had burned down to the filter, to a long gray ash quivering in his fingers, he stubbed out the red glow and sank down next to her, feeling the pain that had begun to seep through the fibers of his mind. He wanted to call back his words, to lock his guilt away and give back her secret to keep safe somewhere inside her.

Joanna lay with her eyes closed. He looked at her hands. One rested at her side, the other across her bare breast. In the quiet paleness of the room, it seemed to him that her long nails glistened, the bloody claws of a tigress who had not yet licked them clean after the kill.

THE REDEMPTION OF LAMAR BILLBERRY

*P*earl stripped off her clothes, the dress and soggy underwear, and hung them on a nail behind the bathroom door. When the telephone rang, she grabbed a towel and threw it around her shoulders before running barefoot down the hall to find out who was calling. She lived on a farm south of Nectar, staying alone in the unpainted four room house that had once belonged to her father. Her nearest neighbors, Olley Mae and Pet, lived more than a mile and a half down Sugar Creek Road, so there was no one to see that she was naked.

"Hello, Pearl?" Olley Mae was going deaf, and her voice was so loud Pearl had to hold the receiver away from her ear. "You finished hoeing yet?"

"I just come in and taken off my sweaty clothes." Pearl pushed back a limp strand of hair. "Lordy, it's hot out there."

"Listen, Pearl, you forget about the weeds in your okra patch until tomorrow. I'm coming over to help you get prettied up. Me and Pet's giving you a home permanent wave."

"What are you talking about? I ain't had a wave put in my hair since tenth grade. You and Pet gone crazy?"

"No, but you'll about go wild when you hear the news. Guess who is coming tomorrow, driving all the way up from Prattville?"

"How would I know? I heard that the Stamps Quartet is coming to sing at the Mount Zion revival, but that's not until Sunday."

"Sit down if you're standing up, Pearl."

"Olley Mae, will you get on with who it is?"

"It's Lamar. Lamar is coming to see you."

"Who?"

"Has the sun baked your brains, Pearl? Lamar Billberry, that's who."

"Why is Lamar Billberry coming to see me?" Pearl felt the blood rush to her face. "I haven't thought about Lamar since Lord knows when."

"Ha, ha, Pearl Elizabeth Appleton. You are lying through your teeth. How come you still keep his picture in the gold locket around your neck?

"Don't yell, Olley Mae. I can hear you. How do you know he is coming tomorrow to see me?"

"He called Floyd Johnson long distance from Prattville last night, and I just this minute found out about it from Floyd's wife. You remember that fist fight him and Floyd had out behind the school, the time Floyd accused Lamar of stealing money from the cash register at Uncle Elmer's filling station where Floyd worked?"

"Lamar didn't take no money" Pearl clutched at the towel as she shifted her weight from one foot to the other. She saw the goose bumps break out on her legs and she felt indecent to be without clothes while she talked on the telephone about Lamar Billberry. "He worked in my daddy's feed store for two years, and Daddy never seen him take so much as a grain of corn."

"Well, the thing is, Pearl, Lamar did steal money from Floyd's Uncle Elmer's cash register. He admitted it last night, said it has weighed on his mind all these years, and he wants to pay back what he took. With interest."

"Why don't he just mail the money to Floyd, since Uncle Elmer's dead and gone?"

"Floyd put that very question to him, offered to forgive him right there on the telephone, but Lamar says he plans to do it face to face. Says he has been born again and is purging hisself of all his old sins."

"But Lamar's coming to see Floyd Johnson, not me."

"I'm getting to that if you'll quit buttin' in. Lamar asked if you still live here on your daddy's place. And Pearl," Olley Mae lowered her voice so Pearl had to press her ear against the receiver, " he asked if you ever got married. Floyd said he seemed real glad to hear you are still a single lady."

"I suppose he could be wanting to drop by just to say hello." Pearl heard her heart pounding in her ears.

"It's clear as can be he wants to purge hisself of the sin he committed when he run off after promising to marry you."

"I told you I never want to talk about it again." Pearl's fingers opened and closed around the locket on the chain around her neck. "You said you'd keep it secret."

"I'll have you know I never breathed a word to a soul except Pet, and maybe one or two others."

"Well, I don't hold it against him no longer," Pearl sighed. "It's been years, and we was just kids."

"But don't you see, Pearl? He's coming back to ask you to be his wife, now that he has repented and joined the church."

"What if he's already got a wife?"

"That's the good part I saved for last. He told Floyd his wife passed last year. Lamar is a widower and he's got a fine job at the Prattville City Water Works."

Pearl was shivering when she hung up the telephone, although perspiration rolled down her neck in little rivulets and disappeared in the candy striped towel she held tightly over her breasts. She hurried back to the bathroom to put on her slippers and red flowered muumuu, then shuffled to the kitchen for a glass of iced tea.

The thought of seeing Lamar Billberry again left her feeling giddy; the tea seemed to float to her head like scuppernong wine as she remembered it had been twenty years since her daddy found her and Lamar together one night in a back room at the feed store. When he had threatened to horsewhip Lamar and send Pearl away to live with her aunt in Jasper, Lamar put his arm around her waist, looked her daddy in the eyes and told him he intended to marry Pearl. He was going to do it soon, he said.

The next day Lamar told Pearl they would get married in a month for sure if there was any need for a quick wedding. Otherwise, he explained, they could wait until fall when he would have saved enough money to reserve the honeymoon suite at the Tutwiler Hotel in Birmingham. She bought a blue taffeta dress with matching pumps and put a black nylon baby doll nightgown in layaway. Before she got a chance to tell him they didn't have to be in no hurry to get married after all, Lamar had left Nectar without so much as a kiss-my-foot.

Pearl was still sipping iced tea and thinking about Lamar when Olley Mae and Pet opend the back door. Olley Mae was fanning herself with a folded newspaper and Pet carried the home permanent wave kit with a bag of extra curlers.

"I don't know as I want a wave," Pearl protested.

"Hush," Olley Mae tied the plastic cape around Pearl's shoulders. "You want Lamar to come catch you looking like a picked chicken?"

"Floyd's wife says Lamar's coming back to Nectar just to let folks know he is a big shot down in Prattville," Pet said.

"Well, it's plain to me the Lord has saved him and he wants to right the wrongs he's done," Olley Mae argued. "He's coming back to ask Pearl to marry him. You mark my words."

Pet watched the clock so she would know when it was time to pour the neutralizer over Pearl's head. Olley Mae tweezed Pearl's eyebrows while her hair was curling; she made her promise to put Maybelline on her lashes before Lamar came.

"You sure are going to look nice, Pearl, when we get done," Olley Mae said. "I'll telephone you tomorrow soon as I see Lamar's new car top the ridge when he is headed back to town. It wouldn't surprise me a bit to see you snuggled right there on the seat beside him."

"Oh hush teasing me, Olley Mae."

"It's the truth, Pearl," Pet said when they were ready to leave. "Lamar won't be able to resist you. Sleep on your back tonight so you won't mash the front of your curls flat."

She didn't sleep. At five-thirty the next morning she was already in the kitchen, polishing the cut class pitcher that had belonged to her mother. She had convinced herself that Olley Mae was right; Lamar was coming back to ask her to marry him. He had never forgotten her, as she had not forgotten him. In the soft thick darkness last night she dared to think about marrying Lamar Billberry and going away to live with him in Prattville. Now with daylight streaking through the windows, she was less certain. But she was not less determined it could happen, would happen.

When she heard the car stop in the driveway, she didn't wait for his knock before opening the door.

"Pearl?" He stared at her for a moment before extending his hand. "Well, Pearl. It sure is good to see you again."

She looked into his eyes and saw that they were still the color of the cornflowers that bloomed each year down by the water well. "Do come in, Lamar," she said, unable to recall the words of the speech she had practiced in front of the mirror. "Did you have a good trip up from Prattville?"

"Smooth as lard. First time I've had my brand new car out on the road. She'll hit a hundred in nothin' flat."

Pearl held the door open, but he didn't make a move to come inside.

"Floyd told me you never got married, so I guess you don't have no children. You never had a child, did you?" He took a step back on the porch.

"No, I never did."

"Well, I'm glad to see you after all these years, and I praise the Lord I have a chance to right a wrong. I'm sorry your daddy passed before I got around to repenting."

"Come on in and have some lemonade while we talk." She opened the door wider and tugged at his sleeve. Bending close to him, she smelled a sweet spiciness that made her tremble. "I know Daddy would be proud you decided to do the right thing."

"Actually, I don't have no time to come sit, Pearl." He reached in his back pocket and took two ten dollar bills from his wallet. "I figure twenty dollars is about right, since it's twice what I took."

"Twenty dollars? You are offering me money for—"

"It was ten I took from your daddy's store. He never knew about it, thought he'd lost it while he unloaded the sacks of feed."

Pearl felt that her body had turned to stone. Lamar took her hand and folded her fingers over the two bills.

"You do forgive me, don't' you, Pearl?"

"It wasn't money you took from me," she said without looking up when he released her hand.

"I didn't take nothing from you except what you gave me." Lamar wiped his eyes on a corner of the lavender handkerchief in the breast pocket of his suit coat. "Why, I accepted a gift from you, Pearl, a wonderful gift of love. What I stole was ten dollars from your daddy. Now that I have made it right, the burden has been lifted from my soul. Praise the Lord. Do you know the Lord, Pearl?"

She didn't answer or lift her head.

Lamar cleared his throat and glanced at his watch. "Well, I guess I'll drive back through town, maybe look up a few folks who'll be surprised to see old Lamar is doing pretty good for hisself."

Her eyes followed the billow of dust that trailed him down Sugar Creek Road. When his car topped the ridge where Olley Mae and Pet lived, she unfastened the gold chain from around her neck. The locket dropped with a soft thud on the wooden floor of the porch and lay like a tiny heart pulsing in the glitter of sunlight before it dropped through a crack between the boards.

She looked down at the two ten dollar bills still clutched in her right hand, opened her fingers and let then flutter away. They dipped and soared, swirling over the planter of boxwood and out across the yard. Pearl was still standing there, watching Lamar Billberry's twenty dollars blow away in the wind when she heard the telephone start to ring.

THE UNIQUENESS OF
AN IMPERFECT DIAMOND

*I*n the dream I am galloping a white stallion through the surf at Waikiki when I hear the sound. It ripples over the water, humming across the waves, and at first I think it is the cry of the gulls who have come to dip and soar around us to pirate away the glints of moonbeams on their wings. But it swells to make impatient jangles in my head and I wake up, fumble for the light switch and the ringing telephone.

Cory, who is heaped in a long rumpled mound next to me under the covers, groans and flops a pillow over his face.

"Darling." It is Mama's voice in my ear, breathy as though she has raced up a long flight of stairs. "I find that I have a break in my schedule and I am simply dying to get acquainted with my beautiful grandchildren." She speaks the words like lyrics of a love poem, and I prop the receiver against my shoulder while I hitch the blanket around me.

My hands shake and I swallow hard to get rid of the lump in my throat. "It's been a long time since I've seen you," I say for openers, but she lets it pass as I knew she would.

The California winter has been cold, she says, drippier than last year, and I see her groping through a San Francisco "fogging", wind whipping her hair like long spikes of autumn wheat. I wonder why she has called, but she doesn't give a clue. She chatters on about the weather; I interrupt to mention that Cory is the new junior partner at Hughes, Gains, Hughes & Hallmark, and I make small talk about the children: Cole sleeps without a two a.m. feeding and Mims is potty trained, finally. I add the word with a laugh. Mama laughs, too, and wonders aloud where the time has gone, with baby Cole born six weeks ago and Mims just turned two and she's never seen either of them.

You choose not to see them, I want to remind her, but instead I blink back tears and reach for the glass slipper I keep on the night stand beside the bed. The slipper is small, no more than two inches long, a reproduction of the style worn around the year 1900. Mama bought it a few years ago when I kept a collection of miniature shoes. She found it in an antique shop in Jackson, Mississippi while she was touring with Texas Jack Sullivan's band. "Of course, the diamond is flawed," she had explained and pointed to the pinpoint of sparkle set in the curve of the heel, "but it lends a uniqueness, sets it apart from the others on the shelf."

I stare at it in my hand, hear her saying now that she has made flight reservations and will arrive Saturday night. She apologies for the late hour. I tell her it doesn't matter; we will pick her up.

Cory watches from under his pillow. I see his eyes, but I look away because the last thing I need from him is another sermon on coping with my feelings for Mama. I have had twenty-five years of practice.

Cory, whose parents still live together in the house where he was born, once described Mama as the prototype free spirit. "So," he had advised when she packed up and moved to California, "give her time to adjust to the idea of becoming a grandmother. Start loving her for what she is and stop trying to change her."

"But she is leaving town practically the minute I tell her I'm pregnant," I cried, and now the sound of her voice on the telephone reminds me of that day.

Cory drags the pillow off his face after I hang up the receiver. He looks wide awake now. I say, "Mama never remembers the difference between Central and Pacific time."

I switch off the light to let him know I don't want to discuss it. He flicks it on again and lies propped on his elbows, watching my fingers rub back and forth across the glass slipper. "You are expecting a genie to pop out and grant three wishes?" he asks.

"Mama says she is coming for a visit. She has bought her ticket, so I think she is actually going to do it this time."

"She's ready for the Grandmother Cycle," he chuckles and slides his arm around my shoulder.

It's true. Mama lives her life in cycles. I have names for each of them. First, there was Save The World, followed by Basic Establishment, then Good Ole Girl. She was into her current period, Intellect & Culture, when I dropped the bomb about being pregnant with Mims.

"How would you like to be earth's most sexy grandparent?" I had asked and braced myself for hugs and squeals and all of the so-my-little-girl-is-having-a-baby cliches, but the expression on her face didn't change except for the faint crease of a frown while she finished filling out a check to the Alabama Symphony.

"Don't be droll, Holly." She looked up and fingered the clasp on the single strand of pearls, milky white against her jade silk blouse. "What about your plans to enter law school next semester?"

"We've decided to have our family first," I managed to say, just as I had rehearsed it.

"But I'm not–you're not ready for babies yet. Good grief, tell me you are not already pregnant!"

Cory interrupts my thoughts about Mama. He scratches up and down my leg with a long snaggy toenail, says, "So, if you don't want to talk about it, turn out the light and let's get some sleep."

I slide the glass slipper back in its place on the night stand and make the room dark again. When I move close to him, I feel the slow rhythm of Cory's heartbeat against me. He strokes my hair, tells me, "Come on, honey. You know you're dying to patch up the fight with your mother."

"There never was a fight," I sigh. "How can I fight with a person who has no logic?"

We kiss goodnight and I close my eyes, but they are like the lens of a camera blinking impressions of Mama as she must have looked tonight, drumming her long fingernails against the telephone, waiting for my sleepy hello.

She has called, sometimes as often as once a week since she moved to California, and each summer she makes long range plans to come for a visit during the holidays. "I'll be there for Thanksgiving," she promises, but in mid-November she postpones her trip until Christmas. Usually it is a couple of weeks into December when she calls to say she can't possibly get away until spring break. So she sends gifts: magazine subscriptions renewals to *Sports Illustrated* and *Southern Living*, English smocked dresses and dolls for Mims, stuffed bear and six month supply of disposable diapers for Cole.

The toys and other gifts to the children are always tagged "to the sweet babies with kisses, kisses," but she does not sign a name that I should teach them to call her.

"Definitely *not* grandmother," she parries via telephone if I remind her that Mims squeals "Gamma, Gamma!" when Cory's mother scoops her up in her arms. "We'll think of something later."

Cory tells me to be patient and wait for Mama's next Cycle. He claims she is a latent grandparent.

I watch him as he sleeps now, with only brown tufts of his hair poking from under the blanket. I try to drift back to Waikiki, to the white stallion and surf, but they are gone. Two-thirty. No cries yet from Cole.

I slip out of bed and into the nursery to see if he is covered. His hands are warm and he has rolled himself into a ball around Bear. Bear's painted eyes glow in the darkness like a pair of amorous fireflies. Mims stirs in her bed next to the crib. I gather her to me, a woolly heap of pink, and set her on her potty seat. She flinches when her bottom touches the cold surface, the tinkle of her small waterfall breaks the stillness. I tuck her in again and stand for a moment to pat her until she dozes off.

Light from the night lamp smears a wavy brightness across a mirror on the wall in front of me. I study my reflection, remember that Mama used to tell me that I inherited my father's best features: his dark curly hair, hazel eyes and "thank God, nothing more." I turn to stand sideways, suck in my stomach and wonder if, when she sees me, Mama will say I need to lose ten pounds. I am not yet flat since Cole was born.

Mims doesn't fret when I stop patting, so I creep away to wriggle back inside my own warm spot. Two forty-five, forty-six. Minutes skip past like the pages of the letter Mama wrote to me almost three years ago.

Darling, life is so stimulating for me. God. the brilliant humanity here at Berkeley! I had reached a dead end in my life back in Alabama, but now I feel that I am sitting at the feet of the masters and the world has its arms open to me. I work days and go to evening classes. I have decided on the field of psychiatric counseling. After all these years of not knowing what I want, I have found my niche at last!

Mama has been searching for her "niche" for as long as I can remember. She must have thought she'd found it when, after my father deserted us, she married Raoul Haverlich and began her Save The World cycle.

Raoul was into Causes, especially the United Neighborhood Coalition For Peace, Social Tolerance & Harmony, and in the 1960s we moved from our house on the south side of Birmingham to an integrated housing complex in Atlanta. Mama began her work with Raoul by changing her hair from beehive to Joplin frizzy. She wore love beads and tie-dyed skirts and picked her guitar at freedom rallies in the city parks.

One day when she and Raoul joined a group of demonstrators blocking the entrance to the Fulton County Court House, the police hauled them off to jail. That afternoon a social worker met me at kindergarten and took me to the juvenile home. When Mama came for me, she told me that Raoul was leaving for Canada and we were going back to Birmingham to live with Aunt Margaret until Mama found a job.

She went to work as a bank teller and became Basic Establishment the next year when she met and married Harold MacPhearson, a driver for the Greyhound Bus Company. Harold was a bachelor, a deacon in the Baptist Church and twenty-five years older than Mama. We went to live with him in the house he shared with his mother until she fell and broke her hip and he had to put her in a nursing home. Every Sunday after church, Harold took us to lunch at Alma Murphy's cafeteria before we went to visit his mother in the long red brick building that smelled old and sad, like bouquets of withering carnations.

While she was married to Harold and still into Basic Establishment, Mama joined the PTA, drove the bloodmobile for Red Cross and had her hair shampooed and teased at the beauty parlor every Friday. She stopped smoking when Harold was around, baked brownies from scratch and allowed me to invite my girl friends to spend-the-night-parties at our house.

Harold left one night to be gone for a week on a charter run from Birmingham to Denver, and the next morning Mama told me we were moving to Nashville. Without Harold. An old friend had telephoned and promised her a job, picking with Texas Jack Sullivan's band at the Grand Ole Opery. "It's something I've always wanted to do, honey," she said when I burst into tears. "This is what I really, really want to do with my life, so please try to understand."

Her Good Ole Girl Cycle began when she married Texas Jack and went on the road with him to tour the Southeast. I went back to live with Aunt Margaret and go to school.

Aunt Margaret used to put her arms around me when she found me in my room, holding the little glass slipper and crying over the 8x10 glossy of Mama in her white leather and rhinestone suit. "Listen, girl," she would say and gather me to her, "your Mama is different and always will be, I suppose. I remember your grandpa used to look at her, shake his head and say, 'I don't understand this child, but by God, don't she shine?'"

I was a senior in college and married to Cory when Mama's career in country music ended. Texas Jack and two members of his band were killed when their car broadsided a gasoline truck near New Orleans. Mama came back to Birmingham and got a job with the Chamber Of Commerce. She enrolled in night courses in political science and art appreciation and went straight into Intellect & Culture.

It is Saturday morning and I have waited all week for the call from Mama saying her plans have changed. She will tell me she has decided to wait until spring, or come on July Fourth, for sure. When the telephone rings, I jump and spill the raspberry Jello I am mixing with fruit cocktail in a copper mold shaped to resemble a pineapple. The call is from a man who does tree trimming service in the neighborhood. He also checks for beetles and pine borers. I hang up and stare at the ugly bruised stain seeping across the kitchen counter.

Both babies have developed sniffles. Cole is in his basket. He is crying and making bubbly gurgles in his nose. Mims clings like lint to the leg of my jeans. "Gamma coming!" she repeats singsong and I tell her no, not Gamma but another lady is coming all the way from California just to see Mims and Cole and isn't that nice? She falls on the floor and begins kicking the door on the dishwasher.

An hour before I am supposed to leave for the airport, I check the schedule again. Mama's flight is due to arrive at 11:30. Cory, who is staying home with the children, helps me on with my coat when it is time to go. He kisses the tip of my nose, promises to check Cole's temperature in an hour, tells me to drive carefully.

I have dropped the glass slipper in my pocket, but I don't know why.

I arrive at the terminal half an hour early, stop by the snack bar and buy a Hershey with almonds; I have finished eating it by the time I walk to the gate where Mama's flight comes in. An old man in the waiting area gets up, hobbles off. I take his seat by the windows.

Beyond the glass the night is a black velvet mushroom. I squint to search the sky, catch a deep breath as a tiny pinpoint of light grows to sweep the runway with brightness. I picture Mama unbuckling the seat belt before the big craft comes to a stop, see her perched on the edge of her seat, running a comb through her long blond hair and fishing for lipstick somewhere in the bottom of her purse.

The roar of engines shuts off, the room swells with a stream of people, dwindles to a trickle. But she does not appear. A salty ache fills my throat and I start to turn away. Then I see her.

She is the last to come down the ramp, walking behind two flight attendants whose feet move in rhythm. Right, left. Right, left. Mama is walking left, right. Left, right. Her eyes quick check the room, signal she has found me. They sparkle misty blue as she runs toward me, calling my name. Her face is shiny. She is without lipstick and her hair is twisted into a mousey brown bun on the top of her head; a pair of granny glasses dangle near the end of her nose.

I touch the glass slipper in my pocket, press my fingers hard against the diamond in the heel and then I reach out my arms to her.

"Hello, Mama," I say.

CIAO, ELVIS

*T*he night her mother went off to get married again, Phoenix got picked up downtown on suspicion of soliciting and for attempted assault while resisting an officer.

"We were just saying some stuff like we hear on TV", her best friend Marilyn protested when two cops wheeled up and caught them talking to some guys in this black Mercedes parked at the curb.

"How old are you two girls?" The cop with the thin red moustache stepped out of the patrol car.

"Eighteen," Phoenix inhaled, setting off a shimmer in the sequins hugging the bodice of her dress.

"Uh huh." He wrote something down in his book and let the beam of his flashlight wiggle cross her face. She felt like there was a frog starting to jump around inside her stomach. Winnie was going to kill her if she got in trouble with the law; Winnie was who she lived with when her mother, Amanda, was between husbands.

It was the first time Phoenix ever rode in a patrol car or went inside the police station. They stood around in this little room for awhile. Then the cops let the guys go, after they swore they had just stopped at the curb to ask directions to the airport, and since they didn't hear what it was Marilyn asked, how could they know if she propositioned them?

Pretty soon Marilyn's sister came for her, then Winnie marched in, her hair flying like red warning flags. Phoenix hunched down on a stool under the light that kept blinking like the bulb wasn't screwed in tight. To keep from making eye contact with Winnie, she studied a run slithering down the leg of her silver tights and crossed her legs so she couldn't feel how bad she needed to pee.

Winnie got right in the face of this big cop standing next to Phoenix. Her gold bracelets sparkled under the lights and made tiny jangling sounds because she waved her arms around when she got excited.

"I know it's election year and a big clean-up campaign's going on down here," she said, "but rounding up two little girls who happened to be standing on a street corner, children–"

The big cop rolled his eyes at Phoenix, and Winnie's voice trailed. Then he said maybe he had over-reacted, but if the kids pulled another stunt like this he would give them something to think about.

On the way home, Phoenix tossed her long blond hair over her shoulders and scooted down in the car, praying Winnie wouldn't wreck them with her wild crazy driving.

"It was Marilyn that took a swing at that cop." She had to yell in Winnie's ear because the car made loud wheezing noises when it flew flat out. "I shot him a bird, that's all, and it was after he said I looked like a trashy little slut."

"Well, what did you expect?" Winnie ran straight through a red light in front of a Federal Express van. "Look at you. You must have cleaned K Mart out of mascara, and where in God's name did you get those shoes and that so-called dress that don't cover half your ass-end?"

"From the sitter that keeps Marilyn's brother."

"You told me you were going over to Marilyn's to study."

"Well, I got to thinking about things and got all shook and so we just went downtown to relax and have some fun; we weren't really going to do nothing with those guys."

A flash of bright headlights sparked through the windshield, spotlighting Winnie's freckles that always reminded Phoenix of a trail of little brown ants running across her nose. Winnie was a real mess when she didn't have her stage make-up on. Phoenix hoped she wasn't going to make things worse by starting to cry.

"You want to go to jail?" Winnie yelled. "You want me to have to come see you on visiting day down at Julia Tutwiler Prison? You are not even fourteen-years old; you got your whole life in front of you."

"Tell me about it," Phoenix yelled back.

She had moved in with Winnie lots of times for as long as she could remember. Every time she came back with her belongings stuffed in her backpack, Winnie always stopped what she was doing and put some milk on the stove to heat while she fished around in the cabinet for the box of Hershey's cocoa. Sometimes in the evenings when they waited for the sitter to come stay with Phoenix while Winnie went to sing at the club, she plopped a couple of marshmallows in their cups and they drew gooey white moustaches under each other's noses. At night, when the sitter put her to bed, she used to try to stay awake until after midnight to hear the click of Winnie's key in the lock and then the swishing of the shower, scrubbing away the smells of beer and cigarette smoke that came from the customers at the club.

After Winnie was done screeching about how Phoenix was likely to end up at Julia Tutwiler, they rode the rest of the way home in silence. Phoenix felt beads of sweat start popping out on the back of her neck. She had already made big wet circles under the arms of this dress she borrowed. Boy, if she ruined the dress, Marilyn would kill her if Winnie didn't do it first.

The lights of Winnie's Toyota swept across the purple and yellow mums bunched at the entrance to the apartment building. Before Winnie had time to switch off the ignition, Phoenix scooted out and up the stairs two at a time.

"You are lucky it's my night off," Winnie puffed right behind her, giving a hard push when Phoenix tried to slam the door to her room. "Otherwise, you would be cooling your heels in a jail cell."

"So I owe you one." Phoenix kicked off the red patent shoes and slung them against the wall.

Winnie leaned on the light switch and stood glaring at her in the sudden brightness. "Who do you think you are?"

"Well, I'm not your kid. That's who." Phoenix put her hands on her hips and glared back. "Amanda's coming for me soon as she gets back off her honeymoon, and this time she'll keep me for always. Besides, you and her used to live in the back of a car, doing pot and follow around after Elvis, so where do you get off coming down on me?"

"Where I get off is I'm not sitting back watching you mess up the way we did." Winnie's strong fingers caught the bodice of the gold sequined dress. Before Phoenix could put her hands over her breasts, Winnie snatched the wads of Kleenex out of her bra and threw them on the floor.

Phoenix lay awake in the dark, wondering what Amanda's new husband was like. Her real father got shot to death in a bar in El Paso, Amanda told her once, and Phoenix never learned to pronounce the name of the new guy Amanda married. But she didn't stay with him long enough for it to matter anyhow.

Then there was Bill Morris. When Phoenix was eleven, he backed her up against the bathroom wall one day while Amanda was at work. He started kissing her hard on the lips, so she kicked him in the balls where Winnie had told her you could really hurt a guy. Soon as Amanda got home that night, she packed Phoenixs' stuff and took her to Winnie again. After she divorced Bill Morris, she went by herself down to Montgomery and got a job in the office of some congressman.

"Where'd she meet this new guy?" Phoenix asked Winnie one Sunday while they were driving back from seeing Amanda.

"Beats me," Winnie gave the finger to the driver of a red pick up poking along in the fast lane. "His name is John Conners and he's asked her to marry him. She says he's loaded, big lumber businessman from Memphis."

"I bet she met him last summer at Graceland. Boy, she still gets it going with Elvis."

"Well," Winnie sighed, "Elvis was magic, you know? Like a dream you want to hold on to. I guess that's why some of us don't want to believe he is dead."

Winnie opened the kitchen curtains so the afternoon sunlight left bright little squiggles on the table where they sat drinking diet Pepsi and looking at the pictures Amanda sent to Phoenix.

"Her letter says Hawaii is a really neat place to spend a honeymoon. She says they swim naked every day at John's private beach on Maui and eat pig roasted in banana leaves. They're coming back to live in Memphis. What's in Memphis, besides Elvis?" Phoenix looked up at Winnie.

"The Mississippi River," Winnie said as Phoenix knocked over the chair when she jumped up to answer the telephone.

She was wearing her new denim jacket when she walked back through the kitchen and started out the door.

"You got a short memory," Winnie called as she set her drink down with a loud thump. "You are grounded, missy. Remember?"

"Get serious. I said I'm sorry about getting picked up by the cops." Phoenix snatched Amanda's letter off the table and waved it in front of Winnie. "I didn't read it all to you. She wants me to come live with them. John wants me, too, and he's sending me a plane ticket to Memphis."

Winnie's chair made a scraping sound when she pushed it back and went to stand at the sink. "Maybe we'd better talk about it."

"What's to talk about? I don't belong to you, Winnie, and I don't need you clucking over me like a mama hen. You got to realize I can take care of myself and I'm not a kid anymore."

"You are a snot nose kid and you don't know beans."

"And you're turning into a weird old lady, Winnie."

"Yeah," Winnie said, "a weird old lady."

Phoenix didn't know the airport at Memphis was so big. Amanda had said she would wait for her at the snack bar closest to the gate where her flight came in. As she started walking towards an empty table, she knew right off the man watching her was John Conners. He was worse than his pictures; pot belly, thick glasses and hair like it was glued to his head. Boy, Amanda always picked losers, but at least they looked good. This guy had better have big bucks coming out his ears.

"You must be Phoenix."

She hoped he wasn't going to try to hug her or anything, so she nodded and took a step back and asked, "where's Amanda?"

He looked down and picked at a thread on the pocket of his pale blue shirt, then dug an envelope out of his hip pocket. "She couldn't come; she said give this to you."

As soon as Phoenix finished reading the letter, John pulled back a chair and waited for her to sit down before he went to get some coffee and a coke.

"I don't understand it, her fixing up this room for you, then running out like this." After he sat down across from her, he spread his big hands out flat on the table and looked at Phoenix. "You're taking it real nice. Seems like you ought to cry or something."

"You get used to shit happening." She stirred her drink with the straw and watched all the little bubbles pop around the top of the cup.

"Well, it don't seem right, you turning around and heading straight back," he said. "Say, we could go over to Graceland before you leave. I bet you never been to Elvis' house."

"Amanda and some people brought me one time, but I don't remember nothing but the guitars on the gates."

"Seems like there's always something happening over there. It's like Elvis is still alive, people coming and going all the time."

"I gotta go check out the schedule." She glanced at her watch, picked up her backpack from beside her chair. "Thanks for, you know, the coke and bringing me Amanda's letter."

"Well, maybe I'll see you again, maybe Amanda will come back pretty soon and we can be a real family." John cleared his throat and his eyes filled. "You don't believe that any more than I do; I can tell. But I keep thinking, Phoenix, she is your mama, so she's bound to love you."

"Sure," Phoenix said, "like a dog loves fleas."

She fastened her seat belt and opened the envelope again; the flight attendant smiled and handed her a pack of honey roasted peanuts. Phoenix opened the silver foil with her teeth and tasted salt and sweet on her lips. She shook the nuts out in her hand, counting them as they dropped. Twenty-four; there had been twenty-six on the flight coming up. She shrugged and flipped on the light above her seat so she could read Amanda's writing without squinting:

I don't know how to begin this letter, Phoenix, except to say I'm scared and all I know to do is run because it is what I do best, isn't it? Marrying John–I thought it would work out, but being tied down to a rich old man is no different from being tied down to a poor one, except for wrinkles and bad breath. Money don't matter when every day is deadly dullness chipping away at my brain.

Last night I got to thinking that I don't know a thing about you, Phoenix. I've never bothered to find out what you like for breakfast, if you have ever had measles or if you got your first period yet. After you read this, you'll know I am a terrible person, but I have to tell you I have never felt anything for you. That's the way it is and I guess you are old enough to hear it now.

It was Winnie that talked me out of an abortion; she wanted to adopt you and at first I said okay. Then after you were born, this woman from one of those do-good groups came by and said even a bitch dog mothered what she brought into the world. So I tried, I really did, and I tried to stay married but it's like drowning if I can't be free.

John wants a big family. You're still young, he says. Well, you bet I am, and chasing after a pack of wet smelly babies and a teen-age kid ain't the way I plan to grow old. So I'm running again. It's a rotten way to treat you, but hey it's a rotten world and you are better off with Winnie. She tells me you are a good kid.

Phoenix pushed her way to the front of the line filing off the plane.

She picked up the nearest phone inside the terminal and braced herself against the wall when she heard Winnie's voice because it was like the floor was coming up to hit her in the face.

"Winnie," she said, "I'm here at the airport. Can you come pick me up?"

"You are lucky it's my night off."

"I guess I don't know beans. She never wanted me, Winnie."

"You wait for me inside the front door, you hear? I got to make a stop at the Quick Mart for a box of cocoa. I think we're out of marshmallows, too."

"Winnie, are you crying?"

"Yeah, I guess."

Phoenix ran to the ladies room and locked herself in the toilet. She threw up all over the place, and then she had to use a whole roll of tissue to keep blowing her nose. Boy, she couldn't remember when she had carried on like this. Before she unlocked the door, she tore the letter in about a thousand pieces, dropped them and flushed. She just stood there and watched Amanda's words jumble all together and disappear with a loud gurgle.

She decided she had better go on downstairs and wait where Winnie said. A dark haired boy passed her in the corridor, and Phoenix got to looking at the way a crazy streak of light danced and wiggled on the guitar strapped on his back. She wondered if he was going up to Memphis. There was probably a lot happening tonight at Graceland.

ONE LAST DANCE

*H*e walks with her to the park across the street from where it happened, where moments ago he snatched her out of the path of a car hurtling down upon her. Sidewalk strollers, the nocturnal people of the city who stopped to watch her struggle to resist his help, have moved on to melt into the foggy darkness at the end of the block. The two strangers are left alone.

"Suicide isn't always the easy way out," he is saying. "Sometimes it fails because of poor planning or a sudden rush of panic at the last split second."

"It was a good plan. I didn't panic." Her voice echoes the dead sound of the leaves rustling overhead. She drops down on a rough stone bench, slides away from him to sit on the opposite end. "I stepped into the street at the right time. It would all be over now if you hadn't interfered. I just want to die, damn you, so who said you could play God with my life?"

He waits without speaking while she starts to cry softly, wiping her face with the long strands of her pale hair. Smoke curls from the glow of his cigarette; he holds it out to her between his thumb and forefinger. She shakes her head.

"Look," he shrugs, "you're nothing to me. It's just that I have a hangup about seeing people do stupid things. Jumping off the curb in front of a compact Chevy is stupid, no guarantee you get more than a broken pelvis or a couple of weeks in the hospital with a fractured skull. Next time go stand in the middle of the interstate and look into the high beams of an eighteen wheeler coming at you at ninety, ninety-five miles an hour. That's the way to do it right."

"You some kind of expert?"

"Could be I've given it some thought. The hotel room I rented for tonight is thirty stories up. No canopies, nothing but empty space between the window ledge and a beautiful concrete parking lot. Splat."

The wind swirls around an overflowing trash container, sends a red plastic drink cup skittering across the grass. She turns to look at him. "Please don't patronize me. What are the odds I'm connecting with another potential suicide? Give me a break."

He hunches his shoulders, lights another cigarette. "Whatever you want to believe."

"Why do you want to end your life?"

"I'm tired of running and I'm not going back to prison."

"Were you guilty?"

"I killed some people. My wife and her unborn son."

"A good lawyer can get you off if you have money. Do you have money?"

"Four twenties and some change."

"How about your family?"

"A mother somewhere in California."

"Well, I got nobody, at least nobody who cares. If I let the doctors keep sticking me with needles," she says, "I get to linger around for two, maybe three more months of pure hell. I want it to be over."

She watches his hand slide into the pocket of his jeans.

"I've paid for my room, so I'm not going to need this after tonight." He fishes out four bills and change, squints at his watch. "Probably a burger joint still doing business after midnight."

They jay-walk across the street, cut through the alley between two tall buildings. She stops, touches his arm.

"Back there, when you went for your wallet, I thought maybe you had a gun in your pocket. You can do it for me, you know. What's one more life on your conscience? Shoot me right here; you owe me."

"I don't own a gun."

A light rain has started to fall. He shakes the water out of his black stocking cap, puts it back on his head. She starts to shiver.

"Let's go find a bar," he says.

They enter a door under a bright red and yellow neon sign and find a table near the back of the room. He orders two bourbons on the rocks.

"It's the cancer," she tells him while they wait. "You name a body part and I got it there."

"Maybe they will find a cure tomorrow." He stirs his drink with the tips of his fingers touching the ice.

"Sure. And maybe your wife and kid will rise from the dead. Your wife–was she pretty?"

"Not after I strangled her. Not pretty at all."

She glances around the room. "I'd like to go some place else, some place where there's music, a juke box. I want to dance one more time. Will you dance with me?"

"I never learned how to dance."

"I will teach you," she says.

THE DUCK MAN

 write this about my husband. They call him the Duck Man.

Most every afternoon along about sunset, he parks his green pickup at Star Lake in Hoover. By the time he gets out, big plastic bag in hand, a flock of wild Mallards, white ducks and Canada geese have already begun to quack and honk the news that supper is on the table. Some come waddling along the bank. Others cut through the water like Olympic champions competing for the first bites of bread he brings.

"Look, Mom," a little boy points out, "there's the Duck Man!"

People who come to exercise on the one third mile distance around the lake sometimes slow down or stop to chat with him while he hunkers down on the ground to hand feed the little white duck who has a crippled foot or the old Mallard with the broken bill.

He always brings enough bread for the fish. The larger ones who had been crafty enough to avoid the angler's hook get their share of stale hamburger buns and hoagie rolls. Occasionally a pair of green heron follow along the shore to gobble down the little brim darting in to feast on the crumbs.

He saves the last of the food for the small birds, the sparrows and jays, and the multi colored parakeet who somewhere along the way flew the coop and came to live a carefree life in the wilds.

When someone asks the Duck Man's name, he tells them he is Wayne Thompson and usually volunteers the information that he is a retired electrical contractor. If they ask why he comes day after day to care for the little inhabitants of the lake, he always has an answer.

"Because it makes me feel good. I guess it's my way of saying thanks for all this," he explains, taking a last look out across the water before he climbs in his truck and heads back up the hill to his house.

THAT CHRISTMAS

*J*he year I turned seven, the Great Depression , a tornado and my brother all went in cahoots to spoil Christmas: Daddy lost his job, the storm tore up our food pantry, and my brother told me there wasn't a Santa Claus.

After the T&P Railroad laid off Daddy's crew of workmen, the late summer storm swirled down in a black-funnel, dipping through the kitchen on the back part of our house. Shelves, lined with Mason jars newly filled with a winter supply of food, sailed through the air like fat crystal kites. Mama's home-canned black-eyed peas and okra, snap beans and thick, brown chicken stew splattered in the slivers of glass that lay shining in the yard.

"Looks like we'll have to tighten our belts until I sell the beef cattle in the fall." Daddy sat looking at figures in his big black ledger one day. "Christmas may be slim pickins' this year."

I had complete faith in Santa, but my brother, who was two years older and wiser than I, said ha ha in a pig's eye. We had gone out to play marbles by the cedar tree and I'd said it didn't matter if Daddy didn't have money because Santa would bring my gun.

I had kept my eye on the shiny black Daisy air rifle in the window at B.D. Appleton's Farm Merchandise & Feed Store for months; it was exactly like the one my brother got last year. With no other little girls to play with, I was a stringy freckled face tomboy competing with my brother at a time and in a place children learned about firearms along with the alphabet. Target practice was our entertainment; a gun of my own would put me on equal terms when my brother let me go with him down to the creek to shoot at tin cans and snakes and frogs.

"Everybody but babies knows their daddy buys the presents," my brother scoffed. "There ain't no Santa."

"You're a liar. We hear the reindeer on the roof every Christmas Eve after we're in bed."

"You ever know Daddy to be in the house when we hear all that racket? Shoot no. He comes stompin' in from outside, yellin' did we hear old Prancer and Dancer on the house top."

"Liar! Big fat liar with warts!" I kicked him in the stomach as hard as I could.

When Mama came to the door and asked if we were fighting again, he hissed: "Tell and I'll never take you shootin' with me no more."

"No ma'am," I called out in unison with him. "We was just playing."

I ran in the house and hid out in the hall closet and cried for hours. Not to believe, not to know there was a Santa was unthinkable. Forgiving my brother was something I planned never to do, but a couple of days later, he got really sick with scarlet fever. He told me if I didn't forgive him before he died, I would go straight to Hell and burn forever. So I said I forgave him, but the hurt didn't go away and he didn't die after all.

When Mrs. Volley Cross canceled her annual piano recital that year, Mama said it was because nobody had money to pay for music lessons. She said Mrs. Cross had taught piano and violin for as long as she remembered. Mama made and sold most of the fancy crepe de Chine dresses worn by the women and little girls for the occasion. Sometimes late at night when I looked out the door of my room, I saw her, bent over the big mahogany dining room table. Yellow light from the Aladdin lamp shone across her hair and on yards of pink and green and lavender fabric delicate as butterflies pinned to patterns she had carefully measured and traced on large pieces of butcher's paper.

"Well, there goes my snuff money," Mama sighed when she told Daddy about Mrs. Cross. She called it her snuff money because she always squirreled it away in one of Grandma's old Garrett's snuff tins. "Guess there won't be no more comin' in from my sewing."

My brother told me I might as well forget about the Daisy air rifle.

"I sure ain't countin' on no catcher's mitt," he said. "We'll be lucky to get some apples and peppermint sticks."

I stopped going by Appleton's Store on my way home from school. Mama said I was looking peaked and maybe I needed a dose of castor oil.

It was close to Thanksgiving when Daddy loaded up the beef cattle to take to market. All afternoon I sat out on the screened-in porch so I would be first to see his old black truck careen around the bend in the dirt road, its wheels belching out the clouds of thick red dust that powdered the scrub oak trees and high tin roof of the barn.

I ran out to meet him as soon as the truck wheezed to a stop by the clothesline. A pair of white Leghorn hens came squawking with a loud ra-a-a-k out of the honeysuckle bush and fluttered to safety under the fence. Daddy got out and patted my head without looking at me, without stooping to sweep me up in the air or letting me search his pockets for candy and cherry flavored bubble gum. I heard a scuffling sound in the truck bed and looked over to see one of the calves still there.

Mama came to the kitchen door, drying her hands on the front of her green checked apron. She stood looking at Daddy and then told me to run on out to the wood pile to rake up more chips for the fire. Her face looked stiff, like she held her lips tight to keep from crying.

After supper Daddy explained that he had to sell the cattle at a loss. Then he told my brother to come help him unload the calf he brought back. "No point in givin' it away," he said. "I figure he can find enough feed to get him through til spring. Maybe beef will bring a better price by then."

When it was time to chop the Christmas tree that year, Daddy went out in the pasture and cut down the tallest one he could find, a cedar with fat bushy branches. I wondered why, since there would be no presents under it.

Mama and Daddy always decorated the tree on Christmas Eve after we were in bed. I went to my room early, without being sent, and lay for what seemed like hours with the pillow thrown over my head. Footsteps creaked back and forth across the front room floor. I uncovered my face, listening to Mama's laughter seep through the darkness just as a couple of loud thumps rattled the ceiling.

After awhile Daddy charged through the door, swinging the red lantern he carried when he went outside at night.

"Old Prancer and Dancer, clopping right across our roof," he whispered. "You hear 'em?"

The flicker of the lantern light swam in the pools squeezed hard against my closed eyelids. I didn't move or answer, and then I heard him tiptoe away.

It seemed like it was still night, but morning had begun to streak the windows when my brother came to shake me awake. I sat up and saw long icicles glistening on the pump handle at the well, and I wished it would snow and make it be like Christmas.

"Hurry up," he called and ran towards the front room.

The house smelled of cedar and of the nutmeg and cinnamon bubbling in the apple dumplings already in the oven. A log in the fireplace cracked, spitting a handful of sparks on the hearth. Green woolly stockings, bulging with apples and stick candy, hung on each side of the mantel. And under the tree that Mama had draped in white paper chains and the long strands of popcorn, there was a Blue Willow tea pot for her, a pair of sheep skin lined gloves for Daddy, a catcher's mitt for my brother and the shiny black Daisy air rifle from B.D. Appleton's store.

I never knew until many years later that Daddy swapped the beef calf to B.D. for the gifts, and I soon forgot to be angry at my brother for telling me there wasn't a Santa Claus. But I still remember standing in front of the tree on that Christmas morning, a moment of magic when I believed again in all the wondrous workings of a child's universe

WORM MONEY SATURDAY NIGHT

*O*dessa pulled Hoot's old blue poncho over her sweater and ran towards the clothesline in the back yard where snow covered the bare earth like frosting on a chocolate cake. During the night the wind had spooned it in dollops along the fence where a sign read: Hoots Fishing Camp Closed For The Winter. She saw the clouds drifting east and reasoned that rain would come by the end of the week and the spring thaw begin. Tonight she was going to tell Hoot that he was driving her to town on Saturday.

The sheets she had put to dry on the line were frozen, Hoot's overalls hung stiff and unyielding as though his contrary body remained trapped inside the faded denim. Odessa sighed as she dropped the pins into the canvas bag she carried tied around her waist on wash days. She must spread newspapers on the floor to let the clothes thaw by the fire while supper cooked; Hoot would be home in an hour.

She stood close to the kitchen stove and rubbed her hands together until the heat made her fingers tingle. Reaching behind the sugar jar on the shelf above the oven, she took down the Prince Albert tobacco can that held the jumble of bills and coins she saved last summer. Her worm money, Odessa called it. She earned it selling mealy worms, crickets and night crawlers to the fisherman who stopped to buy bait. Hoot said it all belonged to her and while she waited for the stew to simmer, she counted it again.

She unwrinkled and turned each bill so the pictures of George Washington and Abraham Lincoln faced in the same direction.

When she heard the sound of Hoot's old pickup truck, she smoothed the skirt of her dress and touched the frizz of curls around her face. Odessa hoped tonight he would look up from his plate long enough to notice she wore her red dress and see she put a home permanent wave in her hair. Hoot didn't talk when there was food in front of him. They ate without speaking until he sopped the crust of biscuit around the rim of the dish to catch the last drop of gravy from the stew.

"Did you get the nets patched today?"

He nodded. "Still got plenty to do before camp open next month."

"It'll be nice having folks come around again. I ain't seen hardly a soul since we closed for the winter." She looked at him and noticed his eyes were beginning to droop. *Just like a baby when he gets his belly warm and full, so I may as well come right out and tell him while he is still awake.*

"Hoot," she said, "You're driving me to town on Saturday."

"What in thunder for?" he blinked and stared at her. "I got our supplies last month when I went for lumber to build the shed."

"I'm taking my worm money to the furniture store to buy a new porch swing."

"I told you a hundred times I'll fix the old one. I ain't got time to go traipsing off to town and lose a whole day, not with all I got to do."

Odessa learned in the twenty years she'd been married to Hoot that it was best to keep quiet while he was having his say. When he stopped for breath she took him by his hand and pulled him towards the front door.

"No need to drag me out in the night air," he protested. "I know what a broke swing looks like."

It lay upside down in the far corner of the porch. The wooden slats had rotted and the chains that anchored it to the ceiling dangled in empty rhythm with the wind.

"I aim to have me a place to sit in the shade this summer. Waterman's Furniture has got their spring sale on porch swings." She took a piece of newspaper from her pocket and held it close to his face. "You see? It's got green cushions printed with white flowers and I'm gonna go buy it, even if I have to get there without you."

She saw his shoulders sag as though he remembered another time when she threatened to drive herself to town.

"You don't know nothing about mechanical things," he had raged as he stood gawking at the sight of Odessa and the truck sitting bogged down in the tomato patch.

"But I was aiming it frontwards. I didn't know it was gonna back up and run over the garden."

"Damn machine don't know what you're thinking. If you put her in reverse, she's gonna go backwards, no matter what".

After awhile he grew quiet and stood looking at the plants buried in the ruts. She saw his shoulders droop as they did now when she showed him the picture of the swing, and she knew Hoot was driving her to town on Saturday. Tomorrow she would sew the hem in the yellow dress she planned to wear.

She heard the spatter of rain on the roof when she woke up and looked at the clock. Odessa sat down on the side of the bed and began to slide her stockings over her feet, careful not to snag them with her toenails.

"Hoot," she called softly at first, then louder, "Hoot."

She forgot to tell him they were leaving early. The only light in the room was from the lamp beside the wash stand.

He bolted upright, squinting to see her standing over him.

"It's four thirty. Time to get started."

"Well, I ain't leaving out in the middle of the night."

Odessa tied a woolen scarf over her hat and dropped the picture of the swing in the pocket of her Sunday coat. "I aim to be in town to get a place in line before the store opens. I'll wait outside in the truck."

She slammed the door behind her. Hoot followed, digging sleep from his eyes and buttoning his pants as he crawled behind the steering wheel. He craned his neck to peer through the darkness.

"Lucky if I can get her started," he grumbled. "Battery's about gone dead. If we'd of waited til a decent hour I wouldn't have to turn on no lights."

"If we'd of waited til a decent hour the swing might be already sold."

The truck slid sideways in the road and bounced across a chug hole. Odessa tied her handkerchief around the can of worm money so the lid wouldn't fly open when they hit the next bump. She hoped Hoot would drive faster when it got light enough to see the bad spots in front of the wheels. It seemed to her that the truck stood still while shadows of the scrubby trees on each side of the road crawled backwards. She jumped at the sudden rumble of thunder and watched the rain pattern the windshield with dots and splashes, then sweep across the landscape.

Hoot slapped his foot on the brake. The truck wobbled off the road and one of the rear wheels sank over the edge of a gully.

"Why'd you stop?"

"Can't see the road. Fool wiper won't work and now we're stuck in the mud."

"Well, drive on. We can't set here in the middle of nowhere."

"Now how in thunderation can I drive on when I'm stuck and can't see where I'm driving on to?"

"Maybe we're not stuck too deep." She took off her scarf and adjusted her hat.

She watched the muscles in Hoot's jaws work up and down as he tried to coax the truck forward. Each time the wheels spun, they settled back in the soft oozy clay.

He slammed the door when he got out and walked around to the back of the truck. "I think a push will get her out," he called, so you move over in my seat and do like I tell you."

"But I'd rather push. You know I'm scared to death of this thing."

"Do like I say. When I holler for you to give her the gas, you mash down easy, easy, you hear me? And you keep on mashing til I say stop."

He showed her once more how to let out the clutch and push the accelerator. Odessa's knees shook so hard she couldn't keep her feet where they belonged.

"Now! Give her the gas!"

She closed her eyes and tried to remember his instructions. The old pickup shot forward, and suddenly she was aware that it was careening down the road, leaving Hoot waving his arms and running after it.

"I couldn't hear you holler to stop mashing," she explained when he got back inside and sat glaring at her. "Anyway, the rain's slacking and we can stop to have some breakfast at Jack's diner." She knew the thought of food would improve his humor.

Water dripped from Hoot's hair and trickled through the dark patch of stubble on his cheeks. His mouth was clamped in a tight line, but when they reached the café he pulled to a stop between two Jeeps.

"Now don't go asking for no fancy cured ham and orange juice," he warned. " I ain't made of money."

"Anything will be fine," she said, "just so somebody besides me has cooked it."

She kept her eyes turned away from the group of National Guard soldiers at the counter. She did not want to give Hoot cause to accuse her of flirting, a reason to say Odessa Suggs put on a yellow dress and curled her hair so the men in town would take notice of her. The smell of coffee filled her with a warm contentment as she ate the food, cutting each bite gently as though she did not wish to inflict pain on a stack of pancakes.

"I ought to of asked about new wiper blades at that filling station back yonder," Hoot said when they were on the road again.

"Rain's most likely over." Odessa leaned her head against the seat and let her thoughts fly. She could almost see the tall dark man who sold tickets in the booth out front of the picture show. He would smile at her when she stopped to look at the billboard. She thought of closing her eyes for a little nap when she heard the hissing noise and saw a cloud of steam.

Hoot grabbed her scarf off the seat and wound it around his hand as he jumped out of the truck.

"She's hotter'n a firecracker!" he shouted. "Got a leak in the radiator."

"We can get it fixed at the filling station back yonder," Odessa said.

"Shoot fire, they ain't got no mechanic. They's no place between here and town to get her patched up."

"They's water in the side ditches if we had something to tote it in." Odessa scratched through the tangle of fishing lines and corks under the seat until she found an empty coffee can. "We'll keep filling it with the ditch water til we get to town."

Mr. Waterman was near the front door of the furniture store when Hoot and Odessa came in.

"What can I do for you folks this morning? I haven't seen you in town since about this time last year." He backed away when he glanced down at the mud on Hoot's overalls.

"We come to buy the porch swing." Odessa showed him the picture she carried, then untied her handkerchief from around the can of worm money. "I can pay cash."

Mr. Waterman pointed to a row of wooden swings propped against the back wall.

"They ain't what I expected." Odessa stood with her hands on her hips, walking from one to another. "The paper says they got green cushions with white flowers. These cushions is just plain green."

"They're the very kind you wanted last year," Mr. Waterman sighed. "I remember you wanted plain green and I didn't have nothing but flowered. Well, this time I got both. I got the plain green and I got the flowered, so if you folks will step to the back room with me I'll show you a car load of porch swings with flowered cushions."

"Actually," Odessa shook her head, "they won't do. None of them look stout enough to hold a large woman like me." She started to walk towards the door. "You coming, Hoot?"

"We have gliders," Mr. Waterman called, "good metal ones that hold up to five hundred pounds."

Hoot fell in step with her on the sidewalk.

"You can fix our old swing good as new, can't you, Hoot?"

"Sure can." He gazed across the street at the neon sign flashing above the door of the pool hall.

Next to the pool hall, Odessa saw the billboard out front of the movie theater. It said there was a Saturday afternoon matinee with Betty Grable and Dan Dailey Junior.

She saw Hoot still looking toward the pool hall, his eyes bright, mouth hanging open. *It's the same hungry look as when he watches me set a bowl of warm blueberry cobbler in front of him.*

"Morning's half gone." She nudged Hoot to move along. "The radiator might not be fixed until it's too late to drive home."

"Tell you what," he said. "You go on down to the hotel and get us a room. I believe I'll mosey across the street and see what's going on."

She waited until she saw the beginnings of the smile tucked away in the corners of his mouth. *Like a sly ole hound dog that's dug up a juicy bone.*

"I want a room for me and my husband," Odessa said to the man behind the desk in the hotel lobby. "We will be leaving out around daylight tomorrow, so I'll pay now."

He watched while she opened the Prince Albert tobacco can and began counting the money. "Say, didn't you folks stay here last year along about this time?"

She nodded and picked up the key.

"Come to think of it, I believe you have stayed overnight with us several times."

Odessa didn't hear his last words. She saw herself standing in front of the ticket booth at the picture show. The tall dark man smiled when he handed her the change from her ten dollar bill. While the marque lights shimmered on the skirt of her yellow dress, Betty Grable and Dan Dailey Junior danced inside her head.

COPPER PENNIES AND SUNNY DEW COLA

After Elvie was gone and he had lived alone for a year, Jim Henry started talking to the house.

At first he mumbled under his breath, directing his words to a window that refused to open, a door knob falling off in his hands or the leaky roof that dripped circles of yellowish stain across the ceiling in the hall. He hobbled from room to room, the tail of his old gray bathrobe trailing behind him, his arms extended as though evoking an invisible spirit.

Later, when he began to speak in coherent sentences, he sometimes flinched at the sound of his voice shattering the silence around him like a blow of his hammer against the fat hickory nuts he had cracked for Elvie's Christmas cakes.

"Walls," he said one evening after the sun had kindled its fire behind the low branches of the scrub pines, "maybe I'll just set right here in my chair and watch you fall down around me before I can get up and open my can of soup." Then, to the floor: "You got so much trash piled on you I better find me another place to step."

The house set in the middle of ten acres of red clay soil near Pine Knot, Alabama where it is claimed a man with a good arm can throw a rock and hit the Georgia state line. Two years before Jim Henry was born, his father built the rambling white structure with dark green shutters and a veranda stretching along the front. Although the paint had begun to crack and peel since its last renovation, the building was still strong and solid when the tornado came the next week after Elvie died.

The black funnel cloud hop-scotched over the edge of the town of Pine Knot, doubled back and touched down in the middle of Jim Henry's property. It uprooted trees, shredding their branches into kindling wood as the swirling winds sucked his house from its foundation, shifted it so it seemed to tilt in all directions. Since then, it had given up all pretenses of standing upright. If Jim Henry accidentally dropped a potato on the kitchen floor, it sometimes rolled all the way across the room and lodged under his chair in front of the TV.

Now, when he lay alone in his bed at night, his mind could not separate the sounds of the tornado from the roar of the red pickup truck that ran Elvie down that day in Atlanta when she started to cross the street. It had served no purpose to curse the soul of the driver who died shortly afterwards when he lost control of the vehicle, so Jim Henry sometimes muttered curses at the house, accusing it of going in cahoots with Nate.

Nate was his and Elvie's boy. He had been after his daddy to sell the house; as soon as he heard about the tornado, he began saying Jim Henry better get out of the place before it fell down around his head. Nate lived in a big fancy apartment near Atlanta with that girl Julie. He seldom came back to Pine Knot except for the times when the telephone company people disconnected Jim Henry because he forgot to pay his bill. That always brought Nate storming in because he had promised Elvie he would call his daddy every week.

After the last time the phone was shut off, Nate came walking in through the kitchen one Sunday afternoon while Jim Henry was sitting at the table, squinting into a tattered cardboard box.

"I'm going to make arrangements to take care of paying your utilities from now on." Nate stopped in front of his father to examine the assorted rusty screwdrivers, pliers and balls of twine jumbled together in the box.

"I'm looking to find my wrench so I can fix the water heater, if you'll move out of my light so I can see what I'm doing," Jim Henry greeted him.

Nate pushed back his cap, the one that had Blue Lake Country Club lettered on the bill, and slid into the one chair that wasn't piled with old newspapers. He sat drumming his fingers on the edge of the cluttered Lazy Susan in the center of the table, eyeing a pill bottle with the cotton still undisturbed in the top.

"You staying on your blood pressure medicine?"

"Don't need the stuff. Doctor's a quack."

"How are you doing on groceries? The store still making deliveries?"

"I'm on the goddam witness stand or something?" Jim Henry slammed his fist against the table, upsetting the salt shaker and sending it sliding under the telephone stand in the corner.

A loud flapping sound drifted from down the hall and he followed Nate's gaze to where a whole strip of blue and white striped wallpaper had suddenly broken loose and sagged down to the floor.

"Jesus," Nate whistled through his teeth, "the place ought to be condemned."

Jim Henry went on scratching inside the cardboard box searching for his wrench. It was starting to get dark outside but he didn't offer to turn on a light; it would be like an invitation to Nate for finding fault with the door that had warped off its hinges or the dark wet spot where the cabinet was starting to pull away from the sink

"Pop," Nate said after awhile, "you know you got to make up your mind to get out of this place, maybe find somebody who wants to buy and rebuild."

"You just can't let me live here in peace, can you?"

"This is not living, Pop." Nate stood up, tears glistening in the corners of his eyes. "You know Mom wouldn't want it to be like this for you. I can get a nice little apartment in Atlanta or maybe help you find another place right here in Pine Knot, hire someone to come cook and clean for you."

"I ain't asking you for nothing, so mind your own business. And while you are about it, leave my utilities alone. Go on back to Atlanta and sleep with that girl you ain't married to."

"God, you just never let up, do you? It's my life."

"And this is mine, so keep your nose out of my business."

Jim Henry waited until he heard the car door slam before he got up and went to look out the window. He pressed his face close to the panes to watch the long thread of dust unwind behind the red glow of the tail lights. He turned away for a moment, heaving a long sigh and thinking if Elvie was here she would go and open some bottles of Sunny Dew Cola and tell the two of them to shut up if they couldn't do no better that hurl angry words like stones at each other's heads.

He had known all along that Elvie was the glue holding them together for all the years the boy was growing up, a fragile bonding that snapped when Jim Henry said, "I'd sooner forget you're my son."

It happened on a Friday night a couple of years ago when Nate came home for a visit and brought that girl Julie with him. Elvie had stood on the top step of the ladder to dust the shelves in the book case and scrubbed the floors until they were clean enough to eat off of. When she was done, she asked Jim Henry to please hold his tongue this time, not get into a fight with Nate.

As soon as Nate's little green sports car pulled up the drive, Jim Henry watched Elvie go flying out the front door, hugging Julie first off and saying "you are just as pretty as Nate said." And Nate, grinning, "She looks a lot like you, Ma. Her hair's the same color as yours when you were her age."

"But I was never pretty," Elvie insisted as they walked, Nate's arm draped around her shoulders, up the steps of the veranda. "Nate got his good looks from his daddy's side, the black hair and bright blue eyes."

After supper, when it was bed time, Nate said he didn't see any point in putting down the couch for him; he said he felt like a hypocrite, knowing he was going to get right up and go slide under the covers with Julie in the spare bedroom soon as the lights were out.

When Jim Henry looked at his boy, standing there with a smirk on his face and acting like sleeping in his own daddy's house with a woman he wasn't married to was how he was raised to behave, he said, "This, by God, ain't no sleazy thirty-minute hotel."

"Aw, come on, Pop." He saw Julie's flushed cheeks and Nate trying to laugh the whole thing off. "You're embarrassing Julie. Nobody makes a big deal out of being married these days."

"Well, I make a big deal out of it and I'll not see you trot in some little whore to wallow around with right under my nose."

"Julie's no whore."

"You're screwing her and I don't see no ring on her finger. I'll not have that going on in my house, under my roof. I'd sooner forget you're my son."

"Then we'll both forget you're my father. If you weren't, I'd knock hell out of you."

Elvie, coming back from the kitchen with four bottles of Sunny Dew Cola, set the tray down and stepped between them like an angry referee at a prize fight.

"This is my house, too, and you'll both say you're sorry for what you said."

And so they had muttered apologies, Jim Henry's a half hearted one and only to appease Elvie; he was certain it was the same with Nate.

After Nate and Julie left to go back to Atlanta that night, Jim Henry saw the tears that snuffed out all the fire in Elvie's eyes.

"He's a grown man," she said, "entitled to his own way of thinking, even if it is different from ours. He's our family, Jim Henry, part you and part me. Nate is what we'll leave in this world after we're gone."

He lay awake that night, staring into the darkness, trying to recall a time when he had not been angry at the boy. Nate had come along when Jim Henry, more that a decade older than Elvie, was looking back over his shoulder at fifty and set in his ways. Somehow, he never got around to feeling how he imagined a man should feel towards a son. He had been content, just living in this house with Elvie had been enough for him, but he guessed it wasn't the same for her. Her face had lit up like a summer sunrise when she held her baby; Jim Henry watched and saw a piece of his world sliding away as she touched each tiny clutching finger.

He had told himself the bond would come. It would come with time, he said. But after a few years, he decided it didn't matter. He was a good provider. Nate wore better clothes than any boy in Pine Knot, lived in a good house and Elvie gave him more than his share of affection, something Jim Henry never got from either of his parents.

Now with Elvie gone and the TV with no sound or picture since the tornado, he sometimes went for a week without hearing another voice except when he talked to the house.

"I'm too damn old to stand up in front of you," he explained one morning to the toilet bowl. "Little whacker's all shriveled up anyhow and I can't aim straight no more, so I'll just set on you like a old woman."

He kept a picture of Elvie in a silver frame on top of the refrigerator. Sometimes he got it down and held it in his hands so he could look at how her hair was like a handful of copper pennies gleaming in the sunshine. She was a feisty little thing, Elvie, always laughing back then. Sometimes he still smelled her perfume, the scent of roses in summer wind. In the picture she wore a dress that was white with pale yellow daisies scattered over the billowing skirt.

It seemed to him that it had been more than a year since she passed. Nate had come back home then, he remembered, and sat with him beside her bed at the hospital.

"Promise me you will check up on him. Promise you'll call him on the telephone every week," she said. "You never know when he'll fall off the roof or a bolt of lightening will strike him out in the field."

When it was over, after the choir had sung the first and last verses of Amazing Grace, father and son sat side by side in the church pew, the shoulders of their dark blue suit coats brushing, yet not really touching. Once, during the closing prayer, Jim Henry felt a terrible need to put his arms around his boy, and later as they walked away from the new mound of red earth, Nate reached out a hand to steady him. Jim Henry leaned on him for a moment before pulling away.

And then the tornado, with Elvie barely cold in the ground, leaving the house unsettled so that every time he walked across the floor the boards moaned like tormented souls crying out for mercy. It wasn't long after that before the sheriff starting driving by and telling Jim Henry the county was going to have to come out and condemn it.

"These walls look like they can't decide whether to stand up or fall down," the sheriff said.

Jim Henry was sleeping the night the back room fell off the house, just dropped away with a loud groan. He jumped at the sound, then began to stir slowly because his arthritis was shooting pains all down his back. When he got his flashlight from under his pillow, he eased himself out of bed and picked his way to see about whatever it was that had happened. He moved the light in front of him, cutting jerky yellow circles through the dust starting to settle on the pile of old lumber and plaster. He swallowed hard, then snapped off the flashlight so the darkness could blot out the sight of the big oak rafter that had come down on Elvie's sewing machine.

"If I had my tent, I'd set it up in the yard and I would lay down in the grass and watch you fall apart," he shouted at the house as he turned and walked back to his bed.

When morning came, he went out to sit on the edge of the top step of the veranda; he felt the floor shudder under his weight. A wisp of cloud, pink with morning sunrise, drifted over the roof top, and out of the corner of his eye he saw the rising puffs of red dust following a car headed in his direction. It was too early for the mailman, Jim Henry decided, but it could be the county sheriff. Somebody might have notified him already about the room falling off his house and the sheriff was coming out to tell him he was condemning it. He watched a glint of light spark against the windshield as the car pulled to a stop in his driveway.

The woman who got out was tall and slim. As she came striding across the yard, Jim Henry recognized it was that girl Julie.

He tried to get up as she came closer, but a quick stab of pain made him wince and sit back down again.

"I got nothing to say to you," he said.

"Well, I have something to say to you." Julie sat down on the bottom step, gathering her long blue skirt under her knees. When she tossed back her hair, Jim Henry saw how it gleamed like copper pennies in the fingers of light reaching through the trees.

"I drove over here to tell you Nate and I are getting married," she said, "and we are doing it because we're ready, not because you think we should. We are going to have a baby and I want Nate to be a father who can love his child."

"Nobody's stopping him, I reckon."

"You are, Jim Henry. You're stopping him and it makes me mad as hell. Nate knows all about how to love a woman, but he has no idea how a father goes about loving a child."

When Jim Henry didn't speak, Julie waited before breaking the silence. "Now me, you can take or leave alone. It's your choice, but I hope you'll find me an acceptable wife for Nate. I love him, but he needs to feel a father's love before he knows how to pass it along. You just never gave him anything to pass along, Jim Henry."

"Maybe I don't know how to start." His words flowed so softly they were like a thought.

"Maybe you just need some practice," she said.

He watched her car until it disappeared around a bend in the road before he pulled himself up and back inside the house. He wiped at the wetness that lay on his cheeks, but there was still more streaming from his eyes as he walked over to the kitchen wall and pressed his face against it.

"House," he whispered, "you and me have grown old and mean and crippled together. If I was put together with lumber and nails, I would be laying in a heap just like you."

After awhile he blew his nose and limped over to Elvie's old roll-top desk to poke through the stack of bills until he found the disconnect notice from the telephone people. He studied it, moving closer to the window where the sunlight lit the page so he could see the date and be sure it was next week when they were coming to cut him off.

Jim Henry sat down in his chair to figure out how was the best way to handle things from here on out.

"First off," he confided to whatever part of the house might be listening, "I'll catch a ride over to Pine Knot and go to the grocery store to get some things I need."

He leaned back in his chair, closed his eyes while he tried to remember the sweet bubbly taste of a Sunny Dew Cola.

CURRENT DAVEY O

*D*avey stood with his thumbs hooked in the corners of his pockets, looking down on her as though his turning sixteen had suddenly diminished her, compacted her into a small insignificant bundle. "But Mom, it's not over until midnight. The rest of the kids–" his words trailed, and it was not what he said that made her bristle; it was the way he seemed to flaunt towering head and neck above her now.

Keeta tilted her face to meet his eyes, gray and neither passive or hostile, but prepared to take on a look of bored amusement if she lost her composure. "One-thirty," she said evenly, "gives you plenty of time to do your thing after the dance is over. I'll not have you out hot rodding the streets all night, mister, so you be home on time or I'll see that your father drives that damn car right back with him to Indianapolis."

"Like you made him take back the motorcycle, right?"

"You were twelve years old, for heavens sake."

The muscles tightened in his jaws the way Big Dave's used to do and Davey said, not shouting, but quietly, as though he'd thought it over, "Maybe I'll just drive back with him."

"Don't threaten me," she started to say, but he was already out the door. As she heard the scrunching of tires in the gravel at the end of the drive, she leaned against the window to watch the tail lights on the Mustang suddenly hunker down to spill red at the stop sign before vanishing in the darkness.

The streets in her neighborhood were sleepy in the early evening, the houses quietly middle aged and guarded by dignified old oak and poplar trees. The breeze against her face was warm, spiced by the crowns of white blossoms on the hedgerow. Keeta took a deep breath and sighed as she realized she was more frustrated than angry at her son. Ol' Current Davey O, she thought, off in his new car too hot for him to handle, off to the spring dance with Marcie Brunson. Marcie called him Current Davey O because, "Davey is a *now* person. You know, current."

Keeta closed the curtains and sat down at her desk in the den. Light from a small goose neck lamp circled the stack of papers she had started to file before dinner. She leafed through a section of pages, pushed them aside and reached for the telephone directory to find the number of the Holiday Inn downtown. Her stomach had begun to churn by the time Big Dave answered, out of breath as though he'd been running.

"It's Keeta," she said.

"Hey, I recognized your voice. How about that?"

"I don't need a smart mouth tonight, Dave."

"Okay. Want me to open the door and come in again? I'll say how are you, and you'll ask, how's your wife and business?"

She tapped a cigarette against her fingers, decided not to light it. "So how is what's her name and what's new with Bubba Speedball's spark plugs?"

"Andretti," a flash of his slow grin crossed her memory when he answered. "It's the Andretti team I work with. Mario Andretti, his son Michael; the famous Indy racers, for God's sake. Ole Davey told you all about it, right?"

"It's all he talked about after he came back from visiting you last summer."

"He's a neat kid. You're doing a great job raising him, in case I haven't remembered to tell you lately."

"I wish you hadn't given him a car."

"That's what got you so fired up, me giving him a car?"

"Just once, Dave, just one time I'd like you to talk it over with me before you materialize on my doorstep with another-- "

"I took the motorcycle back," he interrupted. "I agreed he might be too young, right? But he's legal age to drive a car now. My God, I was dirt track racing when I was his age, so I didn't know I had to ask your permission to give him something to tool around town."

"A brand new Mustang is just something to tool around town?" She lit the cigarette, laid it in the ashtray without taking a puff. "He thinks he can come and go as he pleases now that he doesn't have to borrow my car. He's barely squeaking by English and History. Lord only knows if he'll keep his head from under the hood long enough to crack a book again."

"Hey, a man needs his own wheels when he takes a pretty girl to a dance."

"He wanted to stay out all night and eat breakfast at McDonald's."

"Growing pains," Dave said. "You can handle it. Ground him if he gets too sassy or doesn't keep up his grades. You do great with him."

"Don't keep saying it; just knock it off, will you? Do you think I don't know who has to keep him in line?" She felt the angry tears close but blinked them away. "I guess I don't want to talk any more tonight."

"If it makes your day, I feel pretty rotten about never being around, just seeing the boy during vacations."

"It doesn't make my day, Dave, but I guess the divorce was easier on him than our fighting."

"So how come we're having this civilized conversation?"

"So how is Mary?"

"Blooming, like you did the first couple of years. We fight, but you and I lost the war. We just lost the bloody war. So, how's your job and your friend, the creative one, ole what's his name?"

"Blooming," she said. "Goodbye, Dave." She didn't tell him that she had just signed a contract to do Parker Electronics' winter ad campaign and her creative friend, Bill, got married a year ago last summer.

Keeta hung up the receiver and sat listening to the faint tick of the little onyx clock she'd bought on a shopping trip with Davey after he came home from visiting his father and new stepmother. "A desk clock would make a nice hostess gift for Mary," she had suggested while they browsed through the mall. Davey shrugged, picked a ceramic frog off a shelf, said, "Hey, about I give her this really ugly toad?" They looked at each other and broke up; later they found a box of expensive chocolates for Mary. Keeta bought the clock for herself. Looking at it now, she realized that an hour had gone by.

She made a pot of almond mocha coffee, filled her favorite brown mug and sipped as she wandered from room to room. She plumped the cushions on the couch, turned on the ceiling fan in the hall, stopped to water the jade plant before looking at her reflection in the bathroom mirror. Her face showed pale threads of lines across her brow and at the corners of her mouth

At half past eleven, she settled down to watch TV. The late movie was something about a giant pumpkin that had devoured New York City and was growing its vine in the direction of Chicago. She turned off the set. Leafing through the new issue of *Urban Living*, she noticed six advertisements for liquor, eight for new automobiles. Davey would be leaving the dance soon, she thought, cool and laid back or whatever it is current to be, twirling the shiny keys to his car, antsy to get out on the road.

The sudden cries of sirens made her shiver. So many, she thought as she ran to tune in Davey's police radio. A three-car pile up on the interstate, the announcer said. She wondered if Big Dave had heard the wailing sounds in the night, if he sat in his room at Holiday Inn with his knees turned to putty. Then she remembered he had said he was leaving on the eight o'clock flight.

Keeta emptied what was left of the cup of cold coffee into the sink and turned to see headlights stream up the drive. Davey's car; she had already learned to recognize its low rumbling growl. When she didn't hear the grate of his key at the kitchen door, she turned on the security lights and waited. "He is standing out there working up the courage to face me," she told herself.

"He's had a brush with the cops or he has banged up his car."

She pulled back the curtain and saw him sitting under the dogwood tree, cross legged like a golden guru meditating in the moonlight. He didn't look up when she walked outside and asked, "What are you doing?"

"Look," he said when she hunched down beside him on the grass. He was squinting at the tiny half shell of a bird's egg. "What kind do you think it is?"

She studied his face in silhouette. Almost a man now, betrayed by his bobbing Adam's apple and the zit that didn't show on his chin in the moonlight. "I don't know," she said. "I don't know much about how birds get out of the egg."

"I'll see if I can find the nest tomorrow." He unfolded his long legs and gave her a hand up. "I thought you were going to turn in early."

"I had some work to do. Did you have a good time?"

"Yeah, it was okay. A couple of the kids got sick on the punch, so we didn't do anything afterwards. Mom?"

"What?"

"I was just thinking. Now that I've got my own car, I can run errands for you. Need anything from the store?"

"At midnight, Davey?"

They looked at each other and broke up, the same way they did when Davey said he should send the ugly frog to Mary. Their laughter was like a ripple of happy music, and Keeta ached to pluck this moment from time, clasp it gently, lovingly, the way Davey held the shell of the fragile blue egg.

DEELIE

*L*ong before the accident and the tragedy that changed her life, members of the Tuesday Morning Bible Study Group referred to her as poor Deelie McDougle. While gazing out the windows of the Butte City Tabernacle Holiness Church, they sometimes spotted her bending down to pet the old bobtail tomcat sunning in front of the post office next door, or noticed how skillfully she picked her way around spots where roots of the giant red oak buckled the concrete sidewalk.

"She is quite nimble, for a large girl," one of the ladies might point out. "Poor Deelie.. Martin married her on the rebound after Clarisa broke his heart."

Clarisa had caught the eye of Martin McDougle on the first day she came to work as a teller at Butte City Bank Of Commerce where he was head of Mortgages & Loans. Within the month he escorted the willowy blond girl to the July Fourth fireworks display, and three times they drove across the mountain to Beeville twenty miles away to clog dance.

Martin's mother, Maggie McDougle, confided to the shampoo woman at the hair dressers where she kept a standing ten o'clock Friday morning appointment, that she was not pleased to see her son involved with a young person who was always traipsing off to beauty pageants, a girl living in a double wide with a father who raised thoroughbred horses but admitted he didn't know jack about bringing up a headstrong daughter.

"Still," Mrs. McDougle was quoted as saying, "the two of them could produce fine looking grandchildren."

A tall muscular man, Martin's hazel eyes twinkled when he smiled and he always wore brightly colored bow ties with the dark blue suits his mother picked out for him. He had a gap between his upper front teeth, which some of the older citizens called a mark of virtue.

"You can trust a man with a gap," they said.

By the end of summer, Clarisa agreed to marry Martin, but two days before the wedding she left town with his diamond and emerald ring still sparkling on her finger. She went with the lean swarthy man who came looking for her, claiming to represent a modeling agency in Atlanta. He said he saw her picture in the newspaper the year she was crowned queen of the Miss Crape Myrtle Beauty Pageant.

Clarisa just up and went without a word, deserted Martin in the shadow of the altar, was how his mother described it.

Deelie, a young woman who worked week-ends only at the Tastee Pastry, was hired by the bank as a temporary replacement. She was short, stout and plain as Clarisa was tall, slender and stunning, which prompted an employee in Investments Service to remark that Deelie was not likely to bring home any beauty trophies.

On Martin's thirtieth birthday celebration that year, Maggie McDougle invited a small group of friends to her home to share her traditional chocolate layer cake served with raspberry sherbert and little triangles of wheat bread topped with cream cheese and pineapple. After the last guest left, the maid who came to tidy up said she overheard Mrs. McDougle say to Martin it was time he got down to the business of starting a family.

"She told him she wasn't getting any younger and neither was he. She said if he didn't have a child to carry on the family lineage by the time she passed, his inheritance from her estate would go to the Maggie McDougle Shelter For Abandoned Animals."

Deelie and Martin got acquainted the following week in the snack room at the bank. He sat at a table near the door, waiting until she came in for some nacho chips and a Pepsi. After introducing himself, he asked if she remembered to register downstairs in the lobby for a chance to win two tickets to the John Wayne Film Festival on Saturday night.

"He was my favorite actor," Martin said.

"Mine, too," Deelie smiled. "My very favorite."

They went together to the festival and the next week-end to a folk music concert over in the next county. Before the new year was under way, she accepted his proposal of marriage.

After the wedding ceremony, Mrs. McDougle gifted the couple with money for a down payment on a gray stone house with four bedrooms and a fenced back yard overlooking the valley of silvery spruce pines. Deelie interspersed their pieces of new furniture with heirlooms: an antique corner cupboard, two mahogany drop leaf tables and the blue fainting couch inherited from her great-grandmother.

Maggie McDougle confided to members of her Sunday school class that the new home was indeed tastefully furnished.

In the mornings after Martin kissed Deelie goodbye and left for the office, she sat at her desk in the breakfast nook and looked out the windows at the ridges along the mountains where, in winter, snow lay white and silent. She wrote stories about a dog named Flippo, the dog who meowed like a cat. In the evenings when she heard the rumble of her husband's car in the driveway, she swept the pages into a stack and hid them inside a locked drawer.

Their child, Sarah, was born the second year after they married. As she grew, her hair lay in gold ringlets and her teeth were like little kernels of white corn. Occasionally, upon seeing her, one of the elderly ladies might discretely whisper to another that some day Sarah would become lovelier than Clarisa .

Clarisa began to make trips back to Butte City for Christmas holidays to visit her ailing father. Each time she seemed to grow more supple and radiant than before. Deelie, who had developed a scattering of varicose veins and added weight since giving birth, acknowledged her with a tight lipped smile when they met by chance one night at the Elk Club's winter dance party. Clarisa arrived alone, saying she was no longer with the man who had come to Butte City looking for her, that he had left her in New Orleans.

Two of Martin's co-workers, who stood near the dance floor when Martin and Deelie waltzed by, said Martin didn't seem to notice that Clarisa gazed at him with a hungry sadness in her eyes.

After they left the party, Martin stopped at the Polar Bear Ice Cream & Sandwich Bar. While he picked up Deelie's chocolate malted and double order of fries, she telephoned home to remind the sitter that Sarah's cough medicine was in the refrigerator if she should need it.

On Sarah's fifth birthday, Deelie buckled her in the back seat of the car and headed for Beeville to watch the troop of clowns and acrobats perform in the traveling circus. It was a morning in early autumn. Wispy patches of fog still hovered over the hollows and the first splashes of reds and yellows brushed the tree tops along the high ridges. Later that day, a neighbor recalled waving to Deelie at the stop light before she entered the highway.

The accident happened just outside the town limits of Beeville. An eyewitness to the tragedy said the truck loaded with sheets of plate glass went out of control on the steep downgrade of the mountain road and slammed into the rear of Deelie's car. Sarah, when it was over, still sat upright in her seat. Her head lay on the floor, severed from her body by a jagged piece of glass.

Weeks later Deelie left the hospital with her right arm in a cast and her face laced with rows of angry red stitches. When friends came to bring a potted plant, or if they saw her walking along the street, nobody seemed to know what to say or to look directly into her eyes. Their glances appeared to be unfocused, as though they must greet her quickly and be on their way.

"The poor thing," a woman whispered to a friend one morning while waiting in the check-out line at the grocery store. She wiped the tears from her eyes at the sight of Deelie pushing an empty shopping cart back and forth past the mound of cabbage heads stacked one on top of another in the produce department.

Clarisa came back to town that year for the annual Christmas dance at the Elk's Club. She wore a red sheath dress that accentuated her thinness and the pale skin low on her back. Deelie insisted on going, despite Martin's protests that she needed to rest. She covered her scars with a heavy application of medium beige concealer and drank three double vodka martinis at the club bar before Martin took her home and put her to bed.

Deelie began to write again, more stories about the dog named Flippo, and hiding them in the drawer with the other pages. One day when the holidays were over, she put away her typewriter, dropped a sharp knife and a hairbrush in her pocket and drove across town to the new K-Mart. A clerk who was taking inventory in the toy department said Deelie walked up and down the aisle, starring at the rows of dolls before taking one of the more expensive ones off the shelf.

"She just stood there, brushing its long blond hair," the clerk later told the store manager, "and then she whipped out a knife and chopped off its head."

The officer investigating the incident said Deelie's screams could be heard outside in the parking lot. He said to his wife at supper that it was the saddest sight he ever saw , this poor woman cradling the severed head of a doll against her breast, brushing its long blond curls. And the wailing, he said, the awful sounds of her sorrow.

Later, Maggie McDougle told one of the members of her garden club, when Martin took Deelie away to the New Hope Psychiatric Hospital she hardly carried a thing with her except the clothes on her back and a drawer full of papers. The ladies all agreed he had no choice but to commit her. Poor Deelie was gone, they sighed, and what would happen now since Clarisa moved back to take care of her father?

Clarisa invited Martin for Sunday night suppers at her father's home, and soon afterwards she made an appointment with the dentist to fix the gap between his upper front teeth. He stopped going to see Deelie every weekend, limiting his visits to once a month. By the end of the year he seldom went at all. He mentioned to an employee at the bank that Deelie had been released from the hospital, had taken an apartment in Nashville and enrolled in creative writing at the university.

It was almost three years before she came back to Butte City. The night manager at the Mountain View Inn said the woman traveling with Deelie was the one who sold her work to the New York publishing company. The evening edition of the Carolina Bugle carried the news of her scheduled appearance at The Book Nook to sign copies of her best selling children's story, *FLIPPO, THE DOG WHO MEOWED LIKE A CAT.*

Deelie asked Clarisa to meet her for lunch the day she left for New York City. Several people in the Blue Peacock restaurant where they met mentioned Clarisa's baggy dress and how bright yellow made her skin look sallow and faded. Someone commented wasn't it a shame the way Clarisa let her looks go and Martin became practically a recluse since Maggie McDougle .passed away and left the family money to the abused animal shelter.

Deelie wore a powder blue silk suit with a single strand of pearls. Her hair style was short and smooth, the scars on her face dimmed by time. The young waitress who served the spinach salad whispered to the girl on check-out that Deelie might pass for a movie star or fashion model.

Diners sitting in the booth next to Clarisa and Deelie said they couldn't hear if Deelie explained why she decided to leave Martin for good and set out on her own. Some speculated that coming back to take up her life again would be too painful, or that she had turned out to be one of those modern women bent on proving herself. Others said perhaps Martin was not the man they thought him to be.

"It's only fair you should have him back," a waiter overheard Deelie say to Clarisa as she picked up the check and turned to go. "Martin was, after all, yours in the beginning. But he gave me the best part of him. He gave me Sarah."

DIALOGUE WITH THE Q.O. MAN

When Hovey married Eleanor, he went out and bought the biggest TV in town. In the ten years since their around- the-world honeymoon cruise, he had never once turned off the set.

At night, when he was ready to sleep, he muted the talk show hosts, stand-up comics and televangelists, leaving their voices to spill empty and silent until the late morning program schedule began.

Marriage to Eleanor McNaire, of McNaire Industries, had made it unnecessary for him to go back to his job with an accounting firm, so he was free to sleep until noon, indulge himself for an hour of juvenile pleasure with The Quaker Oats Cartoon Man & His Family as he had done in long sunny days of childhood.

Promptly at one o'clock p.m., cook set his onion and peanut butter sandwich with a bag of potato chips on the tray in front of his chair while he clicked to the Disaster Channel to catch the latest film clips of mass murders, earthquakes and airline crashes. The palm of his right hand had become slightly curved to form a cradle for the remote; a small brown callous was starting to grow on the lower part of his index finger from years of channel surfing.

Eleanor spent her days rushing between CEO power lunches and ground breaking ceremonies with the mayor. Each morning before she hurried away, briefcase in hand, she stopped beside Hovey's bed and brushed her lips in the air next to his cheek. When she returned, she handed the briefcase to a servant and went to her room to study market reports until dinner. Afterwards, if she had not scheduled a fund raising charity ball or an evening at the symphony for the two of them, she sat on the sofa across from Hovey's easy chair in the den and dozed before going to bed.

One night while Eleanor nodded and Hovey surfed during first commercial break on Character Assassination Hour, which had replaced the six o'clock news on Disaster Channel, a sudden brightness zigzagged across the room. Windows rattled and the screen flared like a pool of blood, then returned to its greenish glow as Hovey heard a tap tapping inside the set.

"Good. I have your attention." The Quaker Oats Man laid a silver spoon on the napkin beside the cereal bowl. "I thought we might have a conversation."

"Well, sure," Hovey said, "but I have to tell you right up front that I feel silly talking to a cartoon, although I once thought of you as a real person. I suppose I did talk to you when I was a little boy."

"You were a nice young fellow. How long is it since you and Eleanor got married?"

Hovey closed his eyes for a moment. "A long time."

He followed the Q.O. Man's glance toward the sofa where Eleanor had fallen asleep in an erect position, her chin propped so precariously on her shoulder that her neck seemed in danger of snapping, sending her head rolling across the floor. When he looked back at the television screen, the Q.O. Man had vanished and Tomato Lady appeared in his place.

Tomato Lady was Hovey's favorite farm yard character from Quaker Oats Cartoon Family. Dressed in spiked layers of green leaves, she stood attached to a vine higher than her head .The vine hung heavy with shiny red tomatoes large as grapefruits. She held out a box marked "Organic Fertilizer" and sang a jingle rhyming the words sowing, growing and hoeing.

The screen went fuzzy and the Q.O. man came back.

"Sorry to do a fade out, but T.L. works solo on commercials." He took off his white wig, wiped a thin line of perspiration from his forehead and down the creases of his rosy cheeks. "So what were you saying?"

"I said I have been married for a long time."

"Are you happy?"

"Define happy. I'm content, although come to think of it we haven't had sex since 1997."

"Isn't that a rather strange relationship?"

"Not really. It's a mutual arrangement. We feed off each other's needs. She needs me to be here for her. I'm here because I need her money. It keeps me in the style to which I have enjoyed becoming accustomed." Hovey looked around the room, pointing to the paintings and tapestries on the walls, mahogany display cases filled from floor to ceiling with collections of silver and porcelain. "Eleanor's inheritance. When she goes, it all belongs to charities."

"Does the thought that you could end up with nothing give you a feeling of insecurity?"

"Not at all. I live for the moment, for what is now. Eleanor is several years my junior and so I take my chances she will outlast me. Meanwhile, I earn my keep. I am her puppet, her water boy, and I look great in a tuxedo; I am whatever she wants me to be."

"Does your life have a purpose?"

"Absolutely. A flick of a button and I watch a war while it is being fought: blood soaked body parts sent flying in all directions. I am privy to the filthy little secrets hidden in the closets of preachers, celebrities, university professors and my own governor. It's a wonderful life, as they say, a world right here at my fingertips."

The Q.O. Man said, "I wanted to have this conversation to thank you for your loyalty and to tell you that I have been sold out. I have been sold to Them."

"Them?"

"The Disaster Channel. They own me, they control me now. Think back to when you were a little boy. What did we talk about? What did we do on Cartoon Family?"

"I remember making a kite out of newspapers," Hovey smiled. "We looked for faces of animals in the clouds. I always found a rabbit."

"Starting tomorrow, we will discuss how to deal with mom's boy friend when he tries to rape her," the Q.O. Man said. "I am a lovable little cartoon, Hovey. How can I talk about such things with eight-year old children?"

"Kids have to learn about life," Hovey shrugged, "and from who better than the Quaker Oats Man?"

"Now that I belong to Disaster Channel, I have been given a new persona. You may have noticed that over the years I have developed some human characteristics. I sweat under hot lights. I laugh, feel sad, appreciate the beauty of a sunset. Do you still remember the feeling of emotions, Hovey?"

"I am human. You are ink and paper," Hovey answered. "A cartoon."

"But who's to say who is real, who is the cartoon?" the Q.O. Man asked ."At any rate, I will take on a different personality, whatever They decide."

The next morning Eleanor left a note on his tray to remind him that she would be late for dinner. After her meeting downtown with the Citizens Against Violence Committee, she planned to stop off on Hickory Road for an interview and publicity pictures at the new AIDS Treatment Center.

Cook served breakfast, muffins with black raspberry jam, while he leaned back in his chair to watch the opening credits of the New Cartoon Quaker Oats Man & His Family. Hovey sat up straight and squinted to get a better look..

The familiar Q.O. gleamed in shimmering silver on his bare chest. No longer one dimensional, the jolly roundness gone, he moved as though every part of him vibrated with life. Beads of perspiration clung to his bald head, glinted on the gold rings dangling from his ears and lower lip. The tattoo of a cobra slithered down the muscles of his arm as he grabbed Tomato Lady by her vine and stripped the leaves from her breasts. She started to scream while he dragged her behind the tool shed.

By evening, Hovey had watched an earthquake swallow whole cities, seen maggots feeding in the ooze of decomposing bodies unearthed in a garbage dump. He turned up the volume to hear a local Disaster News bulletin:

An explosion of what is believed to be two bombs has turned an area of the city into an inferno. There appears to be no survivors where the direct hit was made at the new AIDS Treatment Center on Hickory Road.

The remote nestled in his palm while he studied the callous that seemed to have grown larger on the end of his finger. He took a deep breath, touched OFF. The big screen crackled, went black and silent.

As he looked out through the windows, he saw two policemen enter the driveway. Above the trees, clouds shifted, merging into forms and faces of animals. Hovey sat without moving, watching until a gust of wind erased the last rabbit from the sky.

THE NAKED MAN ON MY PORCH

*A*naked man is lying on my front porch.

I have opened a slat in the window blind to peep outside as I always do before leaving the house every morning, and there he is. His eyes are closed, shiny little bubbles of spittle work the corners of his mouth and drizzle down into his beard. His chest is covered with a tattoo of two bear cubs hugging each other; they spread their paws wider with each breath he takes. My eyes wander further down, and right away I decide the tattoo is the only thing he has going for him.

My neighborhood is the low rent district. Two years ago when I joined the staff at the South Side Inner City Clinic, I decided to live close to the people who came to me for counseling "I want to know who they are, what they think," I told my parents. "I want to make a difference."

"But you can afford to live in a better place," my father said. "You don't have to live in squalor."

My dad is a doctor, a cardiologist. Mom plays golf.

I share an old two story house converted to six apartments. Mine is on the ground floor, two rooms with bath down the hall. The front porch, where I keep my plants, faces the busy street that dead ends one block away at Dixie Heaven BBQ & Beer Palace.

Dixie Heaven serves barbecue pork, beer and mixed drinks from noon until two a.m. Patrons who linger until the closing hour sometimes stagger off to sleep in doorways or wherever they can snag a spot. So it isn't unusual to see a body huddled in a wad on my redwood swing that hangs from the porch ceiling, or to hear snoring sounds coming from behind the pot of purple shamrock in the corner. But naked people, no.

The man lying here on the porch looks harmless enough. I ask myself: where would a totally naked person conceal a weapon? Calling 911 is a bad idea because cops aren't in a hurry to come to this part of town, so I take a deep breath, fish the container of pepper spray out of my purse and ease through the door. I am prepared in case he makes a grab for my ankle when I come near him, but he doesn't move a muscle.

"Excuse me." I nudge his upper arm with the toe of my shoe. "Where are your clothes?"

He flops his peppermint striped eyes open, one at a time like a sick old dog. His hands slide across his belly as though they expect to locate a shirt tail. "Beats hell outta me where they are by now. Two guys stole them." He struggles to sit up, rakes a long string of grizzled hair away from his face.

"Wait right there." I push him back down and go inside to get the old green plaid bed sheet I use to cover my plants when the weather turns cold. "I'll be more comfortable if you wrap this around you while we talk. So how come two guys took your clothes?"

He has draped the sheet into a fairly decent toga. "I was drunk, you see, taking a leak behind some bushes by the alley. They must of decided to keep my shirt and pants when they didn't find no money on me." He sways when he stands but his legs manage to keep him upright.

"Listen," I say. "I'm on my way to work, so can I give you a lift or drop you off some place?"

But he has already turned to go, lurching down the street in the direction of Dixie Heaven.

When I get to the clinic, parked in my space is this blue Chevy pickup with a Jesus Loves Me sticker on the bumper. After driving around the block a couple of times I leave my car in the off-street free parking, hoping nobody steals the stereo or slashes the tires like they did last time I put it there.

The phone is ringing when I walk into my cubical. A man's voice tells me that last night his lady remembered the bottle of gin she had stashed under the mattress. She can't get out of bed to come in for her appointment. So do I make house calls?

A drop-in who comes unannounced from time to time is already waiting to see me. She is an old woman whose chin seems to have melted into the folds on her neck. I watch her hobble in on her cane and lower herself to the edge of a chair. Tears glisten in little rivulets down the wrinkles in her cheeks as she starts to tell me about her husband, dead, she reckons, for about a couple of months.

"At first, I had good dreams about him and I could see him in the room with me." She twists a dirty handkerchief into a knot around her fingers. "But lately, he talks to me. I hear his voice begging me to come to the cemetery and dig him up. He says the worms are crawling over his face."

I stay late to finish some paper work before leaving to get my car. The cleaning man at the day care center across the street pokes his head out the door when I walk by, says he chased a pair of mean looking boys out of the parking lot.

I give him a thumbs up as I drive away.

When I get home, the women in the apartment upstairs are screaming at each other and throwing things again. Books and papers lie scattered in the yard, a pillow comes sailing through the window. I run inside, turn up the TV and just when it gets quiet above my head, the couple across the hall start to rev up for their usual Friday evening brawl.

After awhile I hear a knock out front and I know before looking. The loser of the fight upstairs is leaning against the door, pressing an ice cube against a strawberry welt under her eye. Can she come in, maybe talk with me?

My work follows me home like a pregnant cat. It has been a long week.

It's Saturday at last, almost noon. I'm still in my pajamas, on my third cup of coffee. I skip the front section of the morning newspaper and circle a couple of ads in the classifieds. *Small cottage for sale, quiet wooded area overlooking pond....Now hiring, qualified mental health therapists, great benefits, pleasant surroundings.*

I go out for pizza and a movie and it's almost dark by the time I get back to my place. As I pull into the driveway, the lights flash on what looks like the aftermath of a tornado. Someone has ripped open the pillow in the yard. White feathers everywhere, sticking to the grass, windows, you name it. My porch is trashed, the redwood swing hangs by one end from the ceiling. The other end rests on the floor. Wind jangles the chain in the space above. The brown remains of my purple shamrock are scattered on the floor. Someone has taken the antique flower pot that had belonged to my grandmother.

That does it. This place is a zoo. I'm disgusted with people who have no conscience, who live like a pack of wild animals. First thing Monday morning I am calling about that cottage overlooking a lake. Maybe I'll check on the job with pleasant surroundings and great benefits.

I go inside to sit on the couch, feeling a sickness churn inside me when I hear a knock, a timid rap like maybe it's a little girl out selling cookies for her scout troop. But who would let a kid out after dark in this place?

I open the door wide enough to see a man standing there. He has red splotches on his cheeks, like he just shaved with a razor that had a nick in the blade. His hair is slicked back in a neat pony tail and then I recognize his eyes. It is the naked man wearing clothes, a bright orange shirt and jeans hugging low on his hips.

"I brought it back." He lays my green plaid sheet, neatly folded, in my hands. My tongue is in limbo until he turns to walk away.

"Wait." Tears sting my eyes. "Please wait."

"It's clean," he calls back over his shoulder. "I washed it for you." He is already about a quarter of a block away before I catch up to him. I can't stop crying.

"What?"

"I've made a decision and I need for you to hug me, that's all."

He looks at me, then reaches out and drapes his big arms around me, holds me for a moment. His shirt is rough against my cheek and smells of beer, yesterday's cigarettes and maybe last week's sweat.

"Thank you," I say.

"No problem." He lumbers off. I watch his neon brightness fade into the crowd.

It's rush hour. Horns honk in the street, the crowd of walkers go around me. They crane their necks to stare. I am standing in the middle of the sidewalk, laughing and crying, my soul stripped naked in front of God and everybody.

I stay until it's so dark I can see only silhouettes of people, my people, scurrying to queue up for the eight o'clock round of free drinks and hot wings at Dixie Heaven BBQ & Beer Palace.

SWEET HONEYSUCKLE MORNING

*P*up lifted his head, his ears quivering at attention to catch the beginning of the sound. It was the wail of the police cars; the strange machines, he called them. They had come again, their eyes flashing red and blue across the fronts of the row houses where he made his home. Sometimes they came while the early morning breeze still splashed the air with silence, and sometimes they returned in the evenings to cry in sad harmony with the music of the alley.

The sun had already dropped from sight, but its glow flamed the city with a maverick fire that danced along the roof tops and its heat clung to the bare ground where Pup sat. He was waiting for the woman. He had not seen her nor heard her voice all day.

The woman was old. She had only one eye and there was a deep empty socket where the other had been. Her hair was white, wooly as an old sheep's back, and her skin was like a night without a moon. She lived alone at the end of a line of wooden houses. Each outside wall sagged and teetered toward the next, giving the look of a dozen giant unpainted dominoes waiting to topple one onto another until they all lay propped in a zigzag pile along the fringes of the alley.

The woman protected Pup from the big redbone hound, the leader of the wild pack who prowled the row in search of food. On her porch she kept a pan filled with fresh water, and close by hung the broom she wielded to chase away those who came to skulk behind the tall clump of privet hedge, waiting to challenge him. In the evenings she sat on one of the rickety steps, sharing the supper from her plate while she sang to him about the big white house on a hill where the sweet perfume of honeysuckle filled the air. Sometimes when there was not enough food to fill his belly, she stroked his fur and crooned in a tinny thin voice:

Times is mighty hard, pup
Now hear what I got to say.
Tomorrow's a honeysuckle morning,
Tomorrow is a honeysuckle day.

But Pup had not seen the woman since yesterday, so now as the sounds of the strange machines grew louder, he trotted up the steps and scratched on the screen to remind her he had not eaten today. He turned his head from side to side to listen for the pit pat of her bare feet, but he heard only the wailing noises of the police cars. And when he saw their eyes flashing, he ran to search for his mother. He knew he would find her under one of the porches at the other end of the row where she spent most of her days now that she waited to give birth to a new family.

"It is wise to know when to be afraid," she said when he inched down, shivering beside her in the darkness under the floor. "The blue men who come in the machines are not always friendly to our kind."

The red clay rubbed cool against his empty belly, and he pressed close to his mother as she spoke. He closed his eyes and thought of how he had once tugged at her breasts that swung almost to the ground when she walked. The taste of her milk had been warm and sweet as it trickled down his puppy throat in a slow lazy stream. He rooted his nose against her now, nudging her flank to ask permission once more, but she growled a warning and shoved him away. He hunkered back and kept still, watching the streaks of red and blue light sweep the porch above his head and leak through the cracks in the boards.

"They have stopped at the woman's house." His mother had moved heavily from her bed and stood squinting to see. "The men are taking her away."

"I must go to her," Pup cried.

His mother sniffed the air with her long thin nose. "Stay. There is nothing you can do. The woman is dead."

"Dead? What is dead?"

"Do you remember the rat I once brought to you from the garbage, the big gray box that sets beside the alley? The rat was dead."

Pup thought about how still the rat lay, remembered watching his mother's teeth tearing into its thick hide. He had turned away when she offered to share the dark pungent meat with him.

"Will the woman be eaten like the rat?" he asked.

"No, more's the pity. She will be buried deep in the ground. It is a human custom," she sighed. "Oh, I imagine the worms will feast on her, but it seems such a waste."

"Who will give me food now that she is gone?"

"You will learn to outwit the pack and to fight for the scraps that come from the big gray box," she snapped. "You will eat the meat of the rats and roaches that scurry nearby. You have been spoiled by the woman; now you must learn to do as the rest of us."

Pup went back to the woman's house the next morning before the sun came up, but he found nothing among the cans and papers scattered in her yard. Already the wild pack knew they need not fear her broom, and they had come in the night to wolf down the pieces of bread and gnaw the bone he might have overlooked yesterday. They had lapped the water from the pan and heisted their legs over it, leaving a murky yellow puddle inside.

He found a hiding place in the tall ragweed blooming gold around the garbage box and crouched down to wait for the men who would come soon to empty it. There might be a scrap of meat come tumbling to the ground when the box was lifted high in the air. He licked beads of drool from his whiskers, his legs taut and ready to spring.

When the grass crackled behind him, he whirled his head to look into the eyes of the red bone hound.

"Leave," the hound commanded. "The box is ours."

"No," Pup said, his feet digging hard into the ground.

"Look around you."

Out of the corner of his eye, Pup saw the circle of faces belonging to the rest of the pack, and at the same time he caught sight of the rat moving through the weeds. He lunged, ripping his teeth into the rat's soft underbelly as the wild pack came snarling down upon him. The redbone slashed his ear and tore the rat from his jaws as the brown one grabbed his neck and flung him high in the air.

When the pack began fighting among themselves, he crawled away and burrowed as far as he could beneath the woman's porch. His ear still dripped blood; he rubbed it back and forth in the dirt until he no longer felt the wetness. Curling himself into a ball, he closed his eyes and knew he would feel nothing while he slept. The woman is dead, he told himself. She is cold and stiff, buried deep in the ground. Later he dreamed that she sat with him on the steps, crooning her song.

By the end of summer, Pup had learned to search for food along the streets far away from the row. In the darkness while the city lay cooling itself in the shadows, he scavenged the big gray boxes behind tall buildings. He drank water from puddles along the gutters and kept clear of the wheels of all machines.

One night when he was sniffing his way back to the alley, he watched a woman get out of a machine that sat under a street light. A dog walked beside her. Pup followed close behind until the woman stopped, turned to look at him. He felt his heart start to race as he stood motionless except for the wagging of his tail. She reached down and patted his head. "Go home, boy," she said. "Go on home now."

Pup chased after her as she drove away and when he could no longer suck enough air to breathe, he lay down by the roadside and waited for her to come back. But the sounds of her faded away and soon there was only the stirring of the wind. His ears picked up the distant calls of the pack who also prowled the darkness.

"I was afraid you might have lost your way. It is not safe to leave the alley," his mother said when he came to look for her during the night. "You found food?"

"A few scraps," Pup said, "but I saw one of our kind walking with a human, a woman."

"I am certain it was not one of our kind," she smiled

"It was white and curly and stood on four feet as I do. It raised its leg against the bushes as I am learning to do."

"Some traits we all have in common," she agreed, "but you must accept that there are those different from you and me and all our kind. They are the ones who never know the meaning of hunger or thirst. They were born to be cared for by humans and to live in fine houses far from the row."

"And why was I born?"

"To roam the alleys and stay where you belong. You were fortunate to have the woman's favor, although she was scarcely better off then we." His mother sighed and made a place for him in the dirt near her bed. "Sleep here for the rest of the night and forget what you cannot change. Tomorrow you may find food enough to bloat your belly."

He lay beside her and listened to the slow rhythm of her breathing as he waited for sleep to come to him She is concerned only with living from today until tomorrow, he thought, so how can she understand?

Light from the new day had not come when he crawled out of bed, careful not to awaken her. She had tossed and moaned during the night and he wondered if her new family would soon be born. He sat looking at her, etching the lump of her heavy body in his mind, for he knew he would not see her again.

When he trotted away, he did not look back until he got to the end of the alley. In the half light he saw the water pan, rusty and dry, overturned near the steps at the woman's house. The green flies would come to buzz in and out of it when the sun brought the morning, and the wild pack would snarl and fight in the weeds around the gray box.

Pup began to run. He ran as though his feet had sprouted wings, ran until he came to the place where the big machines, trucks with many wheels, roared down a wide, wide ribbon of concrete. On the city streets, he knew their ways; he had learned when it was wise to run. But in this place where he had not been before, they came at him from all directions.

He had darted halfway across the wide ribbon when the big wheels roared down on him. As they hissed and spun beside him he looked away, his eyes searching for the hill where the woman waited. He knew she sat on the steps of the big white house, and for one sweet moment he smelled the perfume of a honeysuckle morning

MOON WALK

*T*oro called from California around midnight and told me Roxanne was dead. It's been a half dozen years since they went to live there, Roxanne with her dreams of making it big in the movies, Toro tagging along for the ride.

We've kept in touch. I guess I have filled a shoe box with her press clippings from *The Hollywood Star Gazer*. There's this one picture that just blows me away, the one where she is dancing with a fat old dude, and the caption says: Dixie Beauty Catches Eye Of Studio Boss. The tilt of her chin, the half smile is pure fire and ice.

I hadn't talked with Roxanne lately except to tell her I love her; I didn't know what else to say. Toro had told me how everything was falling apart because her drug habits were starting to get out of control. We talked about *Celebrity Enquirer's* cover story of her latest escapade: Roxanne Redwine stripping naked on the dance floor at Elizabeth Taylor's AIDS Benefit Ball, a wild-eyed Roxanne with hair flying, taking a swing at the camera of a reporter who caught her on film.

But hearing Toro say that she was dead was like a hot iron searing my brain.

"I know it's middle of the night down there in Seep Springs, but I thought you should hear it from me before it leaks out to the media vultures," he said. "Her studio is releasing a statement that she might have died from a virus she caught on location in Mexico, but everybody will know that's bullshit when the coroner's report comes out."

The police discovered her body, he told me, after her maid couldn't rouse Roxanne at dinner time.

"Man, I'm sorry to break it to you like this. You didn't see her lately, so I guess it's a bigger shock to you than to me."

"What was she on?"

"Everything. Anything she could shoot, swallow or snort." His voice broke and the lump in my throat got big as an egg.

I used the silence that hung between us to remember that year Roxanne swept out of town with her head in the clouds and her big lumbering cousin Toro Beauville in tow to protect her from the evils of Hollywood. I thumbed a ride to California later on, a college drop-out at loose ends, hoping to find work as a stunt man in one of her movies soon as she got to be a star.

She was still waiting for the break that hadn't come.

"Paying my dues," was how she described her bit parts and occasional starring roles in porn flicks.

As soon as I saw her again, I knew I was still so damn crazy in love with her I would ask her one more time to marry me, but it was like she read my mind. She reached out, cupped my face in her hands and kissed my cheek.

"Give me more time for my dream," she whispered.

I realized it was Toro's voice I heard now and he had just said something about why didn't I come on back out there for awhile.

"I still have the key to her place on Lake Shasta. We'll sit and look at the water and the mountains and talk about how it was to be rag tag kids from little ole piss ant Seep Springs." His words were still hoarse and shaky. "Hey, remember when we used to build space ships in my back yard and Roxanne was always the one who got to be Neil Armstrong?"

"She walked on the moon," I said.

I promised Toro I'd come soon as I could get time off from work. He said it was lucky I didn't find a job in the movies and the smartest thing I ever did was get my butt back home.

"You staying clean?" He asked before he hung up.

"Nothing stronger than Bud and Juicy Fruit."

What I didn't say was it's no bed of pansies down here in little ole piss ant GA and that I'd been giving serious thought to packing my toothbrush and leaving for good. I sure wouldn't leave much behind–six days a week, minimum wage at Unfinished Furniture Mart.

I got other reasons for wanting out. Number one is to get away, infinity miles away, from Aunt Shirley who lives in Sunrise Manufactured Homes Park with this greasy looking guy. He used to race stock cars until he flipped end over end and the gas tank exploded. The fire left his fingers fused together so he can't grip a steering wheel any more.

Aunt Shirley is my mother.

"So what kind of a kid did I raise?" She asks whenever I bump into her, which turns out to be more often than I like. "You don't hardly ever go out on dates, from what I hear," she says. "You want people to think you turned queer while you were out there in California sniffing after Roxanne Redwine?"

Then she starts riding my back about Jo Nell Vargus, about why don't I marry her and try to make something of myself.

Jo Nell is the other reason I want out.

Back in high school I must have spent half of my last two semesters hiding out in the boy's locker room so I didn't get roped in to taking Jo Nell to some movie or dance. I was in love with Roxanne then, same as now.

Jo Nell is pretty, in a big, blond sort of way. Soft. Everything about her, soft; long corn tassel hair, her voice, a pair of tits the right size to lose your face in. She still stays with her folks in the old two story brick house next to the grammar school and works at the post office except for Saturday mornings when she delivers the Seep Springs weekly newspaper, *The Sentinel.*

I guess I was about eight years old the night my mother told me to call her Aunt Shirley.

I can still see her, perched on the edge of her white wicker vanity stool, her right eye squinted while she glued on a row of thick black lashes. Her tapered nails, flecked with little grains of gold, glinted like purple gem stones in the light reflecting back into the mirror.

I kept thinking she might turn around and give me a hug or maybe say she was counting on me to be her man to watch the house until she got back. "You gonna listen to what I say?" She ran her tongue across the lipstick smear on one of her front teeth. "When this man comes to the door tonight and if he happens to ask who you are, you are to say you are staying with your Aunt Shirley while your mama is sick in the hospital. I am your Aunt Shirley. You gonna remember that?"

One night I didn't remember; I forgot and called her Mama, but I never slipped up again. She got home around midnight, hauled me out of bed and began screaming and slapping hell out of me. When blood started to spurt out of my nose, she commenced to cry and say she didn't mean it. So now when I haven't seen her for awhile and happen to run into her at Wal-Mart or some place, I notice how she sort of sweeps her eyes away from looking directly at my nose. It's like she doesn't want to see how it sets a little off center.

I kept mulling this over in my mind after Toro called because I didn't want to think about Roxanne. It seems I had just dropped off when I heard a loud clang followed by whomp against the front door. Jo Nell looks soft, but she has the arm of a Joe Namath when it comes to firing a rolled up newspaper from the open window of her Impala, over the holly bushes and through the green plastic wind chimes on the stoop.

The news of Roxanne's death was already on TV; it was like a bad dream. But reading the black headlines in *The Sentinel* hit me with reality. Each word seemed to roll across the columns of her hometown newspaper with a keening sound, painting a picture of how it had all come about.

Roxanne was, as the story said, destined to be a Star, for she would have gleamed and twinkled in a cotton patch or under a bale of hay. And so, that time when Halcon Pictures sent a camera crew to shoot Fields Of Home in the dinkiest little Southern town on the map, there was Roxanne. She was seventeen, green eyed and raven haired, and that smart ass casting director never figured out what hit him. First thing any of us knew, he gave her a two-line speaking part in the movie and arranged for Toro to be her personal bodyguard when she went to Hollywood to become famous. It took her six years to get to be an overnight sensation and I guess she committed about every filthy act on record to get there. She was finally close to realizing her dream; she had signed a contract to star in a remake of Waterloo Bridge. But it was too late. She had already crashed and burned.

The night before I left to meet Toro, I cruised around town for awhile and tried to get my head together. I drove past Aunt Shirley's place a couple of times but everything was dark. Her big old yellow mutt Bruno snarled and strained at the end of the heavy chain anchored to the porch railing. I figured Aunt Shirley and what's-his-name had gone over to dance and play bingo at the American Legion Hall.

On the way home, I slowed down by the grammar school, close to the house where Jo Nell and her folks live. I parked at the playground swings, rolled down all the windows and sat watching about a million fireflies blink on and off like strings of Christmas lights in the branches of a big poplar tree in their yard. Sounds of canned TV laughter sifted through the open front door. When a light went on upstairs, Jo Nell's shadow moved back and forth behind white lace curtains. I opened a fresh pack of Juicy Fruit and stuffed the wrapper in my shirt pocket.

I stayed there for a long time, wishing it could all be different. I wondered how it would feel to want to bury myself against her, the warmth of her arms sliding around me, making the pain go away.

Toro had the beer on ice and waiting when I got to Lake Shasta. I followed him inside the house and we sat at the bar in the corner of the game room. I watched the sunset brushing red and gold stripes across the sky outside the windows while we started off with a lot of small talk to catch up; it had been a long time since we'd seen each other. I said I liked the chances of the San Francisco 49ers making it to the Super Bowl next year. He asked if fishing and hunting was still good back home.

I felt a chill run up my back. Roxanne was all around me. Her laughter was painted on the clown face of the rag doll lounging beside the fireplace, her sadness in the eyes of a young girl gazing out of the painting above the mantel.

A lot of what Toro told me that night I would like to forget, but I want to hang on to what he said about me being the only man Roxanne ever really loved. He said he believed it was true.

"She did what she thought she had to do to get where she wanted to go. She was a whore and a junk head and she messed around with dangerous folks." He stopped suddenly and I remembered seeing the same look in the eyes of a deer I once shot and wounded. "But, God, wasn't she beautiful? Maybe it was her beauty that trapped all the ugliness of this stinking entertainment business inside her and she couldn't handle it."

He got up and put on a pot of coffee. While it brewed, he said "I've been thinking about pulling out, maybe coming back to Georgia."

"I suppose there are worse places," I said.

"You still on the outs with Aunt Shirley?"

"I see her around every now and then."

"Hell, man. You gonna pout for the rest of your life?"

"Up yours," I said. "I'm thinking about sending her a Mother's Day card."

We both got a laugh out of that.

We got to talking about stuff like the first time we made it with Betty Lou Washburn, the girl whose daddy hauled the whole Seep Springs football team into court the year Betty Lou got pregnant. Toro said he wondered what ever happened to old Betty Lou.

The next night we sat out on the deck and finished off a case of Bud. We watched a couple of shooting stars blaze across the tree line, and Toro said we ought to fire off a space ship that would make Roxanne proud. So we scrounged around through an open-til-midnight drug store and came up with powdered charcoal, some sulphur and saltpeter. We stuffed it all inside the cardboard core from a roll of paper towels, and after we fooled around with it for awhile it was ready to go.

I watched the flare of the match when Toro lit the fuse and I didn't bother to wipe the tears that started to slide down my face. I guess I was crying for Roxanne and Toro and me, and for Aunt Shirley and Jo Nell. Hell, I was probably crying for the whole world by the time I saw the little missile start to pitch and roll, up and over through the darkness. A plume of fire glowed behind it before it righted itself, burning a path on a straight line to the moon.

It was the biggest, brightest moon I ever saw.

DEAD BUTTERFLIES

*W*hen I was six years old, my favorite person was Uncle Luther. He was my grandpa's brother and the black sheep in Daddy's family because he gambled, chased after women, drank hard liquor and never worked. Actually, Uncle Luther was a bum, but I loved him.

Daddy's mother, who lived with us, predicted that some day he would end up dead in a ditch with nobody to mourn him or put flowers on his grave. If folks came to Luther's funeral, Grandma said, they would just be there to make sure he was dead.

Uncle Luther said he owned a ranch south of Hobbs, New Mexico, but he never seemed to stay there. He drifted in and out of the little towns in our part of West Texas, hopping a freight train from one place to another. When Uncle Luther showed up at our house, Grandma usually packed her suitcase the next day and told Daddy to drive her to the Greyhound bus station.

"Write me a postcard and tell me when you are shed of Luther," were her parting words. "I'm going up to Cisco to stay with Nettie."

Sometimes Aunt Nettie brought her back before Uncle Luther left. Grandma didn't get along well with her sister Nettie for any kind of a long stretch, Mama said.

Once when she was at Aunt Nettie's, I slipped into her room and opened the little pink satin lined box she kept beside the black leather Bible on her dresser. I found a gold locket with a man's picture inside. He had dark eyes and wavy hair and a thick black moustache that curved up past the corners of his mouth. I asked Mama if it was Grandpa, if that's how he looked before he got old and died.

"It's the picture of the man who jilted Grandma before Grandpa came along and saved her pride." Mama looked at me with her mouth half open, like she was trying to suck words back under her tongue. "You are too young to know about such things, so you just tend to your own knitting and don't go poking your nose in your Grandma's things, you hear?"

I didn't know what jilted was, but I figured it must be something bad because Grandma claimed nothing good ever happened to her. She told me the world is evil and God would bring it to an end pretty soon with fire and brimstone. She said she hoped it ended before I reached the age of account-ability. The age of accountability is when you get to be eight or nine years old and you know the difference between right and wrong; it's when you have to get saved or risk spending forever in Hell.

I planned to get saved on the morning of my ninth birthday.

Grandma never told stories or sang songs like Uncle Luther did. He taught me the words to all the verses of "Little Joe The Wrangler" and "I'm Going To See My Mother When The Work's All Done This Fall." He said they were songs that had never been put down on sheet music, so you had to learn them from someone who knew the words and tune by heart. Sometimes he told stories about when he was gored by a longhorn bull down in Concho County. Other times he talked about the house he said he had in New Mexico.

"Back on my ranch," he said, "my dishes are always washed by soap and water. I got a cat named Soap and a dog named Water."

Uncle Luther liked to ride freight trains. He told me he guessed he had hoboed in every empty boxcar that snaked down the tracks between Fort Worth and El Paso. I loved how his words painted a picture of him riding a long shiny snake through the rolling hills, blue with salt cedar, past prairie dog towns and patches of prickly pear full of yellow blooms.

When I thought it was about time for him to show up again, I listened for the whistle of the afternoon train as it rumbled to a stop at the water tank beside the Santa Fe depot. The tracks were maybe a half a mile from our house with no trees to block the view. Once I saw him when he hopped off the boxcar next to the caboose; he was just a little dot when he moved.

"It's Uncle Luther!" I shouted, and when he started to walk, pretty soon I could see the way his boots stirred little puffs of red dust around his feet.

Mama ran out of the kitchen, drying her hands on the front of her big white butcher's apron. "Oh mercy," she said, shading her eyes to squint into the bright sunlight. "He'll be here for a long spell. He's toting his big grip."

Uncle Luther picked me up and swung me high in the air when I ran down the road to meet him. I loved the way his long white moustache tickled my cheek. When we got to the house, he shook hands with Mama and Daddy and asked about Grandma, who had already marched straight to her room to pack.

Uncle Luther and I talked about most everything. He told me that sometimes you have to be in the right frame of mind before you can find a rainbow. The best time to look for one is the very second the sun pops out after a rain shower. He explained why you shouldn't feel sad when you see a dead butterfly. Butterflies are the happiest of God's creatures, he said. They come and go as they please, free to drift with the wind.

When Uncle Luther gave me a goodnight hug, I sniffed the sweet mix of bay rum hair tonic and the tobacco he carried in the little brown sack in his shirt pocket. Sometimes I heard the ticking of his gold watch on the chain looped across his leather vest. He wore handmade cowboy boots, even during The Depression. Once, when Grandma had the flu and was too sick to go to Aunt Nettie's, she asked him did he win his new boots in a poker game or pull them off a dead gambler's feet? He just shook his head and smiled.

Grandma said Uncle Luther was telling a lie about having a ranch near Hobbs, New Mexico, and she claimed he wasn't ever a cowboy down in Concho County, Texas. She said he never hit a lick of honest work in his life and was too trifling to settle down. I didn't believe what she said about him, but she was right about one thing, about how he ended up dead in a ditch.

One day around noon, the sheriff from over in Sweetwater called and told my daddy about the body of an unidentified man there in the county morgue. A rancher found him face down in a drainage ditch and there were two bullet holes in his back. The sheriff, who had jailed Uncle Luther a couple of times for gambling, said his boots and the gold watch and chain were missing when they brought him in. He said he knew for sure it was Luther, but somebody needed to come on up there and take a look and make some arrangements.

It was starting to get dark by the time Daddy drove to Sweetwater and back. I sat out on the back porch to wait for him. The pink and white blooms on the oleander bushes by the steps smelled sweet, like the Sunday perfume on the collar of Mama's blue crepe de Chine dress. I heard Daddy turn off the highway, and as soon as I saw the lights from his truck flash against the side of the house, I ran inside my room and held my hands over my ears because I didn't want to hear that Uncle Luther was dead.

The funeral next day wasn't much; it was just us, the preacher from the First Pentecostal Church, and Coondog Smith. Coondog was a grown man, but Mama told me he would always be like a little boy. Just before he was ready to be born, she said, his mother accidentally looked at a neighbor's deformed child, and that was why his mind wasn't right. Usually, the preacher brought him along when he held a service at the cemetery. Coondog came in handy, he said, when extra chairs needed fetching or if one of the stout ladies fainted and it took a couple of men to haul her to her car. I liked Coondog because he wasn't ever going to grow up and because he got saved twice every summer during revival meeting.

The preacher, Coondog and Mr. Floyd from Floyd's Funeral Parlor, were all there when we arrived. Daddy parked the truck beside a tombstone with an angel carved on top. Mama whispered to me to step careful and not get on any of the graves. The hot sunshine sparkled on the windshield of Mr. Floyd's black hearse.

Sweat dripped off the faces of the two men leaning on the handles of their shovels. They stood up straight when we walked up, and they took off their hats when Mr. Floyd eased around to the back of the hearse and opened the doors. He motioned to them to come help him get Uncle Luther's casket down on the ground. Coondog trotted behind them.

Uncle Luther had never darkened the door of a church house, my grandma said, and all that the preacher knew about him was he gambled, smoked cigarettes, drank whiskey and chased after women. So he read "The Lord Is My Shepherd" and asked God to have mercy on the soul of a poor sinner.

While the preacher reminded God of Uncle Luther's sins, Grandma said "Amen" in a loud voice every time he stopped for breath. She kept her head bowed the whole time, but I saw her take a look at the black clouds starting to boil overhead. She tugged on Mama's sleeve and whispered that she was headed for the truck if lightning got close before they lowered the coffin.

Big drops of rain began to spatter as the men let the casket down in the hole. The preacher told Coondog to run get an extra shovel out of the gravedigger's truck and help fill in before the storm broke.

When I heard the clods of dirt thumping on top of Uncle Luther, I ran into the woods behind the cemetery. Grandma yelled for me to come back before I got struck by lightning, but Mama said let her be.

I sat down on a log out of sight of everybody and started watching a doodle bug drill a hole in a little pile of red sand. I laid my face down on the ground next to it and looked at the way it threw the sand every which way with its feet.

Uncle Luther knew all about how to catch doodle bugs. You take a stick and stir it three times in the sand where the doodle bug is, then you chant the magic words: "Doodle bug, doodle bug, come get your bread and coffee. Your house is on fire."

I scooped up the doodle bug and let it crawl around on my hand. It kept trying to jump through my fingers, so I dug a hole for it and covered it with a big high pile of dirt. After awhile, Daddy called and said I had better come on back. On the way I stopped by a broken Nehi soda bottle and picked a bunch of buffalo clover. The blooms were purple and blue with white in the centers. They smelled like bay rum hair tonic.

Daddy and the preacher stood on one side of the mound of dirt they had shoveled on top of Uncle Luther. The preacher said wasn't it a shame we didn't get more than a piddling little shower out of that big thunderhead. Daddy looked down at the toes of his dusty boots and said it was the driest summer he could remember.

I scattered the clover on the grave, then crawled in the back of the truck. The sun came out and quick as I could, I looked for a rainbow. But I didn't find one.

When we got back home, Mama made a pot of coffee and poured a cup for her and Grandma. Daddy hurried to change out of his good blue serge suit so he go milk the cows. It was getting close to sundown. I heard the freight train whistle when it pulled out of the depot.

I sat down at the kitchen table with Mama and Grandma to hear what they were going to talk about. Grandma was quiet and her hand shook when she picked up her cup. After awhile Mama took a couple of sips and said she wondered if the drops of rain that fell on Uncle Luther's casket were God's tears. Grandma's cup clattered when she set it back in the saucer. She reached down inside the front of her dress where she kept the gold locket wrapped in a white lace handkerchief. She didn't open the locket; she just sat there, turning it over and over, like she wanted to see the way the light sparkled on it.

"I reckon all the hate burned out of me out there at the graveyard." It didn't sound like Grandma's voice saying the words. "It ain't Christian to hold a grudge against the dead."

"That day, just before our wedding, I told him to make a choice. Once and for all, I said, you got to make a choice." She said it soft, like a whisper. "And it was the roaming, the drinking and gambling he loved more than me." Grandma seemed pretty with the tears glistening in her eyes. It was the first time I ever noticed her looking pretty.

I went outside. My shadow stretched all the way from the back porch to the clothesline. A dead butterfly lay on the ground next to a brown twig under the cedar tree. I picked it up and held it on my finger for a long time. It was yellow with little brown dots on its wings.

When Mama called me in, I laid it on a branch of the tree. I pretended I saw it spread its wings, the way butterflies do before they fly away.

The kitchen smelled like cinnamon from the sugar pies Mama had baked and set to cool on the dough board by the stove. It was Daddy's turn to say grace: "Oh Lord, bless this food to the nourishment of our bodies and bless this home, for Jesus sake. Amen."

Grandma said she believed she would just have some corn bread and sweet milk and go on to bed. I said I would save her some sugar pie.

All during supper, I kept thinking about the dead butterfly, how it looked like it wanted to fly away, maybe off somewhere in the bright sunshine. Just flutter its wings and drift free with the wind.

APPLES

She squeezes past the Produce Man in
Golden Yorks
to park her cart beside the pale green mound of
Granny Smiths,
remembering when she was six years old
and ate a worm that writhed and wriggled in
a Jonathan.
On second thought, it might have been
a Winesap, or
perhaps it was
a Pippin.

She ate the worm to prove
her love for Freddy Gildersleeve
who later said she was a dummy to believe
he'd kiss girl who ate a worm.
And so he laughed and ran away, leaving her alone,
alone to retch the undigested peel and seeds,
alone to strew her misery in the grass.
She sees the Produce Man arranging stacks of
Golden Yorks
and wonders if he questions why she drops

a dozen Grannies

in her cart before she wheels away to

Coffee, Tea and Lo Fat Cheese.

She thinks the Produce Man is Freddy Gildersleeve

grown fat and bald. Does he believe

she cannot know about the worm

that lurks inside the core of

Granny Smiths?

WHERE ARE ALL THE CARING PEOPLE?

ood evening. This is Monica Godwin with a wrap of today's news. The search continues for Cynthia Murphy, elderly Oakmont woman reported missing from her home. Described as approximately five feet tall, blue eyes and short gray hair, Ms. Murphy was last seen wearing brown slacks and red sweater. Police recovered her abandoned automobile yesterday but refuse further comment except to say that foul play is suspected.

According to a neighbor, Ms. Murphy lives alone and drives to a nearby park early each morning to walk her dog, a small brown mongrel named Homer. City workers found the dog early today wandering near the baseball field in Willow Park, about three miles from the Murphy home. A spokesman said he will be held at the county shelter until someone claims him or until the next euthanasia of stray animals is scheduled.

Ms. Murphy disappeared three days ago on Easter Sunday.

"What a glorious Easter morning," I said to Homer.

Mist hung like a counterpane of lace over the trees dotting the park. A week of drenching rain had scrubbed the faces of the buildings across the valley and set a gleam in their windowed eyes. I switched off the ignition and sat inside the car for a moment to watch the first bright streaks of light frolic over the sleeping city. My eyes caught a quick movement reflected in the rear view mirror, a motion in the tall clumps of hedge. When I leaned out the window to listen, the branches stilled, and I thought : it is only a small animal in search of food, or the wind has come to frighten an old woman in a lonely place at sunrise. Homer clawed at my arm, his eyes pleading to be off on his morning run. He bounded away towards the little brook that slices through the center of the park as soon as I opened the car door.

The breeze blew warm against my face. A train whistled once, twice, the sound familiar and comforting when I glanced back at the shadowed bushes. But did I see, just as I blinked, did my eyes catch a blurred flash of color among the leaves? Something, someone stirring there? You get a little crazy living alone, watching murder mysteries on TV. I looked around me. The park seemed deserted, silent except for the sound of tolling bells heralding sunrise service.

Easter Sunday. My husband Jack and I used to color eggs for the neighborhood children's baskets, but that was so long ago. He is gone and the young people have grown up and moved away or forgotten me since he died. My telephone never rings except for a wrong number, or when that person from the Home For Battered Women calls to ask for a donation of old clothing. Last week I said to her: "I am wearing my old clothes. How can I afford to buy a new dress when I eke by month to month on Social Security and a piddling pension from Jack's union?"

Well, I told myself, no cause to dwell on what is past. I got out of the car and started to walk in the direction where I last glimpsed Homer's plumy tail as it dropped out of sight in the bed of wild azalea. A twig snapped behind me. When I turned, I saw the man standing between me and my car. He was big, thick as a tree trunk, his legs planted as though ready to spring.

"You all alone out here, Mama?" His words soft and polite, eyes round and moist like a pair of slate grey marbles left outside in the rain.

"My husband has walked to the other side of the park and he will be back any minute." I heard the sounds of the words. Was it my voice?

"You lyin', mama." He wiped his mouth on his sleeve and shuffled closer. "I been watchin' and they ain't nobody here but you and the skinny pup and me. And Clell, right behind you."

The man called Clell moved around in front of me before I had time to turn.

"Well, now," he said.

He was small and pale, wiry, with a purplish scar rutting his left cheek from the corner of his mouth to his ear lobe. His glance darted from me to my car, back to me again. He shook his head and grinned. "I reckon I ain't up to snatching me no old scrawny piece this mornin', so you gonna miss out on a real fine time. What I got to have is a set of wheels and I'm lookin' at your little ole blue automobile."

Talk. Stall for time. "My purse is on the front seat in the car and you can have the money."

"Maybe you got a hearin' problem, mama. Clell didn't ask for no money." The big man's hand flicked out, struck the side of my face.

Trees swayed, earth and sky tilted to meet, settled back again when I heard Homer's shrill bark. I blinked to clear my vision and saw him streaking towards me, his stubby legs whipping beads of water from the grass. He skidded to a stop, his ears quivering at attention.

A gun glinted in the big man's hand. "Want me to shoot him?"

Clell grabbed the pistol, stuffed it in the waistband of his trousers. "Now ain't you the big brain? Somebody hears a gunshot in this nice little park and how many cops you think gonna come runnin'?" He pulled a green bottle from his hip pocket, took a long swig and handed it to the big man. "Finish it off and we'll git on with our business."

I tried to run when the big man turned away for a second, but his hand grabbed my sleeve. He came snarling, the bottle raised above his head. My face exploded. Red everywhere—trees, sky, his eyes close to mine. I remember holding out my hands in front of me, but the blows came again and again. And once again.

Consciousness drifted away, came once more. I heard the rushing of water, the roar of an out of bounds river or creek. Darkness. I lay on my side, knees drawn up under my chin. I was sure my eyes were open but I couldn't see. Pain rolled over me when I tried to move, and then I remembered. That bastard in the park broke a bottle over my head and locked me in the trunk of my car. Perhaps he stopped now to throw me out on the side of the road, the way someone once did to Homer.

The sound of a key grated in a lock. I heard the trunk pop open, felt a clammy breeze brush my face. I lay without moving, feigning death.

"Old bitch still alive." Clell's voice, his lips near my cheek, breath sour with the smell of gin.

"Maybe I drag her over in the woods and finish her off." The big man grabbed my arm. "Want me to whack her again?"

"Naw. The creek'll take care of her. More rain comin' tonight. By morning' she'll end up in Black River.

I felt no pain when they dragged me out by my hair. It seemed the wind cleared a path to let me soar with the birds before the water closed in around me. Dark and cold, swirling. I tried to float to the top, to lie on my back, but the tide spun me around, under and over. My thoughts whirled with it: Jack is gone and there is no one who knows I am alive or dead except the neighbor who says good morning, how's the arthritis today? But she really doesn't give a damn. Homer is all I have. I found him last year, lying broken by the road side where someone tossed him out like a piece of trash. The world seems filled with madness. Where are the caring people?

I don't know how long or how far the rolling water carried me before I let go. There was no bright light, no heavenly visions. Death came quietly like an old friend to hold my hand as I sank to the bottom. Down, whirling, turning. One, two, three. Waltz me around again, Jack old dear.

This is Monica Godwin with the evening news. Volunteer rescue workers recovered the body of Cynthia Murphy today, four days after she was reported missing. Police are holding two men who have confessed to kidnaping the elderly woman in the early morning hours of Easter Sunday, stealing her car and throwing her from a bridge into rain swollen waters of Catclaw Creek. The victim was alive at the time, according to the suspect's statements. A rescue worker discovered her remains lodged among logs and rocks near the creek's bank.

A telephone call to this reporter moments before air time today added a final note to the story. The message was from a woman who works at the animal shelter where Ms. Murphy's dog is held. She said a man, identifying himself as the person who brought Ms.Murphy's remains to shore, came to the shelter early today and adopted Homer.

"I figured the little guy needed a home," she quoted the man as saying, "and I need a dog."

"You should have seen how that little fellow jumped into his arms, just like he had been waiting for him to come," she continued. "That man had tears in his eyes. Such a kind and caring person."

REQUIEM FOR A REFRIGERATOR

*O*ur refrigerator died yesterday. During the morning she made strange gurgling sounds, then abandoned her feeble efforts to freeze ice cubes. In late afternoon she belched a final clatter and expired.

"But you've fixed her so many times," I pleaded with the repairman, "Can't you do it again, whatever it is you always do?"

"I ain't no magician, lady." He shook his head. "What you got here is a wore out appliance, a twenty year old model."

Twenty one. We got her on the day the twins were born. Her shelves were loaded with bottles of baby formula that year.

He looked at numbers on a measuring tape. "We could fit one of our small models in this space."

I used to give summer parties for the kids in the neighborhood. You wouldn't believe how many strawberry and lime popcicles I've made in that dinky freezing compartment.

"A twin door would be nice," he said "Yellow, to match the stove and dishwasher."

Did you ever try to wash lipstick art off the sides of a white refrigerator? Bright red roses and a Mother's Day poem?

"We can get a new one delivered to you tomorrow." He shut the lid on his tool box and looked at his watch.

The poem had two stanzas. I left it here for the longest time, until the words ran together and the lipstick roses got all gooey.

"Be sure and come by the store first thing in the morning to make your selection," he said.

"Yes," I closed the door behind him. "I'll be there early."

BUDDY

*W*e met at the clothesline one rare balmy morning in late December. As I finished hanging the bath towels to flap dry in the wind, he flitted in just above my head and perched on the line an arm's length away. It would be my first experience up close and personal with a mockingbird, this black and gray feathered gun slinger known to attack cats, dogs and even kids on bicycles

I stood for a moment before inching closer, talking to him in a low voice. He fluffed out his feathers, took a hop back but didn't fly away or make a hostile move toward me.

After a few minutes of standing eyeball to eyeball, I walked back inside the house to look for some scraps of food for him. The bird feeder by the kitchen window was filled to the brim with sunflower seeds, but mockingbirds are not primarily seed eaters. Maybe some hamburger meat from the fridge. Wouldn't be as tasty as a fat worm or spider, but it might be worth a try

I pinched off a couple of small bits of the ground beef and dropped them on top of the tall metal storage cabinet that stands beside the sliding glass doors on the patio. When I came back, the hamburger had vanished. The bird sat close by on the picnic table.

By the third day, he was a regular customer, fluttering in as soon as he saw me walking past the doors on my way to the kitchen for my morning cup of coffee. He perched on the edge of the cabinet while I talked to him and dropped the food closer and closer to his feet. Gradually he moved towards me and began to take bits gently from between my fingers. From that moment on, he was hooked and so was I.

He became "Buddy"at the suggestion of a dear little friend who was upset because she had chosen that name for her brand new baby brother. Her parents overruled her idea and called the child Jonathan, but she seemed pleased to have the bird carry the Buddy name.

He found a mate right away and the two settled down to nest building in a tall holly bush. The little female never came to eat with him. She always sat in a tree or on the fence, waiting for him to bring lunch, so suddenly I found myself passing out hamburger like I was on the fast track at McDonalds..I was the designated waitperson, trotting back and forth between fridge and take-out window, sometimes as many as a dozen times a day.

And then, trouble arrived, a real mockingbird badass we named Attila who fought everything in sight—nasty tempered jays, woodpeckers, crows and especially my mild mannered friend. Buddy feathers flew everywhere.

One day I looked out to find Buddy sitting in his usual spot atop the cabinet, his wings dragging, eyes half closed. I saw his chest heaving up and down and I began to stroke his ruffled feathers and talk to him. He snuggled in my hand then flopped down to the ground and dragged himself out of sight behind the barbeque grill. I was certain he was dying, but soon he shook himself and fluttered away and out of sight.

When I opened the curtain next morning there he sat, a few feathers short and one wing drooped a bit lower than the other. Attila was nowhere to be found. Afterwards, his terrorist raids in the yard became fewer and always with Buddy in hot pursuit. Buddy had become top gun at last!

After the big fight, he shared egg sitting with his mate who sometimes took on the task of bringing home the hamburger. She was very skittish of taking it from me and sometime clamped down really hard on my fingers. I never doubted which bird was which. When the two babies hatched, they stayed mostly in the shrubbery or occasionally we spotted their fuzzy little bodies perched on the roof. We never got a close look at them.

When the month of May rolled around, the mockingbird population dwindled as they began their migration from our area. One morning Buddy came early and somehow I knew it was time for him to go. He ate about twice his usual amount of hamburger, stayed for a few extra seconds to allow me to stroke the feathers on his head one more time.

I watched as he swooped away to join his family sitting in the oak tree, waited until I could no longer see their black and white feathers flashing like pinwheels in the sunlight.

Maybe birds are like human after all.. There are good ones and bad ones in all species. Sometimes you have to dig deep, but what a joy when you find that good one!

THE DAY THE PRETTY BIRDS CAME

She opened the car door and shoved a faded denim backpack in his hands. "This is where you get out," she said.

"Ain't I goin' back with you to Mobile?"

"I'm leaving you here where you used to live with your mama." Her hands shook as she fumbled in her purse for a cigarette. "It ain't your fault, Toad. I just can't look after no crazy eighteen year old boy. I can't."

"But where'm I gonna eat and sleep?"

"Around," she said. "You'll find places."

He stood at the side of the road, and when Aunt Lu Billy's car was nothing but a spot on the highway, he started walking toward the big yellow shell above the gas station on the corner. It was where Mr. Leroy worked, he remembered.

Leroy Crutchfield squinted into the bright sunlight when Toad stopped beside him at the gas pumps. "Ain't seen you since last year," he said. "You come back here to live?"

"Yes sir. I been down at that school in Mobile but my mama died."

"I heard." Leroy wiped his hands on a red flannel rag and stuffed it in his hip pocket. "Right now I'm trying to get my station spiffed up so I can win the Maryville Business Club beautification contest and get me a free trip to Disney World."

Toad felt his heart start to pound like there was a hammer inside him.

"I'll help you win it, Mr. Leroy. If you'll let me hang a bird feeder in that tree out front, I can call up the pretty birds to come beautify your station."

"Now whoa right there, Toad. I recall you used to ramble on to everybody in town about how you can whistle up a flock of bright feathered birds to come flying in out of the woods." Leroy folded a stick of Red Dog chewing gum in half and popped it in his mouth. "You even had my old lady believing it, but she believes in everything– speaking in unknown tongues at church service, burying a dish rag under the steps to cure warts, things like that."

Toad felt his face turning hot. He dug at his left eye that started to twitch and cross inward toward his nose, the way it always did when somebody was getting ready to say mean things to him.

"So how come I ain't seen nothing but a bunch of filthy sparrows and pigeons around here? I ain't seen none of them pretty birds."

Toad shifted from one foot to the other. "You ain't never asked me to call 'em."

"And I ain't now," Leroy said. " The contest rules says I can paint and fix up the rest room, plant flower beds and make the grounds around the station look good. Nothing about birds. You know anything about growing marigolds and petunias?"

"Shoot. I can grow flowers big as dinner plates," Toad grinned.

"Well, I plan to win that contest this year, beat out Charley Hunter if it's the last thing I do."

"Mr. Charley still run the place down the road?"

"Self service now and a brand new car wash building." Leroy pushed his cap back and stood looking at Toad. "Tell you what. I need a strong back around here for awhile, so you come back on Monday and I'll think about hiring you to pull them weeds out of the flower beds."

"Boy howdy, Mr. Leroy. Can I come in on Sunday?"

"I'm closed on Sunday. Can't you remember nothing?"

Toad sat hunched over a pile of wood shavings beside the stack of used tires. He felt the hair curl up on the back of his neck when he saw Mr.

Leroy's big feet stop right beside him.

"Are you messing with that feeder again, piddling around when I'm paying you to be working?"

"I am workin. Lunch hour ain't over til the factory whistle blows. You said I can work on my feeder at lunch hour."

"Well, you can thank my old lady. She talked me into letting you hang that box of seeds in the tree. She's as crazy as you."

When he heard the shrill blast of the factory whistle, Toad set the bird feeder down and started digging a hole to set out another clump of petunias. By the time he finished packing dirt around the roots, he barely had time to wipe his hands on his shirt tail before Mr.. Leroy stalked over from the pumps and pointed across the street. "Not one weed in the marigolds around them golden arches, and you can bet your butt every business place in town is going after that award this year. A free week-end at Disney ain't to be sneezed at."

"You think Mr. Charley Hunter gonna win again? How many times has he done it, Mr. Leroy?"

"Too many."

Toad picked up the feeder and held it at arm's length, his stubby thumb and forefinger gripping the metal hook on top. "The pretty birds will come to beautify your station. You'll see."

"Now Toad, you know and I know you can't whistle up no flock of birds to come put on a show when them contest judges come here. It's just a story you read some place."

"I can't read, Mr. Leroy."

"Well, I got brains enough to figure out it ain't gonna happen. I'm letting you hang that contraption in my tree to keep peace with my old woman. She's took a big shine to you since you been inviting yourself over to our house for Sunday morning breakfast." He frowned as he lit a cigarette and flipped the match in the direction of the trash barrel. "Somehow, I got this feeling Charley Hunter has got a trick up his sleeve this time. He's been driving by real slow, eying that feeder and smirking."

"Miz Leroy says you got to throw in something extra to beat him."

"Don't remind me. That woman won't let up."

"Miz Leroy can carry on, that's for sure," Toad agreed. "She says I can come back again next Sunday."

"Can't you ever go eat no place else on my day off?"

He had waited in Mr.and Miz Leroy's back yard since daylight, dozing on the stoop with his head propped against the screen door until he sniffed the smell of bacon frying in the kitchen. "Mornin', Miz Leroy," he said when she answered his three quick raps. "Cookin sure smells good. I been sittin here hearin the pretty birds chirpin out in the woods."

She unlatched the screen and told him to wipe the dew off his feet and go wash his face and hands.

"I was just telling Leroy again he has got to come up with something extra to catch the judges eye," she explained when Toad sat down in the place she fixed for him. "It seems like if McDonald's don't win that contest, Charley Hunter does. That man can grow dahlias big as mixing bowls, but I guess Leroy ain't got no green thumb."

"Charley Hunter's thumb is green because he's got time to piddle around, snipping off old blooms and setting out bait to kill the slugs." Leroy glared at her. "Hell, Charley Hunter's got a boy to help him run the station."

"I could do that, Mr. Leroy, help you run your station." When Toad looked up, his elbow slipped off the edge of the table and sent his spoon clattering against the sugar bowl.

Miz Leroy ran and got a wet sponge to clean up the blackberry jelly that dropped beside his glass of milk. She dabbed at the tablecloth with quick circular motions that made the skin on her fleshy upper arm sway in rhythm with the movements of her hand. "That's an idea, Leroy," she said. "Why don't you hire Toad to help you wait on the customers?"

Leroy pointed his fork at the wet purple stain seeping across the tablecloth. "That give you any clue why? That boy can't walk and pick his nose at the same time without" —

"I'll do it without no pay," Toad interrupted, "if you'll let me come sleep sometimes in your old trailer house in the back yard."

"And what about eating? Where you gonna eat if I don't pay you no money?"

"Same places as always. Around." Toad's grin split his freckled face in half.

While Miz Leroy banged the knives and forks against the dishes in the sink, Mr. Leroy pushed back his chair and sat looking at him. Toad felt his tongue turn to butter, the way it did when he figured Mr. Leroy was thinking up a mean thing to say to him. Mr. Leroy wasn't like the man who taught in the woodwork shop at that school in Mobile. The man in Mobile said he believed God had given Toad the gift to call the pretty birds from the woods.

"You think you can have them flower beds ready when the judges come?" Mr. Leroy asked.

"Oh yes sir. And I could help you run the station if I had a cap and some green pants."

"Now listen here, Toad. You got to remember you ain't the brightest boy in town." Mr. Leroy made clucking noises with his tongue and shook his head. "You can't expect me to dress you up in a cap and uniform and turn you loose in my station."

"Oh no sir, I ain't expectin *that*. I was just thinkin maybe you can learn me to be smart like you and *then* I can get me a visor cap and some green pants."

"I reckon I ought to get some use out of you." Mr. Leroy rubbed the grizzly stubble on his   cheek. "Lord knows, you're under foot at breakfast time every Sunday."

"Ain't got no other place to go. Mr. Mac locks up the feed store on Sunday, so I just come on over here and see you and Miz Leroy."

"Well, nobody's using my mama-in-law's old trailer, so you can sleep out there when you ain't got no other place, and I reckon you can come help me with the customers on Saturday."

"Boy howdy. Can I start today?"

"Today is Sunday, Toad. Can't you keep nothing straight?"

Miz Leroy set the bucket of Lysol water on the trailer house steps and walked inside. Toad followed, carrying a brown shopping bag and a shoe box filled with sunflower seeds. She stopped to look at a sampler on the wall, the words God Bless Our Home cross stitched in variegated shades of blue. "I had to pack up Mama's things after she passed, but I never come back and took down the pictures and hangings," she sighed.

"It's nice." Toad fingered the edge of the taffeta curtain moving in the breeze. "Mr. Mac ain't got no windows in back of his place where I sleep sometimes."

"You sleep in MacGruder's feed store with all them rats?"

"Rats ain't mean, not if you feed and take care of 'em. And Mr. Mac, after I sweep up the floor, lets me have the seeds for my birds." He opened the shopping bag and took out a pale green box built like an A-frame house with a glass front and hinged roof.

"Why, Toad," she touched it with the tips of her fingers, "it's beautiful. Where did you get it?"

"Built it. The man in Mobile learned me how and Mr. Marvin at the lumber yard gives me scraps of wood and glass when I help him load the trucks."

She brought a pitcher of lemonade from the kitchen and they sat together on the steps.

"You got no other people here since Lu Billy run off and left you?"

"No ma'am," he shook his head. "Ma before she died give some money to Aunt Lu Billy so I could keep goin to school, but Aunt Lu Billy said she wasn't puttin up no more with a crazy eighteen year old boy."

"Don't she ever get in touch with you? She ever write you a letter or postcard?"

"Couldn't read it if she did." He picked up a brown twig and made a long straight mark in the dirt, then a shorter one across the top. "But if I was to go back to school in Mobile I could learn how. Learn to write, too. The man said so." He rolled the empty glass in his hands so the ice made a tinkling sound. "I whistled up the pretty birds for him once. You ever seen them?"

"I expect there ain't none in Maryville, Toad."

"Oh yes ma'am, they're here, they sure are." He closed his eyes and hugged his knees against his chest. "Bitty little things, all blue and green and some like gold in the sun, singin like you never heard."

"Toad" she said, "I'm having me a talk with Leroy."

The day before the judges came, Leroy stood watching Toad down on his knees in the flower bed. "Our dahlias is bigger that Charley Hunters," he said.

Toad grinned and wiped the sweat out of his eyes. "Tomorrow when it's judging day, the pretty birds will come."

"It's just a notion you got in your head, Toad. That's all it is." Leroy picked at a piece of white lint on his shirt. "If you are so sure they'll come, why don't you whistle them up right now? Let me see them pretty birds. I'm calling your bluff."

"It ain't time for them to come , Mr. Leroy. They're waitin out in the woods. Tomorrow when its judging day they'll be here."

"Well," Leroy said, "you can get ready for that box of seeds to come down the minute them judges leave, soon as my old woman finds out she is as crazy as you."

Toad came early the next morning to water the flowers before they wilted in the sun The air was heavy with the stickiness of late summer and the breeze stirred without cooling, blending the scents of diesel fuel and oleander blossoms. Toad sat down under the tree, listening for Mr. Leroy's truck when it came down the road. He closed his eyes and let his head roll against his chest. The sounds he made were low at first, a soft keening, then high and piercing as he clamped his hands over his ears. Now he was silent, without moving, as still as the rock he sat on, waiting. When he opened his eyes he saw the first flash of color in the leaves above him. Another, after another and then he heard the rumble of Mr. Leroy's tow truck in the driveway.

"They're here!" he cried and ran to meet him.

"Lord Almighty!" Mr. Leroy's eyes bulged as he looked wildly around. "The judges here already?"

"It's the pretty birds that's here, Mr. Leroy, just like I said! Come look."

Leroy jumped out of the truck and slammed the door. "It don't matter none if a flock of your damn birds sets around and whistles Yankee Doodle Dandy in the judges ears. Charley Hunter's found a way that's sure to beat me again."

"How's he done it, Mr. Leroy?"

"A big red plastic picnic table with benches along the sides, sitting right out front by the dahlias, and free balloons and Kool-Aid for the kids. That's how he's done it." He spit in the driveway and rubbed the toe of his shoe across it. "I figured Charley Hunter was pulling a fast one. I seen him one day last week driving by, eye balling you out here working in the flowers and grinning at that box of seeds hanging in the tree, so I went by his place just now. He's beat me for sure."

"But our flowers is more pretty than his this year," Toad said. Tears spilled out of the corners of his eyes. He didn't bother to wipe them away, didn't bother to remind Mr. Leroy again about the pretty birds.

"For once my place looked better than his and a hell of a lot better than McDonalds." Mr. Leroy's voice got louder. "But I had to listen to my old woman. 'Throw in something extra to catch the judges eye', she says. Well, I throwed in a bird feeder and Charley Hunter won't never let me live it down."

"Yoohoo, Leroy." Toad shaded his eyes to see who was calling, coming down the road at a half trot.

"Great gulliver, it's my old woman," Mr. Leroy said. "That's all I need."

"Am I in time to see Toad's pretty birds?" she gasped, wiping the sweat from her face. "The neighbors will be along directly."

"They're here, Miz Leroy!" Toad began to jump up and down. "They've come, just like I said!"

Mr. Leroy threw his cap on the ground.

Toad looked at his feet and started to back away. "Want me to water the flowers some more?"

A man driving a silver and blue Chevrolet beeped the horn and parked in front of the Coke machine. He held the door while three ladies got out.

"Just go somewhere out of sight and keep out of my way while these judges is here," Leroy hissed in Toad's ear while he straightened his bow tie.

Toad dropped down by the tree, hugging his knees with his hands clasped together. Miz Leroy came over to stand behind him. Now the pretty birds tumbled out of the branches to swarm the feeder with puffs of rainbow colors, darting, flitting, and when they began to sing it was like all the bells on Christmas morning. Toad heard Miz Leroy catch her breath but he didn't dare to move. The pretty birds fluttered everywhere, blue and green and gold, so many he couldn't count them even if he knew how. Their colors swam in front of his eyes. When he looked up he saw the man and the three women with Mr. Leroy, but their faces were blurred because he was crying and Miz Leroy was hugging him.

"The pretty birds have come to beautify Mr. Leroy's station," he said softly but it was loud enough for everyone to hear, and then he turned away to watch how the sunlight shimmered against their breasts. He could hear, above their singing, the mummer of voices gathering behind him, the squealing of tires against the pavement, the running of feet. He didn't look up when the three women and the man came over to say goodbye nor hear what Miz Leroy had to say to Mr. Leroy before she went home.

One by one, the pretty birds flew away and the grey brown sparrows, joined by the pigeons, drifted back. Toad shook himself and went to get his sandwich out of the cooler in Mr. Leroy's office.

Mr. Leroy was leaned back with his chair against the wall and his feet crossed on top of his desk.

"Hell no, the boy ain't looking for no other job," he said into the telephone. "Besides, my old woman's took a shine to him, and now it don't look like she's gonna let up on me until I get him back in the school in Mobile. I reckon I'll have to jump right on that soon as we fly back from Disney World." He lit a cigarette and coughed. "What do you mean it was a dirty trick?"

When he hung up the phone, he began to laugh.

"That Charley Hunter," he said to Toad, "is a piss poor looser."

THE WINNOWING

"The Winnowing" is set one hundred years in the future when Earth's population has skyrocketed with multiple births of babies. Deaths of the elderly has plummeted to near zero due to the advance of medical science. In order to decrease the population, the Government has created the Mandatory Office of Winnowing of the US@MOWUS.GOV which decrees that all persons who have reached the age of 120 years must be sent to the Winnowing Chambers. The story opens with Sam and Emma Edwards waiting for their instructions.

The message would come this morning at precisely eight o'clock. Sam Edwards steeled himself to watch the bright red letters scroll across the screen stretched from wall to wall in the bed room. He turned his head on the pillow to look at Emma as she slept, mouth slightly open, little beads of spittle bubbling in the corners of her mouth.

We're a lucky couple, he mused, born six months apart in the same year, married for a whole century. Now we will leave the world together, not with one taken away and the other left behind as has happened to friends in neighboring towns.

"Has it come yet?" Emma's eyes seemed to pop open like shutters when she sat up.

Glancing at his watch, he felt a tightness grip his throat. "Still five minutes to go," he said.

A series of loud beeps signaled the incoming letter:

Subj: Winnowing

Date: 5/14/2105

From: Mandatory Office of Winnowing of the US @MOWUS.GOV

To: samandemma@fedcontrolledcomm.gov

The winnowing of Crystal City citizens who have/or will have reached their 120th birthday in the year 2104 is scheduled for tomorrow, 15 May, 2105 at Crystal City Population Appraisal Bldg. A MOWUS vehicle will pick up at your complex. You should be prepared for boarding at 09:00. Please be prompt. Omit breakfast and do take care of personal hygiene obligations before boarding time. Do not wear jewelry or dentures. As of this message, all means of travel in/out of town are closed until further notice. The Crystal City Winnowing completes the National program for the current year. It is scheduled to resume at a later date as need arises.

MOWUS regrets the necessity of this decision. Population on earth has reached critical proportions due to high increase in multiple births, i.e. sextuple, octuple, etc. while, in the last century, deaths of the aged tumbled to near zero. The growth and successful transplants of vital organs such as hearts, lungs, memory cell boosters, kidneys and bladders, combined with manufactured parts—legs, arms, hips, etc. has extended lives many decades beyond original calculations. When added to funding of research programs, doctors, drugs and hospital care, the cost has spiraled out of control. Also, our country's lengthy engagement in the current Martian War has depleted emergency funds reserved for transfer to this program.

Again, we regret this decision and we endeavor to make it as stress free as possible. For the past year, the drug Klenderstadt has been injected into your prescription medications, which has enabled your mind to accept death as a necessary procedure.

As you enter the Winnowing Chamber, all unpleasant thoughts are deleted from your brain pool. You will feel no physical or mental pain. The experience will be over in nano seconds.

Please note: The word GOD is also erased from your memory bank. However, if requested, a brief period of aroma therapy and psychiatric counseling is available.

They lay under the covers, hands clasped, eyes fixed on the screen now gone dark. Emma broke the silence. "I'm wondering about the number of manufactured replacements and organ transplants you and I have."

"I can't recall for certain." Sam propped himself on his elbow. "Three hearts for me, a couple of kidneys, my left eye, both hips and knees. I have very few original parts."

"I've lost count of my bladders," she said.

He kept silent for a moment, watching the bright shards of sunlight crawl along the windows. "Do you regret," he asked, "that we put off doing so many things we planned? We were too busy to take that trip to Jupiter, never looked down on Earth from Mars. We let so many things slip away."

"We didn't let the important thing slip away," she said. "We loved each other."

Sam looked at her for a long time before he reached behind his pillow and flicked a button in the headboard of the bed.

"Crystal City weather update," a soft voice floated through the room. "Bright sunlight, no rain, gentle winds. Have a good day."

"So how do you want to spend it, this wonderful last day?" he asked.

"You go first." She sat up, brushed a strand of brown hair from her face.

"I would like to see you smile today," he said. "I would like to hear the sound of your laughter."

"You know," she nodded, "there *is* something I would like to do today, but it sounds so ridiculous."

"Tell me."

"Do you recall the childhood game of hop scotch? Someone took a piece of chalk and drew a series of single and double squares on the sidewalk. The object was to hop, plant one foot in the single, then both feet, one in each side of the double. I was the best in my neighborhood." She paused to catch her breath. "Well, lately I have been trying to think how to maneuver a hop. Back before I turned one hundred I could do it, but lately I find

I have forgotten. Do you recall how it is done?"

"Hopping was for girls," he said. "I never learned, but no time like now I suppose. So let's go outside and give it a whirl."

"It's daylight and people will be watching. I would feel so foolish."

"I doubt it matters what people think. I'll be there to catch you if you fall."

They rode the slow track sidewalk to the Fitness & Well Being Center, a low stone building surrounded by a pink marble patio. He held her hand while she lifted one foot to attempt a small hop on the other, haltingly at first.

"Turn loose!" she cried after a few moments. "It's all come back! I can hop!"

Sam sat down on one of the benches as he watched her movements grow sure and agile. It seemed to him he saw her face begin to beam like that of a smiling child at play. Bright sunlight glinted on the tears welling in his eyes when she stopped to reach for his hand.

"An old woman hopping about," she said. "What a silly sight I must have been."

And Emma begin to laugh.

ABOUT THE AUTHOR

*A*yleene Archer Thompson was born in the second year of the Roaring Twenties and grew up in Buffalo Gap, a tiny speck on the Texas map between Fort Worth and El Paso. After marrying Wayne Thompson, her high school sweetheart, the couple moved to Birmingham, Alabama. Her short stories have won awards in literary competitions and several are published in anthologies including *The Alalitcom, Oktoberfest* and *Magnolia Quarterly*. She has contributed free lance articles to *The Birmingham News*, also short fiction to *Good Reading* Magazine. Mrs. Thompson has two children, Patricia and Wayne Evan, three grandchildren, two great grans and one great-great on the way. She lives in Hoover, Alabama with her husband; a flock of ducks and a three-legged dog named Cassie.